W9-BNP-459

Praise for *Tall, Dark, and Vampire*

"Shines with fascinating new characters… Readers will not want to wait for more from the very talented Humphreys!"

—*RT Book Reviews* Top Pick of the Month, 4.5 Stars

"Engaging… Humphreys skillfully blends intrigue and romance."

—*Publishers Weekly*

"Refreshing…rousing romantic urban fantasy. The sleuthing is terrific…but it is the second chance at love that enhances this entertaining thriller."

—*Midwest Book Review*

"Riveting… I found Ms. Humphreys's writing and characters fresh and exciting."

—*Anna's Book Blog*

"Outstandingly written, it will possess the hearts of readers. A must-read for all vampire lovers."

—*Bitten By Love Reviews*

"The world building and passion will leave readers breathless."

—*The Romance Reviews*

"Mystery, action, intrigue, and hot love scenes…will literally get your blood moving."

—*BookLoons*

Also by Sara Humphreys

The Amoveo Legend

Unleashed

Untouched

Undenied (novella)

Untamed

Undone

Unclaimed

Dead in the City

Tall, Dark, and Vampire

Vampire Trouble

30 July 2014.

SARA HUMPHREYS

sourcebooks
casablanca

Copyright © 2014 by Sara Humphreys
Cover and internal design © 2014 by Sourcebooks, Inc.
Cover design by Jamie Warren
Cover photos © imagebroker/Alamy; John Fox/Getty Images

Sourcebooks and the colophon are registered trademarks of Sourcebooks, Inc.

All rights reserved. No part of this book may be reproduced in any form or by any electronic or mechanical means including information storage and retrieval systems—except in the case of brief quotations embodied in critical articles or reviews—without permission in writing from its publisher, Sourcebooks, Inc.

The characters and events portrayed in this book are fictitious or are used fictitiously. Any similarity to real persons, living or dead, is purely coincidental and not intended by the author.

Published by Sourcebooks Casablanca, an imprint of Sourcebooks, Inc.
P.O. Box 4410, Naperville, Illinois 60567-4410
(630) 961-3900
Fax: (630) 961-2168
www.sourcebooks.com

Printed and bound in Canada.
WC 10 9 8 7 6 5 4 3 2 1

For my family...

"When you look at your life, the greatest happinesses are family happinesses."

—Dr. Joyce Brothers

Chapter 1

THE AIR AROUND HIM WAS VOID OF THE NORMALLY INCESSANT sound of fluttering human heartbeats or the typical noises of New York City nightlife. No honking horns. No inane human conversation. Nothing.

For a split second, Shane thought he'd awakened somewhere other than his apartment within the Presidium's New York facility. Standing ramrod straight, fangs bared and senses sharp, he surveyed the empty, hauntingly quiet Manhattan street.

Shane Quesada hadn't been blanketed by silence like this in more than four hundred years, not since that fateful summer night so long ago. Though it had been centuries, he still recalled that hot August evening with vivid clarity. The mysterious woman visiting his village seduced him, turned him and then after toying with Shane for a century, Selena left the way she'd found him. Broken and alone.

That man—the one who wept for the woman who abandoned him—no longer existed, and Shane knew this particular moment was certainly not the time to revisit that period of weakness. Shutting down the unpleasant memory with the cold, calculating demeanor of a vampire sentry, he focused on figuring out where in the hell he was.

As he struggled to understand what was happening, his hands balled into fists and his jaw clenched. He could see he was standing outside The Coven, the club owned by one of the new czars of New York City, Olivia Hollingsworth. He'd frequented the place most nights over the past several months, but certainly not for the ear-shattering music, the stench of sweating humans, or the undrinkable swill that was served.

Instead, the blond, youngling vampire bartender had captured Shane's interest and drawn him there night after night. Most evenings he wouldn't stay long, only a few minutes before or after his sweeps of the city, but he'd discovered that skipping even one night made him surprisingly agitated. Even if only a moment or two, he simply had to have a glimpse of her. Maya Robertson, the flirtatious beauty who had a penchant for toying with human men, had become both the bane of his existence and the object of his long-dormant desire.

It had been years since he actually wanted a woman for more than her blood. However, the moment Shane encountered the curvaceous beauty with the compelling blue eyes, lust gnawed at him. His sudden and instant attraction to the beautiful little vampire was highly unsettling. The nagging, pulsing need for her clawed relentlessly, deep in his gut, and even though he wanted nothing more than to claim her, Shane resisted.

He had no time for an emotional entanglement, let alone with one of the czar's progeny. Emotions were dangerous and distracting. He was known as one of the finest and most focused sentries within the Presidium's ranks, and he had no interest in losing his position or getting sloppy.

Aside from the fact that Maya was a youngling, only turned five years ago, she was reckless. And if there was one thing Shane couldn't abide, it was recklessness. Maya had a fondness for human men, and from what he could tell, she'd taken many of them to her bed. His jaw clenched and anger fired through him at the mere thought of her with another man.

Shaking his head, he set his mouth in a tight line and fought to remove the image of her gorgeous oval-shaped face from his mind. Her skin was fair with not a freckle on it, and the only things more alluring than her hourglass figure were her enormous blue eyes. They were almost lavender, and she seemed fully aware of their hypnotic power. Maya might not be able to glamour Shane or any other vampire the way she could a human, but she certainly seemed to have him under her spell.

The woman had become a distraction, and in his line of work, things like that could get a vampire dusted. Shane sharpened his focus and tried to concentrate on the matter at hand—where the fuck he was and why the city had suddenly fallen silent.

What he found even more perplexing than the unsettling quiet was that the world around him was painted in black and white. Normally, with the night vision of a vampire, he would see the colorful world in varying shades of sepia tones, but not now. He blinked and turned slowly, surveying the familiar neighborhood, but things remained colorless and mute, as though he'd stepped into a silent film. There wasn't a flicker of color anywhere, and the only sound was from his bare feet as he moved along the sidewalk.

Shane stopped.

Bare feet?

He looked down to find that he wasn't wearing his

sentry uniform, only a thin pair of cotton pajama pants. The same ones he'd put on before going to sleep for the day. He held his arms out and looked disapprovingly at his outright state of undress.

Pajamas?

What the hell was going on? He would never in his right mind leave his apartment in only his pajamas. As a sentry and well-known soldier for the Presidium, he had made far too many enemies over the years to leave his home unarmed—let alone half-naked.

Shane stilled when the realization of where he was washed over him.

A dream.

He was walking in the dreamscape for the first time in almost four hundred years. A smile cracked his face and he ran both hands through his dark, thick hair while looking around in pure awe. The absence of dreams was something he'd grown accustomed to and hadn't particularly missed. When he'd finally stopped dreaming, about ten years after being turned, it was the last step to letting go of his human life.

His smile faded when the gravity of what this might mean settled over him. Was he ill? Had he been bewitched in some way? Why now, after all this time, would he suddenly begin to dream again?

With those unanswered questions rattling through his mind, he saw two humans rounding the corner ahead of him. Shane stepped back into the shadows as they approached, but he kept his sights on them. The man had his arm wrapped tightly around the blond woman, who stumbled and was behaving as though she were highly intoxicated. Her hair fell over her face and she was shaking her head, trying to push the man away.

Shane stilled, uncertain of what to do. Could they see him? Were they merely a part of his dream, or were they sentient dreamwalkers like he was? It became abundantly clear that neither of them could see him when the human male tugged the young woman against him and started kissing her. She pushed him away, telling her aggressor to stop, but her words fell on deaf ears.

She struggled harder, which only infuriated the man. I bought you dinner and fed you drinks all fucking night. We both know where that leads.

The brute spun the blond around and tried to kiss her again, but she continued to refuse.

No, *Shane heard her whimper.* I want to go home.

I don't think so. *The man looked around, certain no one was in sight, and started dragging her into the alley next to the club.* I own your ass.

Fury shot up Shane's back at the increasingly violent scene, and any restraint he felt shattered when he got a glimpse of the woman's face. A pair of terrified and familiar lavender-blue eyes locked with his just before she was dragged into the alley. Maya.

Rage consumed him as Maya's desperate pleas from one of the darkest corners of the city filled his head. Shane bellowed ferociously and flew out of the shadows toward the tortured cries for help. He tore ahead, expecting to find Maya with her attacker, but the tunnel of darkness seemed to go on forever.

Shane flew faster, extended his sonar-like senses in search of Maya and her whimpering calls, but all he found was a limitless void. The tunnel of darkness went on forever, with no end in sight. No sign of Maya, the city, or the bastard who attacked her. Nothing except screams in the dark.

Shane woke with a start and leaped from his bed with Maya's name on his lips. Body tense, senses alert, and eyes wild, he stood motionless in the sparsely furnished but familiar bedroom, attempting to regain his bearings. He was no longer flying through darkness surrounded by Maya's pain but standing alone in his studio apartment and very much awake.

Shane went to the bathroom and switched on the shower, waiting for it to become almost painfully hot. As he stood with his fingers under the steaming streams of water, anger flared at the memory of what he witnessed. Doug Paxton, Olivia's mate and the other Czar of New York, had told Shane that Maya was brutalized on the last night of her human life, but nothing could have prepared Shane for what he saw in the dream. Knowing about it was one thing. Witnessing it and not being able to stop it—well, that was entirely another.

The empty glass bottle skittered across the mahogany bar and the beer, slick with condensation, slid easily into Maya's hand. She winked at the handsome, young human male when he slapped down a twenty-dollar bill with black-painted fingernails and a cocky smirk. Maya made quick work of getting him a fresh drink while giving him the coquettish looks she knew he wanted.

Tonight's boy toy was big, studly, arrogant, horny,

and not the sharpest tool in the shed. Just the way she liked them. Maya tended to the two other customers at her end of the bar but didn't miss the scolding look from Trixie, the other bartender.

Lay off, would ya? Trixie's voice touched Maya's mind with the familiar ease of a fellow coven member. Her coworker glanced over her shoulder and nodded toward Olivia, who was the head of their coven, their maker, and owner of the nightclub. Olivia was making her rounds before closing and like always, she kept one eye on Maya.

You know how much Olivia hates it when you mess with the customers. Trixie's voice, edged with irritation, filled Maya's head.

Jeez, I'm not a child, Trixie. Maya's voice touched Trixie's mind with an exasperated sigh, and she rolled her eyes. *Leave me alone and mind your own business*.

Yeah? Then you leave him *alone*. Trixie kept their telepathic conversation moving while tending the three customers at the other end of the bar. *Come on, girl. Olivia is gonna fucking flip out if you try to feed on this guy. No more live feeds from any customers at The Coven, remember? Like it or lump it. That's the new rule, and it's not that new. It's been almost six months, so I don't know why you're looking to break it and catch a world of shit*.

Yeah? Maya flipped her long, blond hair over a bare shoulder and shot Trixie a narrow-eyed look. *Well, maybe I'm sick of the rules and having everyone in my business*.

Maya slammed her mind shut, preventing any further communication, which clearly annoyed Trixie.

She flipped Maya the bird with a ring-studded hand and shook her head disapprovingly. Maya was so aggravated, she wanted to fly over there and yank Trixie's pink, spiked hair right out of her head. For a girl who looked like a punk-rock rebel, Trixie was sure stuck on following the rules—and unfortunately, even in the world of vampires, there were rules and limitations.

Can't go in the sun or risk turning to dust.

No more sterling silver jewelry because it burns like a bitch.

No feeding on customers from the club.

Blah, blah, blah.

Maya was getting sick and tired of other vampires telling her what to do at *every* turn. It was starting to make her crazy. So what if she liked to play with human men? She fed on them and teased them a little. She took them right to the brink of sex and then denied them the one thing they wanted—but she never hurt them. Hell, after she glamoured them, they never even remembered being with her.

Like all live feeds, Maya absorbed blood memories of her prey, and every time it confirmed her suspicions about what kind of men they were. She had a knack for picking boys who liked to hurt girls, and their blood memories always proved what her gut instinct told her. Most of the men she fed on thrived on dominating women in and out of the bedroom.

In her experience, all men wanted sex and most were driven by lust and desire. The majority of the guys Maya toyed with had used violence at some point in their lives to get sexual gratification. Sex and sexual power were all they wanted, and Maya swore she would never give that to another man again.

Nor would she let anyone take it.

Maya didn't want to kill these men or even hurt them. She simply wanted to know she had control and possessed power she'd never had as a human woman. None of the men she had dallied with had any real memories of their time with her, but Maya did—and it was the only thing that helped quiet the nightmares.

After Olivia turned Maya, she told her that within the first ten years of being changed, all vampires stop dreaming. Maya couldn't wait for that particular part of being a vamp to kick in because she was still having dreams.

Well, not dreams exactly. They were more like nightmares.

She let out a short laugh and punched buttons on the touch screen of the register. *Dreams?* Far from it. The dreams she had as a human would have been a welcome respite from the dark, frightening memory that haunted her sleep more days than she cared to count.

Maya's final mortal night, the last terrifying minutes before she died, replayed when she slept. No matter what she did, regardless of how much she begged and pleaded, her attacker didn't stop. In fact, her cries seemed to excite him more. No one heard her screams for help or her whimpering pleas from the alley, at least not until it was too late.

That's where Olivia had found her five years ago. Raped, beaten, and a heartbeat away from death in the alley behind the club. Left there like garbage by a man who treated her like less than nothing. He was like so many other men who passed through this club night after night, looking for a woman to use and abuse with no second thoughts, no remorse.

During the first few days after Maya was turned, she didn't remember what had happened. In fact, most of her human life was a fuzzy blur. But about a week after she became a vamp, the nightmares started and horrifying terror came with them. She never felt safe, but more than anything else, she loathed feeling like a victim.

Before Maya moved into her own apartment beneath the club, she'd stayed in the guest room of Olivia's place. Some nights Maya's cries woke her maker and she would come running. Olivia would always ask Maya about the dream, but she'd pretend that she couldn't remember and insist it was nothing.

To speak of it with anyone would only feed the fear. The only thing that helped ease Maya's anxiety and gave her some semblance of control was to dominate the human boys who attempted to seduce her. Sometimes, it would even keep the nightmare away for a sleep or two, but eventually the dark memory always came back.

Maya closed out Spike's tab and slid his receipt to him with one pink manicured nail. She smiled, knowing how easily his human mind could be manipulated by the glamour of a vampire. Male or female, no human was a match for her kind, which meant Maya could play all she wanted. There was never any question about who would come out on top, and that was just how she liked it.

Spike was babbling on and on about his motorcycle and how hot she would think it was to ride on it. Maya smiled and fiddled with the teardrop-shaped emerald in her gold necklace, playing up the dumb-blond bit, pretending to be impressed by his blathering.

The smooth, cool stone whispered beneath her

fingers, and she fiddled with the ropy gold chain. Though she wore the necklace every day, there was always something soothing about holding the heirloom in her hands. She had no idea why. Her foggy, jumbled memories of her human life were like puzzle pieces scattered on the floor.

However, she suspected the necklace had been in her human family for generations. When she concentrated and really focused, Maya could picture a smiling, elderly lady wearing the necklace. Her gut instinct told her it was her grandmother, and most of the disjointed memories she had included this woman.

The sad truth was that she had no clue who her family had been or who *she* had been. When Olivia found Maya, she carried no identification, and in the days following the incident, there were no missing persons reports on the news with her picture. Olivia even did an extensive search online but nothing showed up. Even Maya's blood memories were limited to the night she was killed, and the only other piece of information Olivia was able to get was Maya's name.

It was as though Maya never existed until the night she became a vampire.

Tears pricked the back of her eyes at the reality of what that meant. It was heartbreaking to realize that no one was looking for her. What kind of person had she been? Apparently, she wasn't one worth finding.

"So, you wanna take a ride?" Spike asked, bringing Maya back from her thoughts.

Maya let out a sigh and nestled the stone safely in her ample cleavage. No point in dwelling on things or people that no longer made any difference. Her human life was behind her, and the powerful existence of a vampire was the only world that mattered. The gnawing hunger tugged at her gut while she smiled at the human. She was itching for closing time and running out of patience. Thankfully, the place had almost totally emptied out and she wouldn't have to wait much longer.

"Sure, baby. I'd love to take a ride with you." Maya ran one manicured nail over his fingers that clutched the beer. "Just gotta take care of a few things and then I'm all yours."

Maya glanced past her would-be suitor and caught a glimpse of Olivia's long, curly red hair as she ushered out the stragglers. She shot Maya a disapproving look and pointed at her while mouthing, "Stay there."

Maya suppressed a satisfied smile. Normally, vampires could telepath with their makers, siblings, or progeny. However, ever since Olivia found her bloodmate, Doug, more than a few changes had taken place. There was one side effect of Olivia and Doug's unique mating that impacted the rest of the coven, at least aside from her mood swings. Ever since she mated with Doug, Olivia could *only* telepath with him.

To complicate matters for the coven even further, Olivia and Doug were now the Czars of New York City, and both of them had become daywalkers. But the real kicker, the cherry on top, was Olivia's pregnancy.

Jeez, and she thought Olivia was cranky *before* she got pregnant.

Not having the comforting connection of telepathy with her maker had been unsettling at first, but at moments like this, it was a blessing. At least the scolding was limited to verbal lashings.

"Last call, sweetie." Maya winked a long-lashed eye at Spike and leaned on the bar, a move she knew would accentuate her ample cleavage.

The black leather bustier did a fine job on its own, but a little extra pop couldn't hurt. She noted that Spike's lascivious gaze flicked to the sizable emerald in her necklace. With any luck, he'd try to steal it and give her an excuse to kick his ass. Maya never hurt the men she toyed with, not only because it would cause trouble for the coven, but also because violence like that just wasn't in her nature.

Being violent was almost as frightening as being victimized.

"Is there anything else I can *do* for you?"

"Sure," Spike said with a lopsided grin. He took a long pull off his beer and leered at her over the bottle. "Come with me after you get out of here, and I'll get you off about ten minutes after that."

Maya suppressed an eye roll but kept a smile plastered on her face. Just when she was about to tell Spike she'd meet him outside, a dark shadow loomed large next to the young man and a powerful wave of energy wafted over her.

Shane.

Maya flicked her gaze to the hulking form that appeared out of nowhere. Though Shane wasn't looking at her, and his energy was tuned into the human, she was still transfixed.

Shane Quesada was one of the sentry soldiers for the Presidium in New York. He also was easily the best-looking specimen of a man she'd ever laid eyes on. Maya was only five foot five, and he loomed over her at well past six feet. He had gorgeous olive-toned skin, a thick muscular build, and a head of wavy, chestnut brown hair that looked silky soft.

The man was a feast for the eyes, and the only thing hotter than how he looked was how he sounded. Something about the deep, rich baritone of his voice made her weak with desire, but after meeting him a few months ago, she quickly discovered that Shane was about as much fun as a nun at a keg party.

He was totally uptight, all about following the rules, and she was fairly sure he left his sense of humor in another century. Not only that, but he moved like a ghost and had developed the nasty habit of messing up her dates like it was part of his freaking job.

"It's time for you to go." Shane's voice, quiet and powerful, captured Spike's attention.

Spike held the bottle in midair and stared straight ahead, wavering slightly when the glamour effect took hold. Watching the scene unfold, it dawned on her that Shane wasn't making eye contact with the kid and was glamouring the human with only the sound of his voice. Maya swallowed and took an involuntary step back, unnerved by the scope of Shane's power.

The combination of Shane's inescapable presence and the unsettling attraction she felt for him created an overall feeling of unease. It made Maya feel out of control and vulnerable—two things she loathed. Since becoming a vampire, the only other time she felt that way was when she relived the attack in her dreams.

"You did not enjoy yourself here, and therefore, you won't return." Shane leaned closer, his voice dropping to almost inaudible tones before he flicked his dark, piercing gaze at Maya and whispered, "Never again."

Maya's stomach fluttered, and when his eyes locked with hers, an odd sense of recognition crept into her mind. From the deep corners of her memory, an image of that dark, piercing stare ran through her mind, and in a rush of panic...*she remembered.*

Shane had been in her nightmare.

Those deep brown eyes—intense, laser sharp, and full of fury—had been in her nightmare yesterday. Her brow furrowed. Shane had been there, lurking in the shadows of her nightmare. *Watching*. Maya's body tensed and shook with confusion as the gravity of this revelation settled over her.

Shane's eyes narrowed and he stared back at her, but his hulking form didn't flinch. Was that really possible, or was she imagining it? Could Shane have been in the dreamscape? Was he so powerful a vampire that he'd found a way to infiltrate the dreams of a youngling vampire like her?

Maya's jaw set. The how wasn't important, but the *why* was. Why would he spy on her and watch her being attacked while doing nothing to help? What kind of sick, evil son of a bitch gets off on watching something like that? Not only that, but who the hell gave him permission to spy on her in the dreamscape or right here in the bar?

Anger and confusion flashing, she shoved herself away from the bar and glared at him. Shane didn't retreat but simply held her stare with his usual calm arrogance. Was it arrogance or was it something else... distaste? Did he think she was a whore for flirting with this human and others like him? Did Shane think she deserved what happened to her that night?

Maya bit back tears, refusing to cry in front of him even though the accusing voice of shame kept rolling around in her head. The truth was, Shane wasn't the one saying those things, *she* was. She *had* been drunk that fateful night and had flirted with her date from minute one.

Maybe she had asked for it.

"This place sucks." The boy blinked and put his beer down while giving Maya a wary look. He took cash out of his back pocket and tossed it on the bar before mumbling something inaudible and walking away. "I'm outta here."

"Good riddance," Shane murmured as he watched the boy leave.

"You're a killjoy," Maya said, scooping up the money, turning her back on Shane, and closing out the sale. "What's your deal, anyway? Do you get off by ruining my fun?"

She slammed the register drawer shut, grabbed a wet rag from the sink, and started wiping down the bar. She had to create busywork for herself and get out from under the weight of Shane's accusing gaze. She was remarkably unsettled by that flashing memory of his eyes in her nightmare but determined to shake off the feeling. She refused to allow this stodgy, old vampire to steal the tiny bit of sanity she clung to.

Maya swallowed the urge to scream and rubbed at the bar faster. She glanced at Shane. He was walking slowly along the opposite side of the bar, keeping his eyes on her with his hands at his sides.

It was ridiculous. How could Shane have been in her dream…unless?

What if he had actually *been* there that night five years ago? What if he was there, outside that alley, and witnessed what happened but did nothing to help her? Maybe she'd repressed that part of the memory until now.

Panic, fear, and shame filled her, but she refused to cry.

"That human was beneath you," Shane said quietly. He stood in front of her with his large, dark eyes tracking her every move. His long leather coat, undoubtedly lined with various sentry weapons, hung over his massive frame with almost regal perfection. "You should know that."

"Exactly," Maya said with forced sweetness. She refused to let Shane know how unsettled he'd made her. "That *was* kind of the point."

"Why do you insist on wasting time with these human men?" He cocked his head to one side, the sharp angles of his masculine face and his chin covered by a perpetual five-o'clock shadow revealed in flickers by the strobe lights of the club. "It's not simply for their blood, is it?"

"I'll tell you what it is. It's none of your business." Maya paused mid-swipe and puffed a long, blond strand of hair off her face, wrestling with her waning patience. "Why is everyone so damn concerned with what I'm doing?"

"It may not be my business." Shane stepped closer, so the buckle of the belt on his leather pants clinked against the edge of the bar. He rested both hands on the bar and leaned in, that mesmerizing gaze latched firmly onto hers. "But I'm asking anyway."

She needed to create some distance between herself and the powerful vampire. He unnerved her. Not because she thought he was going to hurt her but simply due to the power he possessed and the way her body reacted to his.

Every time those glittering eyes locked onto hers, she felt like a light switch went off inside her—but she willed away the sensation. What was the point of entertaining feelings like that when she had no intention of acting on them?

However, he was unavoidable, and night after night for the past few months, he'd been coming to the club, staring her down but saying little. His mere presence was unsettling. Shane was centuries older than she was and radiated raw, unadulterated strength.

She'd heard stories about his skills in battle, and the other girls in the coven speculated about his skills in the bedroom. Trixie and Sadie took bets to see who could bed him first, but he seemed oblivious to their advances. He was a warrior. A sentry with hundreds of years of experience, and by all accounts, the man was death incarnate.

Shane moved in between shadows like a phantom. Even for a vampire, he was fast.

"Tell me, Maya." His voice seemed to surround her and pulled her from her thoughts. Her belly quivered as he leaned closer. "Why?"

Chapter 2

Before Maya could answer him, Olivia's all-too-familiar voice interrupted their conversation.

"I'm glad to see you sent that kid on his way." Olivia let out a weary sigh and sat on the bar stool to Shane's right. Her bright green eyes studied Maya carefully. While rubbing her swollen belly, she said, "I'm impressed you showed such restraint. That one was right up your alley."

Maya said nothing. Shrugging, she cast a glance at Shane, who was giving her a smug, satisfied look. It made Maya want to punch him square in the nose. The house lights flicked on brightly, bringing Shane's arrogant grin into full view, and when the music shut off, his voice seemed to fill the entire club.

"Yes." Shane pushed his hands off the bar and folded his arms over his chest. "Impressive, indeed."

"Seriously, Maya." Olivia ran a hand through her long, red curls and smiled. "You've come a long way in the last few months. Listen, I know I've been kind of bitchy and cranky, but this pregnancy has me all screwed up. Do you know I actually ate food the other day? Actual *human* food. I made Doug go out in the middle of the afternoon to get me a hot dog."

"A hot dog?" Shane asked with more than a little disgust. "I won't even eat the hot dog vendor because of the stench."

"I didn't realize you were such a snob," Maya teased.

"I prefer to think that I have high standards," Shane responded with a lopsided grin.

"Sounds snobby to me." Trixie hoisted herself up onto the bar and sat behind Olivia. "Doug was probably just happy to have an excuse to go out in the sun." Trixie cracked her knuckles and stretched her arms over her pink-haired head. "Damn. I'm not much for monogamy, but if I have a bloodmate out there, he better get his ass to New York quick. I'd love to feel the sun on my skin again—but I could do without getting knocked up and eating hot dogs. Gross."

"Yeah." Olivia made a face. "Don't ask me why or how, but I ate the whole thing. The worst part is that I freaking loved it—or the baby did. Anyway," she said on a sigh, "I'm sorry if I've been tough on everyone, but you know how important it is that we leave the customers alone. It's in the best interest of the coven. My weirdo pregnancy is drawing enough attention from the supernaturals." She rolled her eyes and let out a short laugh. "This is the pregnancy heard round the world, and apparently it's high on the list of things to discuss at this year's summit in Geneva."

"Why do they even have that stupid meeting every year?" Trixie snorted. "Were, Amoveo, and vamp stuffed shirts all in one place? Sounds like a fuckin' bore."

"And the Fae, the Brotherhood, and the Witches," Olivia added. "Don't forget them."

"They gather to share information and keep the lines of communication open." Shane's voice cut through the room. "It started centuries ago. The first summit was the catalyst for the truce between our race and the werewolves."

"Truce or no truce, I still don't trust the wolves." Olivia's tone grew serious. "I think it's ridiculous that a pregnant vampire warrants attention from the world's supernatural leaders." She shrugged. "Whatever."

"Why are they even going to discuss it?" Maya's brows knit together with concern. Olivia may be bossy and a killjoy, but she was also Maya's maker and her friend. No matter what rules she made Maya follow, she'd love Olivia like a mother for her entire existence. "What are they worried about?"

"Human politicians aren't the only ones who waste time and money." Olivia's words were laced with exasperation. "The other supernaturals probably want reassurance from the Emperor that he's not plotting some kind of master vampire race or something."

"Will they all be in attendance?" Shane asked casually. Maya noticed the way his body seemed tightly wound and ready for action at all times. "I assume the Emperor has a sentry attending with him?"

"Yes and yes. King Heinrich of the wolves, Prince Richard Muldavi of the Amoveo, Zemi the Fae queen, and Willow from the Witches' Council. I heard the Brotherhood is being represented by Asmodeus. Anyway, thanks again, Maya, for sending that guy on his way. I like to avoid trouble with humans on a regular day—and especially during the stupid summit week."

"Actually, I didn't send him away." Maya tossed the rag into the sink without taking her eyes off Shane. She jutted her chin toward him and leaned back against the register. "He did."

"Really?" Olivia's red brows flew up and she looked from Shane to Maya. Running one hand over her rounded belly, she said, "Then I should be thanking Shane while I remind *you* of the rules."

"Maybe I'm sick of the rules," Maya snapped, frustration crawling up her back. Olivia said nothing but arched one eyebrow in response. "Maybe I'm tired of living and working under a damn microscope all the time with every vampire in Manhattan trying to control me and tell me what to do."

"No one is trying to control you, Maya." Olivia's tone softened and she looked at Maya with something akin to pity, which only made it worse. Nobody else knew the extent of the attack Maya suffered like Olivia did, and whenever she gave Maya that look, it made her feel pathetic.

"This is not just about you, Maya, and you know it. Everyone has had to adjust to the new rules, and really, it's only *one* new rule. No feeding on customers in the club. We live in a big city with millions of able-bodied people. Why are you fighting me on this?"

"I'm tired of everyone butting into my life. Maybe I just want to be able to go to work without feeling like my every move is being watched."

"What are you saying?" Olivia asked with genuine curiosity. "I thought you liked working at The Coven."

"I do—I mean, I did—but it's just too much, Olivia." Maya kept her attention on Olivia but could feel the weight of everyone else's stares. Even Damien had come in from his position bouncing at the door and now stood by Shane. "All of us working together all night and living right next door in the apartments downstairs. Besides, with everything going on, I thought you'd be happy to be rid of me for a while."

"You're one to complain," Trixie interjected. "If I have to listen to one more Celine Dion song, I might scream. That shit seeps through the apartment walls and makes me crazy, but you don't hear me complaining."

"Trixie." Olivia held up one hand but kept her concerned expression on Maya. "Let her finish."

Maya straightened her back, finally voicing the frustration she'd been feeling over the past few months.

"I mean it's different for you and Doug, Olivia. You guys are mates and have your own place at the Presidium's offices, but…I don't know…living and working together…it's too much. I feel like I'm suffocating and the walls are closing in on me."

Before Maya could respond, an unfamiliar voice boomed through the club.

"This isn't the only joint in town, kid."

Irritation flickered over Shane's face at the sound of Rat's voice slithering into the club. Maya didn't have to look at Olivia to know how displeased she was by the vampire's arrival.

"Hello, Rat," Olivia said wearily.

"Dude, your timing sucks," Trixie said, laughing.

"To what do we owe the pleasure?" Shane murmured, turning slightly to his left and peering down at their unwelcome visitor.

Rat was short and bald with a wiry build, and while he was stronger than any human, he was no match for Shane. The guy owned a strip club in the city that catered to both humans and vampires, but everyone knew it was a cover for a prostitution ring. Maya gave Rat a quick smile and fiddled with the emerald in her necklace. She didn't miss the look of disapproval from Shane, but of course, that only encouraged her. Maya knew Rat found her attractive, and even though she wasn't interested, if flirting with him would annoy Shane, then she was all for it.

"Don't you have your own club to tend to?" Shane said tightly.

"Nice to see you too, Quesada." Rat sat on a bar stool to Shane's left and winked at Maya. When he grinned, his two gold front teeth glinted at her. His bald head gleamed like a lightbulb, and the tattoo of a viper slithered out from beneath his collar, around his neck, and up the back of his skull. "You're a barrel of laughs, Quesada. I'm starvin'. You got anything back there for your nonhuman clientele, blondie?"

"Her name is Maya," Shane interjected before Maya could respond, while sending a glance toward her. "You would do well to address her like you would a lady."

A lady? Yeah, right. Maya almost scoffed out loud. She nestled the necklace in her cleavage before plastering on a big smile.

"Don't you pay any attention to him, Rat. You can call me whatever you like. Shane may be the sentry of the city, but he's not my maker, my daddy, or my husband." Maya smiled broadly at Rat, reached beneath the bar, and pulled out a bottle of blood. It was common practice for all vampire establishments to keep blood on hand, just in case. Leaning both elbows on the bar, she wiggled the bottle at Rat, and if she didn't know better, she'd swear she heard a growl coming from Shane. "Shall I heat it up for you?"

"No, that's okay, *Maya*," Rat said dramatically as he took the bottle from her. "Room temp is just fine."

Shane watched Rat remove the cap and drink the blood greedily while keeping his beady eyes on Maya or, more specifically, her cleavage. Shane pulled out a stool and sat between Rat and Olivia and directly in front of Maya.

"I may not be Maya's maker, but I am in charge of keeping order in this city among our kind." Folding his hands on the bar, he didn't miss the face Maya made before pushing herself away from the counter. Shane smirked and flicked his attention back to Rat. "State your business or be on your way, because as you can see, the club is closed. I'm sure Damien and the ladies have things they need to be doing."

"I came by to see the czar, not you, so how about if you go fuck yourself? As far as the ladies are concerned," he said with a wink to Maya, "I have plenty of things they can *do*."

"Not with you." Trixie cringed.

"Oh please." Olivia sighed.

In a blink, Shane grabbed Rat by the neck, stood from his seat, and held him in midair like a rag doll. The smaller, younger vampire flailed his legs uselessly, bared his fangs, and clawed at Shane's hand, but it was no use. Standing away from the bar, Shane continued to dangle Rat a foot off the ground with absolute ease. Maya didn't realize she was backing away until her butt hit the register. Trixie hopped off the bar and linked her arm through Maya's in a reassuring gesture.

That is one badass vampire. Trixie's voice, laced with awe and admiration, flickered into Maya's mind.

More like bossy, Maya shot back.

And sexy. Trixie bumped her hip against Maya's

playfully. *Damn, girl. Can't forget sexy. I'd give my left fang to take a tumble with him, but if you ask me, he's got it bad for you.*

No way. Maya didn't want to admit that she thought Shane was sexy. She locked eyes with Shane and her stomach flip-flopped, reminding her, briefly, of what it was like to be human.

His lips lifted at the corners briefly before he looked back at Rat.

"You try my patience." Shane's tone, low and deadly, filled the club, which had fallen silent. Sadie, the club's DJ and Olivia's oldest coven member, flew down from the DJ platform and stood in a protective position next to Olivia. "As you can see, the rest of Maya's coven is not in the mood for you and your misogynistic attitude, either."

"Misogynistic?" Sadie folded her arms over her breasts, nodding her approval. "I'm impressed. You're full of surprises, Shane."

"No surprise how bossy he is," Maya muttered.

Shane slanted a doubtful look in Maya's direction before turning his attention back to Rat. "Olivia is the czar of this district, and when you are in my presence, you will treat her and every other woman you encounter with respect." He put Rat back on his feet, yanked him close, and growled in his ear. "Or you will deal with me."

"Let him go, Quesada," Olivia said evenly. "We'll give him three minutes to say what he came to say and then he'll be leaving. Won't you, Rat?"

Maya did her best to stop staring at Shane, but it was an effort in futility. In spite of his annoyingly overbearing nature, he was magnetic, powerful, and frightening all at once. Maya's fingers drifted to the necklace again as she studied him. It was no secret that Rat was a troublemaker and would probably stab Olivia in the back in a hot minute, so she couldn't really blame Shane for his reaction.

"Yes," Rat gurgled and his eyes bugged out.

"Speak." Shane released him but stood ready to take further action. He glanced briefly at Maya. "And choose your words carefully."

"Thanks." Rat rubbed at his neck absently and took a step backward, increasing the distance between himself and Shane, but he backed right into Damien, the club's bouncer. Rat almost jumped out of his skin. "Shit, your coven just seems to come out of the fuckin' woodwork, Olivia."

"Two minutes and thirty seconds," Shane murmured.

"Alright, alright." Rat held his hands up. "I just wanted to let the czars know that we've got some special visitors coming into the city, and given Olivia's *condition*, I thought she'd want a heads-up."

"What visitors?" Olivia asked quietly.

"Werewolves." A smile slithered over his face. A collective groan rose from the group. Wolves and vampires had battled each other since the beginning of time, and even though a treaty was in place, the tension still ran thick beneath the surface. A few lone wolves lived in the city but not an entire pack. "Not just any wolves. It's the prince and his little pack of bachelors."

"Royalty?" Maya asked with genuine curiosity. She'd never met a werewolf, let alone a royal. "That's exciting."

"That is not the word I would choose," Shane murmured.

"What a shocker." Maya rolled her eyes.

Shut up. Trixie elbowed Maya. *Can't you tell how freaked out Olivia is?*

Maya looked at her maker and guilt tugged at her. Trixie was right. Olivia seemed unsettled by Rat's announcement.

"Shit," Olivia groused. "King Heinrich's son? I am in no mood to placate an overprivileged little werewolf punk. Damn it. I'm sure that Emperor Zhao is going to be annoyed," Olivia said, referencing the leader of all vampires.

"Do you think it has to do with your pregnancy?" Sadie asked with concern. She tucked a long strand of brown hair behind her ear and wrapped an arm over Olivia's shoulder. "A pack comes to town right before you give birth? That's just too much of a coincidence for me."

"Do you think they're coming here looking for a fight?" Trixie asked. "Or maybe they're on some kind of recon mission."

"I suppose it's possible, but I doubt it. King Heinrich has always been forthcoming in the past, which is why I'm surprised he didn't mention this visit to the Emperor. I've always gotten a heads-up from the Presidium's main office in Hong Kong before a visit like this. Hell, even the lone wolves or couples who visit here notify us before they arrive, let alone an entire pack."

"And they're coming into the city while we are down a sentry," Shane said. "Pete is not scheduled to return from paternity leave for another month. This sounds more unappealing by the second."

Shane was referring to Pete Castro, a vampire sentry whose mate, an Amoveo shapeshifter, had delivered twins about six months ago. Olivia had granted him time off to be with Marianna and the babies, but it seemed really weird to hear this centuries-old vampire say the words "paternity leave."

"You and Paxton sure have modernized your little corner of the vampire world," Rat said with thinly veiled disgust. "What's next? Sun insurance?"

It was glaringly apparent to Maya that other vampires, as well as other supernaturals, were irked by Olivia's pregnancy. Bloodmates created daywalking vampires, and based on Olivia's pregnancy, they could possibly create daywalking offspring. If more vampires found their bloodmates, then what would that mean for the old-fashioned kind who burst into flames in the sunlight?

"When are they arriving and how long are they staying?" Olivia asked.

"They get here tomorrow night and are planning on staying for a week. I heard they're staying in the Presidential Suite at the Plaza."

A look of concentration settled over Olivia, one that Maya recognized. She could tell Olivia was telepathing with Doug, the other czar and her mate. Olivia's green eyes refocused and flicked back to Rat.

"How did you come across this little tidbit of information, Rat? King Heinrich should have been the one to alert us to his son's visit."

"Viola, one of my familiars," Rat said, referring to the handful of humans who know about the existence of vampires. "She hooked up with one of the prince's flunkies when she was back home in Alaska visiting her mom. Anyway, all of my familiars are loyal to me."

Rat smirked and Maya didn't miss the look of annoyance on Olivia's face. Having too many humans involved in vampire business always made her uncomfortable.

"Viola came in to work tonight blathering on about how her new werewolf boyfriend was coming to the city for a visit. She's a bit of a star-fucker and is moony-eyed that she's banging a guy directly connected to royalty. The king is at the fuckin' summit or something, so I'm getting the feeling that the kid didn't ask Daddy's permission. Otherwise, I'm sure *you* would have known about this before *me*."

"I don't blame Olivia for being concerned," Sadie said. "Our truce with the wolves has been solid for the past two centuries, but it was King Heinrich's great-grandfather who signed the treaty on behalf of the wolves—not him. You also said it's a pack of bachelor wolves, which makes them even more dangerous." Sadie's expression grew dark and her voice wavered. "They're even more vicious when they're unmated."

"Wolves cannot be trusted," Shane said quietly. "We should take every precaution."

"Which son is it?" Olivia's brows knit together. "If memory serves, he has a couple."

"No clue." Rat shrugged. "I told you everything I know."

Yeah, right. Trixie's sharp tone touched Maya's mind. *This guy is such a dirtbag.*

He did come and warn Olivia, Maya responded. *He didn't have to do that.*

"Thank you, Rat." Olivia smiled tightly. "However, next time you have a message for Doug and me—for the czars—I suggest you follow the proper channels and get an appointment at the Presidium. As you and the rest of the community know, Suzie, one of my coven members, is now the Presidium's secretary in New York. No more Presidium business at my nightclub." Her green eyes glittered and she bared her fangs. "Got it?"

"Sure." Rat shrugged. "Whatever you say."

A breeze whisked through the room, and a second later, Doug was standing behind Olivia and glaring at Rat. "That didn't sound very sincere to me," Doug ground out. His hands were placed protectively on Olivia's shoulders as he stared Rat down. A pang of longing struck Maya when she watched the tenderness Doug showed Olivia.

I wonder what it feels like to be loved that way? Maya thought wistfully to no one in particular.

How did it feel to have a man be so loving and protective like that? She swallowed the sudden lump in her throat and glanced at Shane, who to her surprise, was staring back at her with a look of curiosity. Studying her intently, he tilted his head to the left and his eyes narrowed. For a moment, he seemed like he was going to ask her something, but the sound of Rat's voice quickly broke the spell.

"Like I said," Rat said, leering, "they come out of the freaking woodwork. Yeah, I got it. No more politics in the bar. Speaking of which, I better get back to mine. Gotta clean the place up nice for our visitors. I've never had royalty come by The Dollhouse before, and my girls are pretty psyched. Even my vampire dames are giddy."

"Please remind *your dames*," Doug said with mild irritation, "that feeding on werewolves is strictly forbidden. From what I hear, werewolf blood is like a fuckin' drug, so tell them to steer clear."

"That is so weird, man." Trixie snorted and shook her head. "If we get bitten by a werewolf, their saliva can kill us, but if we drink their blood, it gets us fuckin' stoned and hopped up like super-vamps?"

"Well, I don't know why any of this supernatural

crap works the way that it does." Doug looked at each of them earnestly. "All I care about is this coven, my mate, and our baby. I heard about the war with the wolves, and the last thing I want is to rekindle that crap. Especially with Olivia so close to giving birth. So remind your girls there's no feeding on the wolves."

"No problem," Rat said with an insincere smile. His beady eyes flicked to Olivia's swollen belly and he smirked. "Daddy."

"What about the prince?" Maya asked with genuine curiosity. "Is he single?"

"That is irrelevant." Shane's fangs erupted and he sent a dark look in Maya's direction. "You will do well to steer clear of the wolves, Maya. They are savage, unpredictable creatures and aren't the kind of men you want to toy with. Unlike the czar, I *do* remember the war, and it is not one we want to risk starting again."

"Oh really?" Maya seethed. "Well, *old man*, I don't recall asking for your opinion or advice."

Shane arched an eyebrow at her and an amused expression flickered over his face. "Old man?"

"Maybe not," Olivia added. "But I *am* your maker, and I have to agree with Shane." She rose from the bar stool and stepped back so she could look each of her coven members in the eyes. "I would like all of you to refrain from hunting while the wolves are visiting. The last thing we need is trouble, and in my experience, wolves are exactly that."

"So we're grounded again?" Maya asked.

"You're not grounded," Doug said. He smiled and slipped his arm around Olivia. "It's more like self-preservation. Just no hunting while the wolves are here in town and bottle feeds only. We all know that live feeds can get us all charged up."

"In fact, I'm going to send a district-wide email to alert the community." The line between Olivia's eyes deepened. "I'll be asking all vamps in the city to refrain from live feeds and hunting while the wolves are in town. I just hope everyone behaves themselves and does what's requested."

"Shit," Maya whispered. She enjoyed hunting because it was the one time she felt free. "Well, since they're not here yet, can we go out and hunt tonight?"

"Sure." Olivia nodded and smiled at Doug, who placed a large hand on her belly. "Just keep an eye out. Like we've said, the wolves are unpredictable and could decide to come into town earlier than expected."

"There's plenty of blood behind the bar," Shane interjected. He folded his arms over his chest and leveled a stern gaze at Maya. His voice dropped low. "I'm sure that will suffice, but if not, I will accompany Maya on her hunt tonight."

Maya's mouth fell open in shock. After everything she said before, he still insisted on monitoring her every move. She slipped out of Trixie's embrace, holding Shane's stare as she stepped closer to the bar. Leaning both hands on the smooth surface, she met his challenging gaze. "I don't want or need a babysitter."

"I disagree," Shane ground out.

Silence fell over the room again. Even though everyone looked from Shane to Maya, she barely noticed them because she was too pissed.

"Like I said before..." Rat shouted. Maya was so fixated on Shane that she hadn't even noticed that Rat was leaving. "This isn't the only joint in town, Maya. If you want a change of scenery, we could always use a pretty little thing like you over at The Dollhouse. I've got a bartending gig that's all yours if you want it." He tapped the big promotional picture that hung at the front of the club, the one that featured all of the girls dressed in vampire garb and baring their fangs. "I may not have slick advertisements like this, but The Dollhouse is still a fun place. You know where to find me, kid."

Rat breezed out and the doors closed behind him with a muffled thump. A smile spread over Maya's face. Rat had just offered her a job and an opportunity to get some breathing room and maybe even create a life of her own.

"Aww, man," Trixie moaned. "If Maya quits, does that mean we have to do another stupid photo shoot without her? Vampires pretending to be humans pretending to be vampires." She rolled her eyes. "So freakin' lame."

Maya ignored Trixie's comment and smiled at Shane. "Looks like I have another job offer."

"Over my dead body," he murmured.

"Don't you mean undead?"

"You will not work for a piece of slime like him." Shane's jaw set and the muscle flickered beneath his stubble-covered jaw. "Not a chance."

"Like I said before," Maya continued, dropping her voice to a breathy whisper. "I wasn't asking for permission."

"Olivia, can you please talk some sense into her?"

"Our coven is a family, Shane." Olivia's voice, edged with sadness, pulled Maya from her battle of wills with Shane. "Maya isn't a prisoner here. If she needs some space and wants to get a job somewhere else, then while I may not agree with it, I respect her right to choose."

"Really?" Maya's voice was strained.

"Yes." Olivia leaned into Doug's embrace and lifted one shoulder. "I'm not thrilled at the idea of you working for a guy like Rat, but you have every right to make this kind of decision for yourself."

"Thank you." Maya fought back tears and looked around the room at the rest of the coven. All of them looked at her with the same accepting and slightly sad look that Olivia had. Except for Shane. He was visibly furious.

"You would allow her to go work at the very club where a pack of wolves is about to congregate?"

"It doesn't thrill me, but I'll have to trust Maya to behave properly." She leveled a stern gaze at Maya. "And if you do decide to work there, I will expect you to be back at the apartments immediately after work, at least while the wolves are in town."

Without another word, Maya launched herself off the ground and flew over the bar before gathering Olivia in a weepy hug.

"Thank you," she whispered. "Thank you so much, Olivia."

"You're welcome." Olivia pulled back and looked Maya in the eyes. Brushing Maya's blond hair off her face, she cradled Maya's cheek lovingly and her tone grew serious. "Just remember what we've said about the wolves, Maya. They are nothing like human men… Do you understand what I'm getting at?"

You can't glamour a wolf the way you can the human boys. Trixie's voice drifted into Maya's mind with sisterly concern. *You better be careful, girl.*

Have you ever tried it? Maya asked. When Trixie

didn't respond, Maya knew what the answer was. *Don't worry. I know what I'm doing.*

"I understand." Maya nodded and swiped at the tears that fell in spite of her best efforts to stop them. She knew Olivia didn't want her toying with a werewolf the way she did with the humans, and that was fine by Maya. She didn't miss the glare Shane was giving her but avoided catching his eye. "And no live feeds while the wolves are in town. I promise. But tonight…I'm going hunting."

In a blink, Maya flew to the front doors of the club and stopped just before leaving. She spun around, her long, blond hair spilling down her back, and winked at a visibly annoyed Shane. "If you insist on tagging along, then you'll have to catch me first…old man."

"Fine." Pulling on the leather sentry gloves, Shane took a step forward with his sights set firmly on her. "I'll even give you a head start." He took one step closer. "Ready?"

A surge of anticipation mixed with adrenaline shot through Maya and she placed one hand on the massive wooden doors of the club. Her chin titled defiantly and she nodded. "Always."

Shane took another step nearer. "Set."

"Seriously? There are only a couple of hours until sunrise. I won't be out that long." Maya's eyes narrowed, and in spite of her best efforts, she couldn't stop the smile that played at her lips. "Don't you have better things to do?"

Shane shook his head and whispered, "Go."

The last thing Maya saw before flying out into the crisp November night was the sexy smile on Shane's face. Flying swiftly through the dark Manhattan sky with Shane in hot pursuit, one thought kept racing through her mind.

For the first time in a long time, Maya wanted a man to catch her.

Chapter 3

SHANE GAVE MAYA A HEALTHY HEAD START, ALLOWing her the space he knew she so desperately craved, but he never lost her scent. He whisked through the city sky, high above the streets littered with humans squeezing the last bit of life out of the night, and he realized that he was smiling.

Maya Robertson, the youngling vampire with a penchant for troublemaking, was by far the most beguiling vampire he'd encountered in four centuries. She was defiant, impulsive, and flirtatious, but he saw a frighteningly fragile woman hiding behind her blustery bravado.

That was the woman he wanted to discover. No, "wanted" wasn't the right word. Needed. He needed to peel back the mask she wore to reveal the woman buried beneath pain and fear. Memories of seeing her attacked in the dreamscape came roaring to mind. Shane growled and increased his speed when he tuned in to Maya's scent. It was an unmistakable combination of violets and Ivory soap, a clean, fresh scent that stood out in stark contrast to the sharp-tongued vixen she showed to the world.

There was more to Maya than met the eye, and admittedly, there was more between the two of them than trading spirited barbs. Not only had he been pulled into the dreamscape, but at the club, he could have sworn he actually heard her voice in his mind. Her voice full of longing and sadness... *I wonder what it feels like to be loved that way?*

At least he thought he did, but it was so frustratingly brief, Shane wasn't certain if he'd imagined it.

The only other vampires with whom he could still telepath were his two surviving siblings. His maker was long dead and Shane had no progeny. He'd never created another vampire because the responsibility was more than he was prepared to take on. He had always been tied to his work, and until these past few months, that was all he'd been interested in.

Meeting Maya had changed the game.

The sound of light, feminine giggling whistled up from the park below as Maya's scent grew stronger. He could tell she'd found her prey for the night. Shane sharpened his focus and tuned in to the sound of Maya's voice while he made a swift, silent descent into one of the dark, wooded areas of Central Park.

He scanned the darkness of the hauntingly quiet area with both the heightened night vision and the sonar-like senses of a vampire. She was close. The incoherent mumbling of a human man rumbled along with the soft, hypnotic tone of Maya's unmistakable voice. Shane set his mouth in a tight line at the realization that she had glamoured a human man. Again.

He was flooded by a sudden and unexpected wave of jealousy, and his fangs erupted on a growl when he spotted her amid the shadows of the trees. She had pinned the man against the trunk of a massive oak tree, and her blond hair glinted in the moonlight while she held him there easily. The guy couldn't have been more than twenty-five years old, and the disheveled suit he wore looked like it belonged to his father.

Based on the strong scent of booze in the air, the boy

was highly intoxicated and didn't need much glamouring, but Maya clearly didn't mind. His round, youthful face lolled to one side, and a wistful smile bloomed as Maya whispered seductive promises in his ear. Shane moved closer but stayed behind a neighboring tree. Maya hadn't spotted him yet, and for the moment, he wanted to keep it that way. The ability to conceal his presence was one of the unique gifts he'd perfected over time.

Maya loosened the boy's collar, baring the sensitive skin of his throat, and her delicate hand cradled his chin before she tilted his head with her thumb. Shane fought the urge to fly over there and pull her off the incapacitated human to create distance between her flesh and his. The feelings of jealousy were ridiculous, but that didn't make them any less real. He'd watched thousands of vampires feed over the years, even his maker, and had never been rendered so totally and completely out of sorts.

Maya lifted her bare leg and wrapped it around the boy's, which pushed her short skirt to dangerous heights. Her silky-looking blond hair spilled down her back in tempting waves, and Shane's fingers curled at his sides as he imagined what tangling his hands in those long locks would feel like. His body tightened at the mere idea of touching Maya, of brushing his fingertips up her firm, toned legs and discovering what was hidden beneath that little black skirt.

Shane blinked. What the hell was wrong with him? He hadn't thought about a woman in that way in centuries, yet here he was, standing under a tree in Central Park with the beginnings of a hard-on.

The boy moaned and mumbled something incoherent, pulling Shane from his thoughts. Maya pressed her body tightly against the boy, and just before sinking her fangs into the neck of her prey, she whipped her head around, locking gazes with Shane.

He froze. No one had ever spotted him or picked up on his presence unless he allowed it.

Until now.

A fanged grin cracked Maya's face. Winking at Shane, she whispered, "I win."

A growl rumbled low in his chest at the sight of Maya piercing the tender flesh of the boy's neck. The eyes of her prey widened briefly, and his body went limp while Maya fed. After not even a minute, Maya released him, licked his wound closed, whispered a new memory into his ear, and stepped back. The glamoured human mumbled something incoherent, staggered toward the path, and wandered off into the night no worse for wear.

Shane's eyes narrowed. Something far more than the desire for blood was driving her. She'd barely fed and couldn't have gotten enough to sustain herself for long, which could mean only one thing—she would want to hunt again.

Maya adjusted the black leather bustier and repositioned the emerald necklace that was ever present around her long, lovely neck. She ran her hands through her hair and watched the boy disappear into the night, but Shane couldn't take his eyes off her.

Her alabaster skin practically glowed in the moonlight. Shane removed his leather gloves, the ones he wore to protect himself from the silver weapons he used in battle, and shoved them into the pockets of his long coat. He flexed his bare hands and allowed himself to imagine what it would be like to touch her. To run his fingertips along the curve of her shoulder, to trace a line down the length of her neck with his tongue and sink his fangs into the sweet spot beneath her ear. The wickedly decadent images flickered through his mind, making his body tighten further.

In the blink of an eye, and without realizing he'd done it, Shane had closed the distance between them and found himself standing directly behind her. Maya's petite frame was dwarfed by his own and wavered just inches from him.

"I knew you liked to watch." Her voice, quiet and edged with bitterness, cut into the silence of the night. Maya spun around and stormy, dark blue eyes latched onto his. "Do you get off on that?"

"You are the one who challenged me to follow you." Perplexed by her obvious anger at his presence, Shane knit his brows together. He inched closer, his gaze wandering over her face, memorizing every curve. "Or did you forget?"

Maya's eyes widened with every inch of personal space that he invaded, yet she didn't retreat. "I remember telling you and everyone else that I'm tired of having my every move monitored." She placed her hands on her hips and met his challenging stare. "You're a sentry and supposedly some badass warrior, but you're spending the last hours of your night spying on me? What's your deal? Are you trying to get brownie points with Doug and Olivia? Do you get some kind of bonus for following me around and messing with my life?"

"Hardly."

"Then what's your damage, dude?"

"Actually"—Shane tilted his head slightly to one side and folded his arms over his chest—"that was going to be my question for you."

"What?" Maya blinked and took a step back. "Me? What are you talking about?"

"Yes, you." Shane leaned closer and his voice dropped low. "Why do you insist on hunting but barely feed on your prey?" Maya said nothing and took another step backward, but Shane persisted. He dropped his hands and continued moving toward her, even though she moved farther away.

"You only hunt men, and from what I've observed over the past few months, your taste in human men is... Well, let's just say it's questionable. You don't just hunt, Maya. You court, seduce, and lure them in much the way one would with a lover, and yet you clearly don't love them. In fact, I'd say it's quite the opposite."

"I like the hunt." Maya tilted her chin defiantly but gasped when she backed right into the trunk of a massive oak. "What's wrong with that?" she whispered through trembling lips. "Besides, what would a stodgy old vampire like you know about love?"

"Nothing." Shane placed his hands against the tree on either side of Maya, caging her in. He leaned in so his face was just inches from hers. "I know little of love, but I'm well schooled in hunting, whether it's to feed or in battle. It's not what you're doing that intrigues me, Maya, but *why* you're doing it."

"I-I'm hunting, like any other vampire does." Her voice lowered to a whisper, but the anger and defiance had been replaced by fear and uncertainty. "For the blood."

"No." Shane shook his head slowly. Brushing a lock of blond hair off her face, he ran his thumb along her jaw. Her skin was warm and smooth beneath his. Although vampires felt cool to the touch to humans, they were felt warm to other vampires because their body temperatures were the same. But Maya's flesh seemed hotter and more enticing than any Shane had encountered.

He tilted her chin, forcing her to look him in the eye, and to his surprise, she didn't resist. "If it were only about blood, youngling, then you would simply glamour a human, feed, and release him. No." Shane traced the line of her full lower lip with the edge of his thumb, and sadness tugged at whatever was left of his heart. "We both know there is much more at play here than the need for blood."

"Then spill it." Maya's features hardened, and her hands balled into fists at her sides. Dark blue eyes glittered up at him with fierce determination. "What is it that you think I'm after?"

Memories of Maya being dragged into the alley and the look of pure terror and helplessness in her eyes came roaring back—and in that instant he *knew*. He felt like a fool for not realizing it the moment he'd woken from the dreamscape. When the realization dawned, something deep inside him shattered into a million tiny pieces.

"Power," Shane whispered. His fangs burst free, and Maya let out a gasp of pleasure. "Control." He placed a gentle kiss at the corner of her mouth. "Domination."

Maya's body quivered, the subtle vibrations fluttering over Shane in erotic waves, like a siren song, willing him closer. He brushed his cheek along hers and nuzzled her hair to the side, exposing her long, lovely neck. He placed his hand on the trunk of the tree, once again framing Maya's petite frame with his far larger one.

"Do I frighten you?" he asked, taking in every beautiful feature of her face.

"No." A smile played at her lips, and he stilled when her hands found their way to his chest. "You're arrogant and bossy, but no, I'm not afraid of you." Her grin widened and charmed him beyond reason. "Annoyed, not afraid."

Maya giggled, filling his head with the sweet, clean scent of Ivory soap in an almost intoxicating way. A gust of wind wafted over them, bringing with it the thick scent of desire, and he *had* to taste her. Shane's gut clenched hotly with need. Sensing what he wanted, Maya tilted her head, offering herself to him instinctively as one leg slipped enticingly between his.

"I have to taste you, Maya," Shane whispered between kisses down her throat. Her body quaked and she moaned in response. He lifted his lip and gingerly ran the tip of his fang along the curve of her neck, knowing what he needed to do. "Will you let me taste you?"

"Yes," Maya whispered. Her fingers curled around his wrists and her back arched, offering him what he so desperately needed.

On a curse, Shane let his fangs pierce the pristine flesh along her throat. The instant the warm sweetness bathed his tongue, lights burst behind his eyes and the world around him fell away. He'd drunk from humans and vampires, and even a fairy or two, but no one tasted anything like this. Maya's blood was sweet and thick and sent tentacles of power through him like lightning.

He leaned in and drank greedily, and one word ran

through his mind: *bloodmate*. The word repeated over and over like a heartbeat. It thundered through his head relentlessly. Amid the flashes of light, one image came roaring into mind—a smiling old woman who was wearing Maya's necklace.

Who am I?

Maya's mind merged with his like a thunderbolt and Shane reared back, shocked by the sudden and combustible psychic connection. Maya looked up at him through large blue eyes, and Shane watched the two tiny holes on her neck close, leaving no evidence behind.

Running one finger along her jawline, he captured her heavily lidded gaze with his. After tasting her blood, Shane was certain that Maya was far more fragile than she would have anyone believe. She was lost and reminded him of someone fighting her way through the fog with no one else in sight. Alone and frightened.

To his surprise, he was unable to read her blood memories. That was a first. It was as though all of her memories were shrouded in secrecy, hidden from anyone and everyone. The strangest part was that he didn't even think Maya knew she was doing it.

Even though he wanted nothing more than to claim her as his, words of caution ran through his head. For all her bravado, Maya Robertson was clinging to her existence with every ounce of strength she had. She was the most haunted soul he'd ever encountered.

Shane could not take her or tell her about the possibility that they were bloodmates until she knew she was safe with him, and she'd never feel safe until she rid herself of the demons that haunted her. Shane knew all too well about demons. He'd let the memory of his maker haunt him for more years than he cared to admit.

Maya wasn't haunted by her maker. Instead, she was tormented by a human life she could barely remember and a vicious attack she couldn't forget.

She licked her lower lip seductively and slipped her hands under Shane's coat, settling them on his waist. As she tugged his hips to her, a grin cracked her face, widening when the evidence of his desire pressed against her hip.

"You want what all men want." Her honeyed voice wafted over him as her fingers slipped beneath the edge of his shirt and curled temptingly against his flesh. She popped up on her toes and flicked her tongue over his lips, testing every ounce of his resolve. "Don't you, Shane? Do you think I'll let you take it? Taking my blood is one thing, but taking my body is quite another."

He held his ground and admitted to himself that Maya wasn't entirely wrong. Shane wanted her more than any other woman, human or vampire, but the taunting tone of her voice, combined with the familiar look in her eye, gave him pause.

It was the same stone-cold look Maya gave her prey.

"No," he said flatly. Shane abruptly pushed himself off the tree and immediately put distance between them. "You will find that I am nothing like the men you've dallied with, human or vampire. I tasted your blood because that will allow me to track you anywhere, if I have to. With the wolves in town, it will provide an extra measure of security."

It was a partial truth—and a cruel one, at that—but it was the only one he was prepared to reveal at the moment.

"What?" Maya's mouth fell open and her fangs retracted as she stared at him in disbelief.

"And there is something else you will soon realize." Shane pulled his leather gloves out of his pockets and tugged them on, not to protect himself from silver but to resist the urge to touch her again. "No matter how many men you dominate, Maya. No matter how many countless humans you glamour and feed on…" Shane took another step back and whispered, "Nothing will erase what happened that night in the alley."

Maya flinched from the sting of his words and her eyes filled with tears.

"I knew it," she whispered. "You saw the whole thing, didn't you? Just stood there, watched it all happen, and did nothing to stop it." She swiped furiously at the tears that spilled down her cheek, her expression hardening. "Well, since you like to watch, you're in for a treat because I've still got about thirty minutes before the sun starts to rise. Enjoy the show."

Shane's brows knit with confusion, and before he could say another word, Maya shot into the sky like a bullet. Shane grew more and more bewildered, repeating her words in his mind—*I knew it. You just stood there, watched it all happen, and did nothing to stop it*. Did Maya believe he was actually there that night? That he would stand by and watch her be attacked and do nothing, or had she seen him in the dreamscape?

Shane swore under his breath and flew into the sky after her. Keeping his distance, he followed her while she hunted, staying close enough only to assure she was safe. With the werewolves' impending arrival, he had little intention of allowing Maya out of his sight.

Over the next thirty minutes, Maya glamoured and fed on two men, both of whom bore a striking resemblance to her attacker in the dreamscape. As with the man in the park, she spent more time glamouring them than she did feeding on them.

He followed her back to the nightclub and landed silently on top of a building across from The Coven. He watched her fly down to the slate roof of the old church and open the hidden entrance next to the steeple. A gust of brisk wind whistled through the tapestry of buildings, lifting her hair off her shoulders.

Shane expected her to disappear immediately into the building but she didn't. Maya paused and turned her face toward the orange glow of the horizon. He crouched low on the rooftop of the neighboring building and waited for Maya to go inside. She continued to stare at the brightening sky, and the sad, lost look on her face tugged at him.

Panic gripped Shane. He didn't need to look at the sky to know how quickly the sun was rising. An ache deep in his chest warned him of the impending sunrise, and with the growing internal warning came apprehension.

Not for himself but for her.

He was far older and could recuperate from sun exposure with more ease than a youngling like Maya. If she stayed exposed much longer and didn't seek cover, the sun would consume her, turning her to dust. Shane rose to his feet, and just as he was about to call her name, he heard her.

Please, Maya's wavering voice, laced with sadness and regret, drifted into his mind. *No more nightmares.* Eyes closed, her hand went to the necklace nestled safely against her breasts, and Shane's heart tugged in his chest at the sight of tears streaming down her cheeks and the tormented sound of her voice. *Please make it stop.*

Shane's fangs erupted violently and his body tightened from the delicious, erotic effect of their minds connecting. It was like being bathed in desire, longing, and the sweet torture of unfulfilled lust. The flames of desire were extinguished at the sight of the protective shadows shrinking amid growing patches of light.

With the sun creeping up in the sky, the ache in his chest turned to a burning sensation. Just when he thought he'd scream with frustration, Maya dropped out of sight into the building. Jumping from the roof, Shane let out a sound of relief and landed silently in the empty street below.

Normally, he would fly back to the Presidium's offices, but given how close the sun was, even *he* couldn't outrun it. He yanked off a manhole cover and descended into the sewer. Whisking through the network of underground tunnels, he made his way toward the Presidium's offices and his apartment. He couldn't stop thinking about the surprising effects that had engulfed him when her mind touched his.

Maya wasn't his sibling, his maker, or his progeny. He should not be able to hear her in his head, and he knew there could only be one other explanation. Bloodmates. Like all vampires, he had been told the legend not long after he'd been turned. According to the legend, if a vampire found his or her bloodmate and bonded, the two became daywalkers, vampires who could withstand the sun's rays. Olivia and Doug's bonding had not only proven the legend to be true but had revealed far more in the process.

Olivia and Doug could only telepath with each other.

Picking up speed, Shane growled with frustration and swept through the tunnels like a ghost. He hadn't imagined it. Shane definitely heard Maya in his mind. But did that mean she was his bloodmate? That would certainly explain his overwhelming attraction to her and the fact that he was pulled into the dreamscape for the first time in centuries—and not into just any dream, but into Maya's. What about Maya? Would it matter to her if they were bloodmates? As far as Shane could tell, she loathed him, and at the moment, he couldn't blame her.

Maya must have seen him in the dreamscape last night and was now under the misguided impression that Shane had been there that night and had allowed her to be brutalized. He was filled with confusion, anger, and a fair amount of frustration. It was an appalling idea to think that Maya believed him to be that kind of monster.

He swore loudly, his voice echoing through the dark, dank tunnels. He was confused and didn't like it one fucking bit. His life as a sentry had been clear, well defined, and orderly, but ever since he'd come to New York City and met Maya, his life had been anything but.

Shane came to an abrupt halt when he reached the entrance of the Presidium. Without even looking for it, he pressed the rectangular stone along the top of the wall. He made a face at the rats that ran past his feet and let out a sound of relief when the hidden door swung open, revealing the brightly lit halls of the Presidium's New York facility.

He stepped into the sunny yellow hallway and the door closed silently behind him. The sound of his boot-clad feet hitting the red marble floor echoed through the corridor. Crystal chandeliers hung from the ceiling and glittered, giving the hallway the illusion of sunlight. The walls were lined with the portraits of past czars. Olivia and Doug had yet to add theirs, and he suspected they never would. It wasn't their style.

Shane stopped in front of the massive wood-and-steel door and tugged off his gloves. He pressed his thumb against a small black panel, and a moment later, the heavy, medieval door swung open, allowing him entry to the central halls of the Presidium network. He was immediately greeted by Van Helsing, Olivia's German shepherd and the newly appointed guard dog at the Presidium.

"Good morning, Van." Shane scratched the enormous dog behind his ears, and the hall was immediately filled with the insistent meows of a cat. The dog sat on his haunches and watched Shane squat down to give the attention-craving feline a pat on the butt. Purring like a freight train, she rubbed up against Shane's leg and accepted his greeting. "Hello, Oreo. I see that you're keeping Van company again tonight. I'm surprised the two of you aren't parked at Olivia's feet."

"Well, close enough," Olivia said as she came around the corner.

Shane stood up quickly, feeling embarrassed at being caught coddling the animals and for allowing Olivia to sneak up on him. Maya had him off his game in more ways than one. Olivia laughed because Oreo kept brushing herself against Shane's leg, leaving white hairs all over his black pants. Shane made a face, which only elicited a bigger laugh from the czar.

"Sorry." Olivia shrugged and rested both hands on

her belly, which looked even bigger than it had a few hours ago. Dressed in a long, green silk robe, she looked nothing like the Czar of New York City, or at least not what Shane was used to. Most czars were formal and aloof, but Doug and Olivia were the opposite. "I can't sleep and they've been walking the halls with me. Doug wanted to come too, but I insisted he get some rest. With the wolves coming into town, he's going to need to bring his A-game."

"He's not the only one," Shane said with a polite smile. "Everyone is going to have to be on alert. I would be lying if I said I'm not concerned about you in your *condition*."

Olivia didn't respond but simply nodded. She walked with him down the hall toward his apartment with Van and Oreo close behind. He knew she was unsettled by the pregnancy, more so than anyone else, but whatever feelings she had about it she kept to herself.

"You're not the only one who's concerned. Millicent has been combing the Presidium's archives, looking for any scrap of information about anything remotely like this that happened before—but so far nothing."

"Yes, well, Millicent is tenacious and the best record keeper the Presidium has," Shane said firmly. "If anyone can find something, it's her. She must have been one hell of a sentry in her day."

"She was." Olivia smiled. "Millicent trained me when I was a sentry, and don't worry, I'm pregnant, Quesada, not an invalid," she said with a laugh. "I can still kick ass with the best of them, and thanks to Xavier's latest weaponry inventions, we're all armed to the teeth. We can handle whatever the wolves throw at us."

"Have you been able to reach the Emperor yet? Has he spoken with King Heinrich?"

"Yes." Olivia's tone was one of wariness. "Apparently, King Heinrich was equally surprised to hear about Horace's arrival. The poor guy apologized profusely and said if the kid and his pack caused any trouble, he would deal with it at once. He also offered to have his oldest son, Prince Killian, come to the city to keep an eye on his kid brother, but I told him that I didn't think that would be necessary. A pack of six wolves is bad enough, no reason to make it seven. I'm not looking for a fight, and taking the king at his word is a good way to start."

"A wise choice."

"I hope so." Olivia's hands rested on her large belly. "But we have to err on the side of caution, and if something does go down, I want my coven prepared. That said, Doug is going to do some battle training with the girls. Sadie is already well-schooled and Trixie is a natural fighter, but Suzie and Maya need some help. Suzie's afraid of her own shadow, but she has to learn to defend herself. We could always use your input."

"Of course. So…Maya has had no training." Shane kept his voice low, even though his head filled with memories of Maya being dragged into the alley. "No battle experience."

"No." Olivia paused for a moment. "I've tried, but she's shown little interest in any kind of fight training."

"May I ask you something?" Shane kept his gaze straight ahead. "It's…personal."

"Sure," Olivia said with some amusement.

Shane stopped in front of the door that led to his apartment and turned to face Olivia. He clasped his hands behind his back and wrestled against four hundred years of pomp and circumstance.

"It's okay, Shane." Sensing his unease, Olivia smiled and gave him a reassuring pat on the shoulder. "Just ask."

"What can you tell me about Maya?"

"Maya?" Olivia let out a sigh and Van whined at her feet in empathy. "How much time have you got?" Shane's look of confusion elicited a loud laugh from Olivia. "Let's just say that there's a lot more to that girl than meets the eye. I can't tell you Maya's story."

"I understand." Shane nodded. "It's not your story to tell."

"No." Olivia frowned. "Well, the problem is, I don't know her story. Not her full story, anyway."

"But you're her maker. You turned her and drank her blood, which gave you her blood memories. Olivia, you should know more about her than anyone."

"I should," Olivia said quietly, "and to some extent I do. I know what happened on the night she died, and that was pretty fucking horrible, but that's it. For some reason, one I've never been able to figure out, I could only see the night she died. Her entire life before that is a blur, and the only one who will be able to shed any light on Maya's past is Maya."

He nodded his understanding because of his similar experience when he drank Maya's blood. Shane refrained from mentioning that part to the czar. Before he could ask anything else, a gust of wind blew into the hallway and Doug appeared next to Olivia with a look on his face that hovered between concerned and annoyed.

"You're killing me, woman." Doug linked his arm

around her waist and kissed her cheek, which had her smiling wistfully. "You have got to come back to bed and get some rest."

"Fine," Olivia said, feigning an angry tone. She looked back at Shane and gave him a sad smile. "Whatever you do, Shane, go easy. Maya may act tough, but it's all bullshit. Which is one reason I'm less than thrilled she's going to work for Rat."

"No she's not." Shane folded his arms over his chest and ignored the smirk on Doug's face. "I will not allow it."

"Good luck with that 'not allowing it' shit, man." Doug shook his head. Linking Olivia's fingers in his, he started pulling her toward their apartment. "That's a surefire way to piss off any woman, human or vampire."

"It's not up to you, Shane, or me," Olivia said. "Maya is not my property—she's my family. She's got every intention of starting work at Rat's club tomorrow night, and as you know, I gave her my reluctant blessing." Shane opened his mouth to protest, but Olivia held up one hand, silencing him. "I am letting her do this because I'm assigning *you* as her personal babysitter. If it will make you feel better, you can tell her that you're her bodyguard. And I'm only doing this because the wolves will be hanging out there, okay?"

"Good move, babe." Doug tried to pull her down the hall, but she held her ground. "Shane can handle Maya. After all, *she's* a youngling and *he's* older than dirt."

Shane ignored the jab because Doug was even younger than Maya. His angel bloodline and the bloodmate bond with Olivia had not only made his transformation seamless, but had also fast-tracked all of his abilities. Doug may have been turned only a few months ago, but he was one of the most powerful vampires Shane had ever met. "I already told her that was the deal, and she's about as happy about it as you would expect."

"What about my sentry patrols?" Shane asked out of duty, not because he wanted to be away from Maya. "We can't leave the city unprotected."

"Doug can handle things," Olivia said with a wink to her mate. "Besides, the big concern is the wolves, and they'll be hanging out at The Dollhouse. We kill two birds with one stone. You can keep an eye on Maya and the wolves at the same time."

"Bed." Doug swept Olivia off her feet as she shrieked in protest. "Now."

"Remember what I said, Shane," Olivia shouted through a laugh while Doug carried her away. "And don't let her out of your sight around those wolves."

Shane watched the czars disappear down the hallway, with Van and Oreo close behind, and his thoughts immediately went to Maya. He opened the door to his apartment and stepped inside, and when the door closed shut behind him, Shane marveled at the silence. His gaze flicked around the large studio apartment with a new perspective. The place was decorated in shades of gray, void of all color, but this was the first time Shane felt the dullness.

Shedding his clothes, he made his way to the queen-size bed, still unmade from the day before, and slipped between the sheets with one thing on his mind—Maya. If he got pulled into Maya's dreamscape again, he would do a hell of a lot more than watch. He drifted into a quiet slumber, and as his eyes fluttered closed, Shane hoped for the first time in centuries to dream.

Chapter 4

The comforting blanket of darkness ebbed slowly like fog lifting off the ocean, and with it came a rush of bone-chilling fear.

It was happening again.

The world around Maya came into focus with horrifying clarity, bringing a rush of memories she desperately wished she could forget. As she anticipated what was surely about to happen, a pathetic whimper escaped her lips. The same horrible event plagued her sleep night after night, and every time there was no escape, no one to hear her cries for help.

There was no one to save her before, so why would this time be any different?

Fingers, like steel claws, dug into her bicep and her stomach roiled in protest, making her nauseous. The stale taste of booze coated her mouth, and her nostrils were swamped by the stench of her attacker's whiskey-soaked breath. He dragged her down the city sidewalk, and though she tried to fight, it was useless. Heavy and cumbersome from too much drinking, her limbs wouldn't cooperate, and try as she might, she could not extricate herself from his grasp.

His name was Franklin and she vaguely recalled being excited to go on this date, but that was all Maya could remember. The summer air was thick and soupy and stuck to her bare arms like heavy layers of cobwebs.

His face, carved with cruelty, looked particularly evil in the flickering shadows of the city streetlights. How could she not have seen the brutality he was capable of? What kind of woman had she been, to go out with someone like this?

Maya stumbled when her stiletto caught in a crack on the gum-stained sidewalk. Her ankle twisted painfully, making her cry out, and though she fell forward, her date yanked her to her feet and kept walking. They turned a corner and Maya pushed her long, blond hair out of her eyes, looking for someone, anyone who could help her. She was met with no response, and just like every time before, the streets around them were desolate. It was a wretched irony to remain unheard in a city that was brimming with people.

He grabbed her shoulders, pulled her close, and tried to kiss her, but Maya shook her head furiously in protest.

No, please take me home, *Maya whimpered through trembling lips. Her hands found their way to his face, fingers rasping over his beard stubble. She attempted to keep his cruel mouth from hers, but he evaded her easily.*

I bought you dinner and fed you drinks all fucking night. We both know where that leads. *He spun her around and tried to kiss her again, but Maya continued to refuse.*

No, *she whimpered.* I want to go home.

I don't think so. *On a growl of anger, Franklin started dragging her into the alley next to the club.* I own your ass. *Linking his arm around her waist, he laughed cruelly and pulled her into the dank, smelly corridor.*

A wretched feeling of helplessness filled Maya. Her

shoes were knocked off in the struggle, and the bottoms of her bare feet scraped over the rough pavement. She fought harder, because maybe, just maybe, this time would be different, but deep down Maya knew there was no escape.

A few seconds more and the worst of it would begin.

Franklin threw her against the stone wall of the building, knocking the wind out of her and making her see stars. He pressed her there, the bumpy surface biting painfully into her bare shoulders, while he fumbled and reached beneath the skirt of her strapless dress.

One hand curled around her neck, pressing the gold chain of her necklace into her skin, and Maya squeezed her eyes shut. She screamed and braced herself for the invasive, brutal onslaught she was about to experience. What usually came next didn't happen. There was no teeth-clattering blow to the head or humiliating invasion. Instead, a low guttural growl filled the night, and at the same instant, the weight of Franklin's unwelcome body was lifted from hers on a cool breeze.

Time stopped.

Eyes still closed, her body shivering uncontrollably, Maya listened to the exquisite silence. Franklin was gone...but she wasn't alone.

Maya? *The deep, familiar baritone rumbled around her gently.* Are you alright?

Shane? *His name escaped her lips on a shaky whisper edged with disbelief and confusion. Uncertain what was happening, and still afraid that Franklin might come back and continue what he'd started, she kept her eyes screwed shut. Her hands curled into fists at her sides, and she pressed herself against the wall, hoping and wishing she could simply disappear or wake up.* What's happening?

I'm so sorry I wasn't here sooner, but you'll have to forgive an old vampire for being a bit rusty in the dreamscape. *Maya flinched as Shane's large hand cradled her face with surprising tenderness. Her fingers trembled and she placed her hand over his, assuring herself that he was really there and she wasn't imagining this entire experience. Sighing with relief, Maya curled her hand over his and pressed it further against her tearstained cheek.* You are safe, youngling.

Finding her courage, Maya opened her eyes and found herself staring into the dark, intense gaze of Shane Quesada. Her brows knit with confusion because those were definitely the same eyes that had glared at her from the shadows the last time she relived this nightmare.

The line between his brows deepened and the sharp angles of his handsome, masculine face seemed even harsher than they did in the mortal plane. In spite of her situation, she wasn't afraid of him. Even though he was a formidable warrior, the man had gentleness within him that she'd never seen until now.

His wavy, chestnut hair curled temptingly over the collar of the long, leather coat, and his square jaw was covered by that ever-present five-o'clock shadow. Those intense eyes stood out above all else, dark pools of brown, peering at her from beneath thick, furrowed brows. Maya shivered. It was like he saw past all of her mistakes, her bad choices, and her bullshit to the vulnerable part of herself that she never wanted anyone to see again. Her gut instinct was to run but she was too tired. Exhausted from fighting and running...just...tired.

Thank you, *Maya whispered. Tears spilled down her cheeks, and a sob wracked her body. Shane gathered her into his arms and cradled her against the broad expanse of his chest. Weeping, Maya's fingers curled around the lapels of his coat.* Thank you for making it stop.

One strong arm linked around her waist, while his other hand cradled the back of her head, holding her while she cried. Shane said nothing, which was exactly what Maya needed. She didn't need someone to tell her it was okay or that the pain would fade over time or some other load of crap. All she wanted was to be comforted, held, and cherished, to be allowed to weep and let it all out. He rocked her slowly in the shadow of the buildings, and Maya cried until she had nothing left.

Limp and exhausted, she sagged against Shane's much larger form. When her sniffles subsided, she could swear the sound of the ocean was swirling around them. Calm and soothing, the gentle, lapping sound of waves washed over her. Swiping at her sore eyes, she lifted her head to look at Shane and was immediately distracted by their new surroundings.

They were no longer in the dark, dirty alley but standing on a white, sandy beach beneath a cloudless azure sky. Maya let out a sound of wonder, and her hand flew to her mouth in awe. They were in a stunningly exotic location, and the best part was the warmth of the bright yellow sun that blazed over them with balmy warmth. It didn't burn. Letting out a laugh, she tilted her face to the beautiful tropical sky. Maya hadn't thought she missed the sun—until now.

You did this? *Maya looked around in awe.* You made this place?

Yes, but my only regret was not being there sooner, *Shane murmured, taking her hand in his and placing a gentle kiss on her knuckles. Maya's stomach fluttered when his lips brushed over her flesh with the gentlest of strokes, and he held her protectively in the shelter of his body.* I can assure you that won't happen again.

Wh-which part? *Maya asked quietly.* The nightmare…or you watching what happened?

Neither. *Shane's voice dropped to low, dangerous tones and his grip on her tightened. A look similar to shame washed over his face.* You will never go through that again. It has been centuries since I walked in the dreamscape, and until last night, I never thought I would again. I didn't even realize what was happening at first, and by the time I did…you were gone.

So you weren't there the night it actually happened? You don't think I deserved it? *Maya asked in a barely audible voice. She closed her eyes, terrified at what the answer might be.* That I asked for it?

What? *Shane's body tensed against hers. One strong finger brushed along the line of her jaw and settled under her chin.* Maya, look at me. *Maya bit her lip and steeled herself before opening her eyes and forcing herself to look at him. She was prepared to see anger, pity, disgust…but not kindness.*

What that animal did to you was indefensible. I would never stand by and watch a woman victimized like that, human or vampire, and if I had been there that night—*a growl rumbled in his chest*—I would have eviscerated that piece of shit until there was nothing left but a dry husk.

Olivia beat you to it. *Worried that he might vanish,*

Maya curled her fingers tighter around his coat and pulled him closer. She looked out at the blue, rippling ocean that stretched out endlessly before them. She doesn't know that I know, but Trixie told me that Olivia killed him while I was in the transformation sleep.

I'm not surprised. *Shane reached between them and took her hands in his before cradling them to his chest.* Olivia is one of the most responsible makers I've encountered in my four centuries, and that's saying something. I didn't even get the pleasure of ripping his throat out in the dreamscape. The son of bitch vanished into thin air, but then again, it's not really him, is it?

What do you mean? *A feeling of dread crawled up Maya's back as she turned her eyes to Shane's.*

Your nightmare is a ghost, a memory from your human life that you're reliving again and again. Like you said, the man who did this to you is dead. *Shane lifted one shoulder.* The dreamscape is your creation.

Are you saying that I want to go through this? *Anger flared hard and Maya shoved him away from her. To her surprise, he allowed her to slip out of his embrace, and the look on his face was one of acceptance and patience.* You think that I am controlling what happens?

No, at least not intentionally. *Shane's voice was even and calm. He held his arms out and gestured to the beautiful tropical surroundings.* Do you see where we are? It's a far cry from the streets of Manhattan, wouldn't you say? I thought this environment would be a better place for you to distance yourself from what happened. I may have been pulled into your dream last time, but this time the connection was far stronger and I was able to manipulate the dreamscape.

You mean that there's a way to stop the nightmares? *Tears pricked the back of her eyes again.* I can make it stop for good?

Yes. *Shane nodded and closed the distance between them. Taking Maya's hands in his, he pulled her to him.* At least, that is what I suspect. I think that the nightmare will continue until you are the one to eliminate your attacker.

Th-that's impossible, *Maya sputtered.* I—I can't.

You can, *Shane insisted in a gentle tone. His fingers curled around hers and his thumb brushed over the top of her hand.* You have far more control than you think you do, Maya. You crave it. I know that your desire for it drives you when you hunt. You are motivated by the need to dominate, to have power and maintain control over your body and your life. That is what feeds you, youngling. Let me show you, Maya. Let me show you where your true power lies.

He tugged her closer still, the hard planes of his body matching hers in all the right places. Maya's stomach fluttered again, a feeling that reminded her of what it was like to be human—to be alive. He leaned close and kissed her cheek, his lips nuzzling her ear.

Yes, *Maya whispered.*

She allowed her body to lean into Shane, and her eyes fluttered while he trailed kisses down her throat. Her hands wandered up his chest and curled over his shoulders as he murmured seductive promises between kisses. When Shane pulled back, his hand cradled the back of her head gently and the look in his eyes made her wet. The long-forgotten feeling of lust and desire burned low and deep in Maya's belly. The evidence of his need for her pressed against her insistently, which only made her want him more.

She couldn't recall the last time she desired a man sexually or when the very idea didn't scare the shit out of her. Staring into the dark, seemingly endless depths of Shane's eyes, she felt the soul-stirring rumble of desire bubble up and spill over. Maya's fangs erupted on a gasp, and a slow smile cracked Shane's handsome face.

This is your dream, Maya. *A growl rumbled in Shane's chest and reverberated through her. He splayed his other hand across her lower back and his lip lifted, revealing his razor-sharp fangs.* Tell me what you want.

Maya's body tensed and she wrestled with actually asking for what she wanted. Unable to make herself utter the words, she simply acted. After all, this was a dreamscape—not reality—and according to Shane, she had all the control. Maya decided it was time to test that theory.

Popping up on her toes, with sand squishing deliciously beneath her feet, Maya threw a silent prayer to the universe, then retracted her fangs and brushed her lips against Shane's. The kiss was gentle at first, tentative, and she sighed when his firm lips parted and she swept her tongue inside the welcoming cavern of his mouth. He tasted fresh and cool, and reminded Maya of New York City at its best.

Wild and dark.

Maya's tongue touched Shane's, making him groan with pleasure, and the kiss quickly grew in intensity. The desperate need to feel something other than fear burned Maya from the inside out. She tore her hands from his and tangled her fingers in his thick, wavy hair, sighing when the silky strands slid through her hands in such a familiar way, it was like she'd done it a thousand times before. His hands wandered up her arms and over her shoulders, and skimmed down her back. He finally settled them on her hips, gripping her, doing his best to keep some kind of distance between them, but it was no use. Maya couldn't get close enough and doubted she ever would.

Breaking the kiss, Shane pressed his lips against her forehead and Maya closed her eyes. With her arms linked around his neck, she fiddled with the ends of his hair and rested her head against his chest, watching the waves lap gently at the shore. Maya smiled, noticing how easily her body fit with his. Every plane and curve seemed to go together with absolute ease; his body had been made just for her. She reveled in the safety of his embrace and the tranquility that surrounded them. It was as if they were the only two creatures in the universe.

It's time to wake up, youngling. *Shane's voice rumbled in his chest and whispered through Maya's body seductively.* I can feel the sun beginning to set.

How can you tell? *Maya leaned back and looked him in the eye.* Is it because you're so old?

Old? *Shane laughed loudly and kissed the top of her head before brushing her hair off her shoulder.* I suppose it is. With time, you'll learn to recognize the rising and setting of the sun, but that is a lesson for another time.

Fine. *Maya rolled her eyes and placed a kiss at the corner of his mouth.* I do have a big night with my new job and everything. *Shane's expression grew dark.* Relax, I'm just going to tend bar so your bodyguard job with the wolves should be super easy. It's not like I have any plans to strip.

Now his eyes were downright stormy and she noticed that a bank of clouds swept in, swallowing the sun. She wondered if that was on purpose or a side effect of his emotions. She made a note to herself to ask the girls about this dreamscape stuff and see if anything like this happened to them before they stopped dreaming.

S-stripping? *he sputtered.* You will do no such thing. I forbid it.

Shane's command slammed into her like a ton of bricks, sending anger and frustration up Maya's back. She set her jaw, and in a flash she shoved at him, instantly extricating herself from his embrace. You forbid it? *Fangs bared, eyes wild, she glared at Shane with outright fury.*

I am your bloodmate, and it is my right. *The words spilled out in a rush, and Shane looked almost as shocked that he'd said it as she did.* You will not do it.

Your what? *Maya took another step back while disbelief and confusion whipped through her like a tornado.* Like Olivia and Doug? *She shook her head and clutched the pendant.* We are not bloodmates. No way.

How else do you explain the fact that I've been pulled into your dreams after not dreaming for more than three centuries? *Shane folded his arms over his chest, and that calm, arrogant look settled over his face once again.* I will not have my bloodmate prancing around half naked in front of a pack of drooling wolves—or humans, for that matter. It's unacceptable.

Oh, really? First of all, this whole dream thing could be a fluke. *Hands on her hips, she closed the distance between them while Shane held his ground.* Secondly, I don't care who you are or who you *think* you are. You have no right to tell me what to do. *She poked him in the chest with one finger, but he merely arched an eyebrow at her, which was even more infuriating*. And if I want to take off all my clothes and go running through Times Square, then I'll do it. You know why, Shane? Because it's my life—not yours or anyone else's.

You're being silly. *Shane smirked*. We both know you're not going to do any such thing.

You see, now that's where you're wrong. I may not remember much about my human life, *she said in the sweetest tone she could muster*, but I'll tell you one thing: I do like to dance. So maybe I *will* give it a whirl on the dance floor at The Dollhouse, or maybe I'll strip and dance through Times Square naked as a jaybird…but if I do…it will be my decision, Shane. Not yours.

Before Shane could say another word, Maya shot up into the sky. Whisking toward the horizon, she heard Shane's deep voice, edged with sadness, rumbling around her.

Just because you can, Maya, doesn't mean that you should.

Throwing on a pair of her favorite jeans, black knee-high boots, and a formfitting, red V-neck sweater, Maya got up and ready for the night in record time. Normally, she'd take her time and dither over what outfit to wear, but not tonight. She had no idea what Rat would want her to wear to tend bar, and the truth was, she didn't even expect to work tonight. In all likelihood they would only talk about her schedule or something, but one thing was for sure—she would not be stripping. She had no intention of dancing at the club, but when Shane threw out an order, something inside her snapped.

Maya snagged a hairbrush off her dresser and ran it through her hair with furious strokes. Ever since she woke up, all she could think about was Shane and what had happened in the dreamscape. She'd never experienced such a roller coaster of emotions in such a short time.

Fear. Relief. Safety. Passion. Lust. Shock. Fury.

Memories of the gentle way he held her hands, the passionate, insistent feel of his mouth on hers…all of it came flooding back in living color. For the first time since Maya had been turned, fear was drowned out by tenderness and she remembered what it felt like to be desired. To be desired for who she was, not what she looked like.

She fiddled with the handle of the wooden brush as she gazed at her reflection in the large mirror above her white dresser. The human men she hunted were easy prey and wanted her for her body, not that they ever got it, but Shane was different. Maya nibbled her lower lip and smiled wistfully. He wanted her physically, that was for sure, but there was more to it. Shane was concerned about her emotional well-being and her safety, which was evident in the way he intervened in the dreamscape.

The dreamscape. What the hell was he doing there? Not that she wanted to seem ungrateful—after all, he stopped the nightmare—but did his presence there mean what he said it did? Were they bloodmates? Her gut clenched at the mere idea of it and what it would mean.

From what Olivia said, there was a blood exchange and bonding, and then both would become daywalkers.

But while he had tasted her blood, she hadn't tasted his. Daywalking was fine, but Maya couldn't quite get a grip on the whole bonded-for-eternity concept. In fact, the mere idea of it was terrifying. She would be trusting him with her life, and Maya never trusted men, other than Pete or Doug. They were like brothers, and it wasn't the same thing.

A smile played at her lips and her fangs broke free while she recalled the way her stomach fluttered from that look in his eyes. Oh no, there was nothing brotherly about the way Shane made her feel.

Not. At. All.

A sudden knock at Maya's front door captured her attention and tore her from her thoughts. With her brow furrowed, she tossed the brush on the dresser and went into the living room. It was probably Olivia or Doug because they were the only two vamps who had access to the apartments that Maya couldn't telepath with.

Putting on a smile, she gripped the brass doorknob and prayed that they wouldn't see through her bullshit and detect the swirl of confusion inside her. Since Olivia didn't know about the nightmares, bringing up Shane's surprise appearance would take more explanation than Maya was prepared to give at the moment.

Smiling, Maya pulled the door open, ready to greet Olivia or Doug, but to her great surprise she found herself face-to-face with Trixie and Sadie, both of whom looked concerned. The two women exchanged perplexed looks and then pushed past Maya into the apartment.

"Well, gee," Maya said, shutting the door, "come on in? What's your deal? If you two needed to talk to me so badly, why didn't you just telepath?"

Trixie sat on the arm of the overstuffed, pink-and-white polka-dot chair and stared at Maya like she'd just burst into flames, but Sadie paced back and forth while nibbling on her thumb. If she kept it up, she was going to end up eating the fingerless lace gloves she wore.

"What?" Maya threw her hands up. "Why are you two acting so weird?"

"Ha." Swinging her combat-boot-clad feet, Trixie sat perched on the edge of the chair. "You're the one who's gotten weird. Well, weirder."

"You're one to talk," Maya teased good-naturedly. "I'm not the one with hair that looks like an Easter egg."

Trixie smirked and flipped Maya the bird. "Suck it."

"You didn't hear us," Sadie said quietly. She stopped pacing and folded her arms over her breasts. "Trixie and I have been trying to telepath to you for the past half hour, and when you didn't respond, we got worried. We went to the Statue of Liberty and looked in your favorite hiding spot."

"You were worried about me?"

"Well, yeah. So much so that I even flew over the river to check if you were hangin' in Lady Liberty's torch, and you *know* how much I hate the water." Trixie shrugged. "You may have shitty taste in music"—she glanced around the pink and white decor of the apartment—"and pretty much everything else, but we still love ya. I was telepathing to you, trying to find out what time you were going over to Rat's place, mostly to see if I could talk your cute blond butt into *not* going there. When you didn't respond, I thought you were just being *you*."

"Great minds think alike," Sadie interjected. "I was hoping to do the same thing, and when we compared notes…"

"Y-you've been trying to talk to me?" Maya's stomach clenched, and for the first time since being turned into a vampire, she thought she might actually barf. Everything Shane said came rushing into her mind, but *bloodmate* rose above the rest. She tried to remember the last time she telepathed with Trixie and Sadie and realized it was at the club last night—before Shane tasted her blood. If she still breathed, she'd probably have hyperventilated by now. Maya closed her eyes and waved for them to do it again. "Try now."

Silence filled her head. The ticking of the clock in the kitchen echoed through the room like thunder. But in between each tick there was only terrifying silence. Tears pricked the back of Maya's eyes and panic welled.

"Holy shit, you're cut off from us," Trixie whispered. "This is just like what happened when Olivia and Doug—"

"Shut up," Maya shouted. She opened her eyes and pointed at her sisters. "Don't say it. Don't you dare say it. This is not the same thing."

"Is it Quesada?" Sadie leaned both hands on the back of white couch and leveled a serious gaze at Maya. "Something happened with him, didn't it?"

"No." Maya shook her head and went to the closet to grab her black wrap. "Absolutely not."

"If it's not him..." Trixie grimaced and cracked her knuckles. "It's not Rat, is it? He's freaking gross."

"Oh my God, no way." Maya made a face of disgust and kept talking like her life depended on it. She worried that if she stopped, the world around her would cave in. "I'm going to work for him and that's it. Speaking of which, I gotta get going. I'll come see you girls when I get back, and I'm sure everything will be back to normal."

Before she could leave, Sadie flew across the room and grabbed Maya by the arm. Letting out a sigh, Maya turned to face her fellow coven members and fought to keep from crying because deep in her gut, she knew it wasn't just some fluke.

"Maya, you can't run away from this." Sadie was always the one to tell it like it is. She kept her voice gentle but her meaning was clear. She slipped her hand into Maya's and squeezed as Trixie sidled up behind her and rested her chin on Sadie's shoulder.

"Something happened between you and Shane. Come on, spill it. Listen, aside from the fact that the guy has been spending every free minute over the past few months buzzing around you at the bar, he chased you out of the club last night like the horny bastard you've turned him into."

"Truth," Trixie said with a wink. "He's got it bad for you and everybody knows it. C'mon. What happened?"

Staring into the loving faces of her sisters, Maya felt her eyes fill with tears because the silence in her mind was deafening. Closing her eyes, she reached out to them again in one desperate attempt: *Can you hear me now?*

Isn't that a line from a cell phone commercial?

Maya's eyes flew open when Shane's amused voice slipped into her mind with unsettling ease. Her sisters looked at each other and then at Maya, but before they could ask what was happening, someone knocked on the door.

"I thought it would be wise to escort you to the club."

Shane's distinctive baritone boomed from the hallway. "I suggest you hurry up. You wouldn't want to be late for your first day on the job, now would you?"

Maya's jaw set and her eyes narrowed, but Trixie and Sadie looked thoroughly amused. Maya tugged the door open and prepared to give Shane a tongue-lashing, but every coherent thought was driven from her mind when she set eyes on him. He wasn't wearing the usual sentry uniform of head-to-toe leather, and based on the catcall whistle from Trixie, it was a definite improvement.

Clad in a pair of perfectly fitting jeans, brown cowboy boots, a Ralph Lauren button-down, and a brown leather bomber jacket, he looked every inch the sexy male specimen that he was. His thick, wavy hair curled over the collar and the top two buttons of his shirt were open, revealing a dusting of chest hair. Maya swallowed and fought the sudden, sharp pang of desire the flared through her.

The man was absolutely beautiful. Vampire. Warrior. Whatever. Shane Quesada was all man.

"Well," Sadie said through a poorly veiled smile, "at least now we know Maya will stay out of trouble."

"Ha," Trixie snorted. "Don't bet on it."

Chapter 5

MAYA HADN'T SAID MORE THAN TWO WORDS TO SHANE from the moment he arrived at the door of her apartment. He tried to touch her mind again, but she slammed it shut, refusing to allow him entry. She probably hoped that would piss him off, but on the contrary, her refusal to talk to him turned him on. He enjoyed a challenge because after so many years of merely existing, Shane felt like he was finally living. Maya was a fighter, and if he could show her how to harness that power, she would be able to stop fighting herself.

From the look on her face when he'd arrived, his decision to change his attire was a good one. He could have gone to the club in his usual sentry uniform, but based on past experience, he knew that wouldn't have been a good move. If he showed up in battle gear, the wolves might perceive it as an aggressive act by the Presidium and the czars, but dressed like any other clubgoer, he'd be able to convince them more easily that he was only there for the entertainment.

The one item he kept with him from his sentry garb was the semiautomatic pistol filled with silver bullets that was tucked safely inside his jacket. On most nights, it was packed with the ultraviolet ammunition designed by Xavier, the Presidium's resident inventor and weapons master. That ammo could turn a vamp to dust but would prove ineffective on the wolves. Not that he was looking to start a fight and break the truce, but it was prudent to be prepared.

When they rounded the next corner, the blinking purple-and-red neon sign for The Dollhouse came into view as two yellow cabs whizzed past. Like all strip clubs, there were no windows, and a large, bulky fellow named TJ stood outside the door checking IDs and taking the cover charge from eager men. TJ was a vampire, one of Rat's coven members, and though the big brute wasn't the sharpest tool in the shed, he was a good fighter. If Rat was the brains behind his operation, then TJ was definitely the brawn.

"Wait." Maya stopped before they crossed the street and grabbed Shane by the arm. When his eyes locked with hers, she quickly removed her hand. "We need to talk before we go inside."

Shane tilted his head and smirked. "Agreed."

"I know Olivia has hired you to be my babysitter, and she probably told you to say you were my bodyguard, but I'm not stupid. I know you're here to keep an eye on *me* more than the werewolves who may or may not show up."

"No one said you were stupid." He lifted one shoulder. "Stubborn, yes. Stupid, no."

"Fine." Her blue eyes flashed at him while she adjusted her black wrap, which was being whipped around by the cold November wind. "Just keep your distance, okay? Wolves or not, I'd prefer *not* to get fired on my first day because my four-hundred-year-old babysitter is an overbearing nudge."

"A nudge?" Shane's brows flew up. "I don't believe anyone has ever called me that before."

"Maybe not to your face." Maya batted her eyes and smiled sweetly. "Come on."

Cars and taxis whisked by them, and he watched Maya as she waited for an opening in the busy downtown traffic. Her platinum blond hair whipped around her in the wind along with the ends of her wrap, and in this moment, she reminded him of a wild horse. Being spirited and unpredictable was sexy as hell, and it could also be a dangerous combination.

"You have nothing else to say to me?" he asked quietly from where he stood behind her on the sidewalk. Shane's hands curled at his sides while he resisted the urge to brush her hair off her shoulders. "No comment about what happened in the dreamscape?"

Maya stilled but didn't turn around. In a last-ditch effort, Shane reached out to touch her mind with his.

I was there, Maya. It was real.

He waited for what seemed like an eternity for her to respond, and when she finally turned around, the look of sadness on her face made his crusty old heart ache.

"I know you were." She adjusted her wrap and hugged her arms around herself as though she was bracing against the cold. "I—I don't want you to think I'm ungrateful, Shane. I appreciate what you did for me, but I'm not prepared to deal with anything else right now—other than starting my first day of work."

Unable to stop himself, Shane pushed a strand of long, blond hair off Maya's forehead and trailed his finger along the curve of her cheek. She shivered beneath his touch but didn't resist it. Bathed in the light of the city street lamps, her blue eyes shimmered to the almost lavender color he so adored. Shane ran his thumb over her plump bottom lip and whispered, "You can't avoid me forever."

"Sure I can." Maya stepped back and glanced toward the street. "I'm immortal. I've got nothing but time."

Shane watched Maya give him a sassy smile before she ran across the street to the doors of the club. When she disappeared inside, he touched her mind with his. *You and me both, youngling.*

Sitting at a small table in the back of the club and pretending to nurse a beer, Shane had a clear view of Maya and the front door. So far, the wolf pack was a no-show, and since it was already midnight, Shane doubted they would be making an appearance tonight. The flickering lights from the stage were about the only source of illumination in the small space. The stage was at the center of the place, surrounded by round tables that all were filled.

Shane could tell by the scents in the room that a few vamps were mixed in with the humans among the customers and the dancers. To his relief, Maya was working behind the bar and not whirling around a stripper pole half-naked. Although the outfit Rat made her wear could hardly be described as clothing. It was more like a couple scraps of red leather held together by laces up the sides, which made it all too clear that Maya wasn't wearing either a bra or underwear.

The only other item she wore was that emerald and gold necklace. Shane's brow furrowed, recalling the single image he saw when drank Maya's blood. He made a mental note to ask her about the old woman later. Perhaps Maya would feel safer if she could remember more about her past.

"Enjoying the view?" Rat asked. Sitting down at Shane's table, he was clearly annoyed by the sentry's presence.

"What can I do for you?" Shane asked without taking his eyes off Maya.

"Always a great conversationalist, aren't you, Quesada?" Rat leaned back in his chair and laughed. "I thought you'd like to know that I just got a phone call from our wolf friends. They're on their way over."

"A phone call?" Shane's brows knit together. "I didn't realize you were in direct contact with them."

"Viola gave me her boyfriend's phone number so I could make sure I had a table ready when they arrived." Rat's eyes narrowed. "Don't make a big thing out of it."

"Yes, well, since you seem to be their NYC contact, it would be prudent to remind them that they should take time out of their visit to pay their respects to the czars." Shane removed a business card from his shirt pocket and slid it across the table to Rat, who smirked when he picked it up and inspected it. "They can contact the czars' secretary, Suzie, and she will arrange it for them."

"Right." Rat stuck the card in his jacket pocket. "From what Viola tells me, Horace isn't much for pomp and circumstance. He's second in line to the throne, and from what I gather, he leaves that official crap to his older brother. The heir gets all the work and the spare gets to party. You ask me, I'd rather be the spare."

"Be that as it may," Shane said evenly, "not paying their respects to the czars would be frowned upon. I can't imagine King Heinrich would appreciate that. It's bad enough they didn't formally announce their visit."

"I'll be sure to relay the message." Rat ran one hand over his bald head. "It's not like they're sticking to some formal schedule, man. Apparently they got sidetracked and arrived in the city later than they anticipated. I have a few of the girls setting up a VIP table for them now."

Shane turned his gaze to Rat's briefly before glancing at the two women, both human and scantily clad, who were scurrying around and setting up a table for six at the front edge of the stage. They were giggling and whispering to each other while they arranged the chairs. Shane could only assume that one of them was Viola, the woman Rat had mentioned last night, most likely the redhead who kept glancing at the door in clear anticipation.

"Thank you, Rat." Shane turned his attention back to Maya, who was flirting with two human men seated at the bar and giving her their full attention. "I'll be sure to let the czars know how forthcoming you've continued to be."

"Well, it's the least I can do, seeing how Olivia let the hot, little blond come work for me. When word gets out that she's working here, my profits are gonna shoot through the fuckin' roof. If I can get her to dance then I'll make a fortune."

Shane's arm shot out like a lightning bolt, and he grabbed Rat by the lapel of his cheap jacket. Pulling the club owner to his feet, Shane leaned across the table and got right in Rat's face. TJ appeared behind Rat in support of his boss but refrained from making a move when Shane caught the bouncer's eye and shook his head slowly. TJ may have been a strong vampire, but Shane was older and a sentry for the Presidium. Attacking him would have far-reaching ramifications.

"Relax, TJ," Shane murmured without breaking eye contact with Rat. "Your boss needs to hear something, and I need to be absolutely certain he hears it. I wouldn't want there to be any...*miscommunication* between us."

"Jeez, Quesada," Rat said through a nervous laugh. He put his hands up in surrender, but Shane didn't release him. "What are you so damn touchy about?"

"Maya will not dance here and remove what little clothing she is wearing. She is here to tend bar and pour drinks." He lowered his voice to a dangerous level and tightened his grip. "And that's it. Are we clear?"

"Crystal." Rat laughed nervously and looked around the club.

The customers and the employees, including Maya, were looking on with obvious concern. Shane glanced at her briefly to see an annoyed look on her face. Then, like a warm summer breeze, her voice drifted into his mind. *Let him go, Shane. I really hope whatever is going on over there has nothing to do with me.* A gentle, comforting sensation of warmth spread through his chest and radiated down his arms and legs when the sweet sound of her voice filled his head.

"Excellent." Shane released the lapels of Rat's jacket and sat casually in his chair as though nothing had happened. "Now, I think it would be best if you tended to your customers and left me to my business. And I'm sure I don't need to remind you *not* to alert the wolves to my presence. Agreed?"

"Agreed." Rat adjusted his jacket and walked toward the VIP table, with TJ close behind. "Enjoy the show, Quesada."

A new song came blaring through the speakers, and as if on cue, the front door of the club swung open and the pack of werewolves walked through the door.

The one in front was the alpha of the group and had to be Horace. He was short and stocky, probably no more than five foot eight, but he looked to be solid muscle, which was common for their kind. Shane's body went rigid while he studied each of the pack members carefully. But as intent as he was on the wolves, he didn't miss Maya's wide-eyed stare. She watched the six of them stride into the club with awe and, he hoped, a bit of healthy fear.

Rat greeted Horace with a warm, welcoming handshake and pat on the shoulder, like they were old friends. Watching the exchange, Shane's eyes narrowed, and every alarm bell in his head went off. Rat had said he was getting information through the dancer and had only spoken with Horace tonight. But based on the body language, these two men knew each other and had met before. There was a comfort level between the two that left Shane with a strong sense of wariness.

Rat gestured toward the VIP table, and the pack followed him over. Viola, the redhead who set up the table, ran over and practically jumped on the tallest fellow at the back of the group. He greeted her, but not with the warmth of a lover, and when she hugged him, the man locked eyes with Shane. He released the girl and whispered something to Horace. Knowing he'd been made as a vampire, Shane tilted his head and raised his beer bottle. Horace remained stone-faced and turned his attention back to the group at his table.

A few moments later, the lights flickered, music blared, and a young woman took the stage.

As the evening wore on, the wolves ordered copious amounts of alcohol and were clearly getting wasted. The night was proving to be even more aggravating, because Maya had started coming out from behind the bar and hand-delivering the drinks to the VIP table.

Much to Shane's chagrin, Horace had begun paying more attention to Maya than the women who were taking off their clothes. He couldn't really blame the wolf. Maya was beautiful, and every sexy inch of her was accentuated by the miniscule dress and sky-high heels she wore. Her legs seemed to go on forever.

What are you doing? Edged with obvious irritation, Shane's voice touched Maya's mind sharply. *You are supposed to be tending bar, not catering to this pack of animals.*

I'm working, and Rat asked me to do it. Placing a drink in front of Horace, she kept speaking with him. *It's not a big deal. Just relax.*

Shane was about to respond, but when he saw Horace's hand find its way to Maya's ass, any restraint he'd been showing dissolved in a blink. Rising from the table with a growl rumbling in his chest, he swiftly closed the distance between himself and the wolves. If any humans in the club noticed the blinding speed with which he crossed the room, they gave no indication, and even though Shane knew it was risky, he couldn't help himself.

The five members of Horace's pack instantly rose to their feet, and Shane could feel the growls that reverberated in their chests. The sound sent his sonar-like senses off the charts, and though no human could hear it, it sounded to him like freight trains rumbling through the club. Maya must have heard it too, because she looked at the wolves with some of that healthy fear Shane was hoping to see.

"Excuse me, gentlemen." Shane kept his voice even, his hands at his sides, and his eyes on Horace. "I need to speak with Maya for a moment."

"She's busy," Horace said, leering. He tugged Maya closer and squeezed her backside. "I'm just getting started with this one."

Shane let his fangs erupt, not caring if a human saw. Just when he thought he'd lose all self-control and start a bloodbath in the middle of the club, Maya's sweet voice swept between them.

"Now, now," she sang. Maya placed one hand on Shane's shoulder and reached around with the other to grasp Horace's hand and pull it gently but insistently off her butt. "I'm flattered by all this male posturing, but let's not make a big scene in front of all these nice humans."

"I would never argue with a lady." Shane retracted his fangs and glanced at Maya. "I do need to speak with her privately, if you *gentlemen* don't mind."

Bullshit. Maya's lilting laugh filled his head. *I feel like all you do is argue with me*.

"Don't keep her away too long." Raising Maya's hand to his lips, Horace kept his gaze locked with Shane and kissed her fingers. "I have a feeling this one is special."

Seconds later, a bevy of half-naked dancers showed up at the table, obviously sent there by Rat, and each one draped herself over a pack member. Two women, one vamp and one of the human familiars, pushed Maya aside and crawled into Horace's lap. With the girls distracting Horace and his gang, Maya grabbed Shane by the hand and pulled him to the back of the club. She pushed open the door that said "Dancers Only," and without a word, she dragged him through the girls' dressing room and out another door that led them into a dark, narrow hallway.

There was barely enough space for the two of them to stand side by side, and the only light was from the bright-red exit sign above the door to the alley. Shane couldn't help but notice it cast a glow over Maya, making her hair look like it was on fire. In that tiny, red leather dress and with the tinges of fire in her hair, she looked like the little devil that she was.

"Are you crazy?" Maya asked with her hands on her hips.

"I was going to ask you the same question."

"Me?" Maya scoffed. "I'm just doing my job."

Shane leaned closer so that their faces were only a few inches apart. "So am I."

"No, you're not." She poked him in the chest with one finger and met his challenge. "You practically started a big, fat fight with Horace in the middle of the bar, which is not like you. You're acting like some kind of overprotective boyfriend or something."

Shane's mouth set in a grim line and shame washed over him because Maya was right. He showed a remarkable lack of self-control and almost broke the truce with the wolves. His gaze skittered over Maya's face and he realized how much trouble he was actually in. This woman had managed to turn his entire existence upside down, and for the first time in centuries, Shane was unsure of himself.

"He should not have touched you like that." Shane's voice dropped to a low, dangerous tone.

"Oh please, it's not the first time some guy in the bar has grabbed my ass, and in case you suffer from short-term memory loss," she said in a quivering voice, "I've had worse." Her chin jutted forward defiantly. "I can handle myself now. I'm not some stupid, sniveling human girl who doesn't know any better."

"I have no doubt of that." Shane placed both hands on the wall, one on either side of Maya, caging her in. "But I can assure you that no man, vampire or human, will be touching you that way ever again." He inched closer, his lips a breath away from hers. "Except for me. Whether you are willing to acknowledge it or not, I'm your bloodmate, Maya, and the meaning of that goes far beyond 'boyfriend.'"

"I'm well aware of what that would mean, Shane." Her voice shook, but her expression remained resolute. "It means you own me for the rest of my immortal existence."

Shane blinked as though she'd slapped him in the face.

"Is that what you think?" he whispered. "No, youngling. That is nowhere near what it means to be bloodmates."

"Then what does it mean?" Maya folded her arms over her breasts defensively.

"This." Shane placed a gentle kiss at the corner of her mouth. "And this," he murmured, brushing his lips over hers briefly. He remained there, his lips achingly close to hers, and the need to touch her clawed at his gut with brutal insistence. "My one priority for the rest of my existence will be to see to your happiness…and *pleasure*."

"I don't know which end is up with you," Maya whispered. Desire bloomed between them. Maya's lips parted and her hands slipped inside his jacket, settling on his waist. "One minute I want to slap you…and the next…" Maya tugged his hips against hers and moaned softly when his growing erection pressed enticingly against her. "I can't get close enough."

"I am familiar with the feeling, and all I can think about is the taste of you—"

"Shane?" she murmured against his lips, her blue eyes glazed with desire. "Stop talking."

"Gladly," he growled before covering her mouth with his.

Shane dove deep, tasting and teasing her tongue with his as though he'd never get enough. Her lips melded with his and a fire burned in his gut, shattering his restraint. Kissing her deeply, he reached down and grabbed her firm, round ass with both hands, pressing her to him, but it simply wasn't sufficient. She fumbled with his shirt and pulled it from the waist of his jeans before raking her fingers along the bare skin of his lower back.

She smiled against his mouth when he growled with pleasure. Her flesh brushed over his exquisitely while he blazed a trail of kisses down her long, lovely throat. It didn't matter that someone might walk in and see the two of them together. All he cared about was getting closer and tasting every beautiful inch of her porcelain skin.

He nudged the heavy pendant out of the way before pulling down the top of her dress to reveal her full breasts. Cupping one soft mound in his hand, he bent his head and flicked her nipple with his tongue. Maya wrapped one leg around him, writhing against him as she threaded her fingers through his hair and held him to her, urging him on.

"Never stop touching me that way," Maya rasped.

His fangs hummed, begging to be freed so they could pierce that perfect flesh and taste her, but Maya tugged his hair and pulled his mouth to hers. He let her take the lead, allowing her full control in teasing and suckling his tongue. She slowed the pace and kissed him with long, languid strokes before finally suckling his lower lip and breaking the kiss.

A knock at the door made them both freeze. Shane blinked. What the hell was he doing mauling Maya in the back hall of a strip club with a pack of werewolves out there? He'd lost his damn mind.

"Whatever you two are doing in there, finish it up, would ya?" Rat shouted. "I've got a pack of wolves out here that are requesting Maya serve their drinks, and they won't buy another one unless she brings it to them."

Shane opened his mouth to respond, but Maya pressed her finger to his lips and shook her head.

"I'll be right out, Rat."

Shane kissed her finger before brushing her lips gently with his. Helping her put her top back in place, he fought the urge to take it off again. She giggled and playfully pushed his hands away so she could do it herself, and though he'd enjoyed removing the garment, it was almost as sexy to watch her put it back on.

"Tuck in your shirt and keep your hands to yourself, mister."

"As you wish for now, but I make no promises about later." Shane made quick work of putting himself back together, but he was relatively certain his raging hard-on would need time to die down. "We wouldn't want to keep Horace waiting, now would we?"

Maya rolled her eyes and pushed past him, but Shane

took her hand in his, stopping her before she opened the door. She glanced over her shoulder, her blond hair flowing in silken waves down her back, and met his stern stare with her own.

"Watch yourself, Maya." He squeezed her hand. "Horace is not a wolf you want to toy with. He's aggressive, and according to Olivia, he came here without his father's blessing. I suspect he's here to cause trouble. I can't imagine you want to be a part of that."

"You sure know how to ruin a moment, don't you?"

"I have your best interests in mind." His jaw set. "But I also have a job to do."

"You know what? I changed my mind." Maya pulled her hand from his. "I don't need a babysitter or a bodyguard."

Then without another word, she disappeared through the door. Shane swore under his breath and followed her into the club. He took a seat at the bar this time and spent the next three hours watching Maya flit back and forth between the bar and the wolves. To her credit, she managed to stay out of Horace's reach, but no matter where she went, that wolf had his dark, shifty gaze glued to her. Every warning bell Shane had was going off in his head. Whatever Horace's plans were, he clearly wanted Maya to be a part of them.

Chapter 6

Maya couldn't believe how quickly her first night of work at The Dollhouse went, and while she was cleaning up behind the bar, a smile played at her lips. Even with Shane lurking in the club all night doing his broody, staring thing, Maya felt freer than she had in a long time. She got on well with the other girls at The Dollhouse, and Rat let her do her thing behind the bar.

All in all, aside from the one tense moment when Shane overreacted, it was a good night.

I will escort you home when you are finished. Maya's breasts tingled the instant Shane's deep, seductive voice touched her mind, and the unexpected contact almost made her trip over her own feet. It was intimate, erotic, and oddly familiar to have him speak with her like this, but at the same time, the sudden inability to hear her siblings was unsettling. Her world was changing at a breakneck pace, which made her feel unsteady and unsure and gave her an overall feeling of unease. *The sun will rise in just a couple of hours, but we could fly for a while, if you'd like.*

Maya shut her mind without responding and her smile faded. So much for feeling like she had freedom. Snagging a wet rag from the bar sink, she started wiping down her work area and glanced up to see Horace give her a wave. She smiled back and studied him for a moment before looking away. He was handsome—not in the tall, dark, and sexy way that Shane was but in a ruggedly handsome way. There was a wildness about him that she found appealing, and after that one grab-ass moment at the start of the night, he'd been a perfect gentleman.

Maya was wondering what all the fuss was about.

All of the men in his pack behaved while they were at the club. They might have been a little loud, but they weren't acting like the crazy animals everyone warned her about. Horace was actually nice, and there was something about him and all the wolves that intrigued her. Maybe it was because she'd never met any before, but for whatever reason, she was drawn to them.

The rest of the club had cleared out, and the only customers who remained were the wolves. A few of the dancers were obviously leaving with them, and that girl Viola looked so excited, Maya thought she was going to bust. Smiling, Maya grabbed a couple of stray glasses and made quick work of cleaning them before slipping them back in the racks. When she looked up, she came face-to-face with Horace.

"It's about time for us to head out, beautiful." Horace lit a cigarette, even though he wasn't supposed to smoke inside. His gaze wandered over her face and drifted down to her cleavage, lingering on that or her necklace, Maya wasn't sure which. He took a long drag, slipped the stainless-steel lighter back in the pocket of his blazer, and nodded toward his pack, who were all waiting by the door of the club. "I was hoping I could talk you into coming out with us for a little after-party back at our hotel. I promise I'll have you home before sunrise."

Maya opened her mouth to tell him no, but before she could utter a sound, Shane appeared behind Horace and took it upon himself to answer for her.

"Maya will not be able to attend your…festivities." When Shane shifted his gaze to Horace, he had to look down a bit because Horace was so much shorter. "Perhaps another time."

"What are you, her brother?" Horace blew a huge puff of smoke directly into Shane's face, but the sentry didn't flinch.

"Definitely not, and I'm sure if I actually breathed, that smoke would bother me," Shane said evenly, leveling a deadly glare at Horace. "However, your meaning is clear. I do hope you'll show better manners when you visit with the czars."

"Yeah, I'll be sure to do that." Horace took another drag. Waving over his shoulder at Maya, he started to leave. "I'm staying at the Plaza, and you can join us if your boy over here ever lets you off the leash."

Leash? Like a fucking dog? Oh, hell no.

Shane was watching Horace walk away and clearly didn't notice the fury in Maya's face when she grabbed the bag with her clothing from under the bar. She should probably change before leaving, but she was so furious that all she wanted was get the hell out of there.

"I'd love to, Horace." Maya flew across the room in a blur. She linked her arm in his as the front door of the club opened. "Bye, Shane. Tell Olivia I'll be back before sunrise."

"Don't do this, Maya." Shane's voice, cold and curt, filled the club.

"She made her choice, big guy." Horace's eyes

flickered to orange briefly and a growl rumbled through him that sent Maya's sonar-like senses into overdrive, almost making her nauseous. She stilled, thinking she'd made a huge mistake, but his eyes quickly went back to normal and he winked. "I'm all bark and no bite…unless you ask me real nice."

The door swung shut behind them, and the last image she saw was a look of pure, unadulterated fury on Shane's face. Stepping out into the chilly air, Maya was filled with guilt, anger, and frustration. Sensing the change in her demeanor, Horace wrapped one arm around her in an almost protective gesture. Maya smiled at him and noticed that his body temperature was far warmer than any human she'd encountered—even more than someone with a fever—and he smelled different too.

All of the men in his pack had a distinctive scent, a combination of fresh earth and wood smoke. Their scents made her almost dizzy, and for some inexplicable reason, she simply had to go with them. She didn't particularly want to be with Horace, but something deep inside her gut pulled her toward him.

"After you," Horace said with a sweeping gesture.

Maya looked up and saw a massive, white stretch limo waiting at the curb. All of the other couples had piled in, and the human limo driver stood patiently waiting by the open door. Maya looked from the closed door of the club to the limo and back to Horace. She nibbled her lower lip, knowing full well she should get her butt back to her apartment, but one of the other girls, a vamp named Ginger, leaned out the open door and waved.

"Come on, Maya. You've never partied until you

partied with these boys. They're wild," she shrieked just before Marcus, one of Horace's pack members, pulled her back into the limo.

"See," Horace said. "You're perfectly safe with us." He trailed one finger along her jaw, down her throat, and around the necklace. "We're just here to have some fun."

The door to the club swung open and Shane stood in the doorway like the angel of death. If Maya didn't know better, she'd say he'd grown about a foot and a half. In the blink of an eye, Maya slid into the waiting limo, but Horace stopped in the doorway and faced Shane. He waved off the limo driver, who promptly went to get in the driver's seat.

"The lady made her decision, Quesada."

The girls in the car giggled and clung to their dates, but the men kept their eyes on Maya. She gripped her bag tighter and peered out the door past Horace. Her stomach dropped when Shane's eyes met hers.

"Yeah," Horace said on a laugh, "I know who you are. You're a sentry, one of the soldiers that do all the dirty work for the Presidium. So unless you want to break the nice little truce we have going between our races, I'd suggest you back the fuck up. I'd hate to have to tell the czars that you were picking a fight with the heir to the throne."

"Heir? That's funny, I thought you were the spare," Shane murmured, shifting his furious glare from Horace to Maya.

"I'm royalty, and *you* are the fucking help."

Shane said nothing but took a step back. Maya didn't know whether to be relieved or annoyed.

"That's what I thought." Horace flicked his cigarette butt into the gutter and slid into the seat next to Maya.

The limo door slammed shut just before the driver pulled away. Maya turned around to look out the window, but Shane was nowhere to be seen. Her gut clenched and tears stung at the back of her eyes because she knew that she'd hurt him. But when Horace implied that Shane had control of her, that he had her on a leash, she lost it. One thought nagged at her: Had she lost Shane in the process?

Maya leaned on the smooth granite counter of a lavish bathroom that was bigger than some entire NYC apartments. Staring at her reflection in the mirror, she didn't like what she saw one bit. One of the human misconceptions about vamps was that they had no reflection, but that wasn't true. Nope. Maya could see her dumb blond self as clear as day.

How could she have been so stupid?

Once they arrived in the suite, which was one of the most gorgeous spaces Maya had ever seen, she quickly excused herself to go to the bathroom and change. At first she worried that Horace might try to stop her and keep her in the horribly tacky dress from the club, but he didn't. He continued to be a gentleman.

There had been no sign of Shane, and so far, he hadn't tried to telepath with her. Right after the limo pulled away, Maya opened her mind to him and found nothing but silence. Achingly sad silence filled Maya's head and made her long for one of Trixie's jabs about her bad taste in music or one of Suzie's silly newbie vampire questions. At this point, she'd even take a scolding I-told-you-so from Sadie.

She heard none of that. There was only silence because Shane, the one person whom Maya could now telepath with, wasn't speaking to her—and she couldn't blame him. Maya nibbled her lower lip and ran her fingers through her hair, attempting to smooth it as she thought about how upset Olivia was going to be when she heard Maya went with the wolves. However, no matter how angry Olivia got, it would be *nothing* compared to the hurt look on Shane's face when she went with Horace.

"What are you doing?" Maya whispered to her own reflection. She rolled her eyes and shook her head on a growl before answering her own question. "You're going home, you dumb ass."

Grabbing the bag, she opened the bathroom door and was struck by the surprising lack of noise. There was no more chatter or giggling from the girls, and the only sound was the music coming from the sound system hooked up throughout the massive, three-bedroom suite. She reached out with her senses and could tell all three bedrooms were occupied—two of them with more than one couple. Closing her eyes, she sharpened her focus and captured the distinct scent of the wolves mixed with the pungent odor of sex—and blood.

The girls were feeding on the wolves, breaking one of the cardinal rules: no feeding on werewolves. Maya's eyes whipped open and she ran into the main living room of the suite. Panicked and dizzy from the strong, almost overpowering combination of scents, Maya felt her vision blur, and lights flickered behind her eyes. Her skin felt too small for her body and her necklace hung heavy and cumbersome around her neck, like a noose.

If she didn't know better, Maya would think she'd been drugged.

"Wh-what's happening to me?" she whispered. Stumbling, Maya grabbed the back of one of the living-room chairs for support. "I don't feel well… I need to go home."

"You okay?" Horace's voice whisked around her in the air, and he encircled her bicep with his hot, sweaty hand. As Horace helped her to her feet, his face went in and out of focus, and she vaguely noticed him take the bag from her. "Come on, let's go out on the terrace and get you some fresh air."

"But I don't breathe," Maya said absently.

The terrace doors opened and the cold, New York City air hit her, instantly making her feel better. Squeezing her eyes shut, with Horace's hand still firmly around her arm, Maya focused on the sounds and scents in the air that were so distinctly part of the Big Apple.

Car exhaust. Human heartbeats fluttering like a swarm of butterflies. Hot dogs and pretzels. Blood.

Even when her head started to clear a bit, Maya couldn't rid herself of Horace's pungent, intriguing scent of burning wood. That same pulling sensation tugged at her gut and willed her closer to him. It wasn't desire, the way her body yearned for Shane's, but something else…something she couldn't quite decipher. Even though she didn't want him, her body was inexplicably drawn to his like a magnet.

Maya leaned on the railing of the terrace and gave Horace a weak smile. The tugging sensation throbbed in her belly, making her nauseous.

"Feeling better?" Horace asked. He linked his arm around her waist and tugged her against him. She could feel his growing erection pressing against her hip, and that feeling of panic began to bubble up again.

"Not really." Maya laughed nervously. She placed her hands on his shoulders and leaned back, pushing him away while he tried to nuzzle her neck. "It looks like your party isn't happening and everyone went to sleep. Speaking of which, I have to get going." Maya glanced at the glimmer of light on the horizon. The sun was beginning to rise, and her time was running out. "The sun will be up soon, and I'd really rather not use the tunnels to get back, so I should leave now."

"They're not sleeping." Horace's eyes glowed orange and he held her against him with surprising strength. "They're fucking. Which is exactly what I'd like to do with you."

"No." Maya shook her head and tried to extricate herself from his grasp. It should have been easy—she was, after all, a vampire—but to her horror, it wasn't. "Let me go."

"Think you're stronger than me, little vamp? Not a chance," he growled. In a flash, Horace's hand curled around her throat. "I guess your boyfriend didn't school you on our kind. We're even stronger than you bloodsuckers. So you're not going anywhere. You have something I want, and you're not leaving until I get it."

Maya's fangs erupted as anger, fear, and panic filled her, and she locked gazes with Horace. Using every ounce of strength she had, Maya pushed into his mind with hers in an attempt to glamour him. For a moment, just a moment, she thought it had worked. When a slow smile cracked his face and a low, guttural laugh bubbled up…she knew it hadn't. Trixie was right. Werewolves couldn't be glamoured.

"Sorry, baby vamp." Horace yanked her neck so that her face was right next to his, and the orange glow from his eyes was almost blinding. "Didn't they tell you? You can't glamour a wolf."

Horace growled, his teeth extended into the sharp canines of a wolf and his body began to contort and stretch against hers with frightening speed. Maya screamed and struggled to get away from the repulsive feel of his body shifting, but Horace was too strong—it was just like before. Only this time, there would be no Olivia to save her. His claws emerged, ripping her sweater, and Maya prayed for the sun to rise.

His claws sliced across her arms at the same moment that something rocketed out of the sky and sent them both flying to the stone floor of the terrace. Maya wept in a bleeding heap in the corner, frozen by fear. Memories of the past filled her head, and all she could do was pull her knees against her chest, squeeze her eyes shut, and pray for it to end.

Glass breaking. Snarls. Gunshots. Howls. Shrieks.

Maya pressed her hands over her ears and let out a scream just before the darkness consumed her.

Shane had followed them from a distance and stayed on the roof just above the terrace of their suite. He was torn between being absolutely furious with Maya and worried for her safety, although he knew he was partially to blame. He should have let Maya tell Horace "no" all by herself. Instead Shane had blurted it out before he could stop himself.

What. A. Dope.

He swore under his breath and glanced at the brightening horizon. It was yet another moment when he showed an appalling lack of self-control, once again related to Maya. He made a note to himself to speak with Doug and Olivia about the bloodmate legend. He had hoped to keep his suspicions under wraps, but based on the way things were fucking up at every turn, he needed help. Besides, he heard Trixie and Sadie's conversation with Maya about their inability to telepath with her. Odds were that they had already shared that tidbit with the czars.

Squatting on the edge of the roof, elbows resting on his knees and hands clasped, he remained stone still, tuning into Maya's and the wolves' scents. Having tasted her blood, he should be able to find her anywhere, but to his dismay, the scent of the wolves was interfering somehow and making her exact location difficult to pinpoint.

He frowned. That had never happened before.

Over the four centuries of his vampire existence, Shane had battled all kinds of supernatural creatures, including werewolves, but he'd never had their presence interfere with his ability to track. It was a less-than-appealing development and was going to make his job that much harder.

Maya's scent in the air captured his attention, and he looked down to see Horace bringing her outside. Shane's eyes narrowed. Something was wrong with her. He instantly reached out to touch her mind with his, but it was like running into a mass of psychic cobwebs. She wasn't blocking him. He'd felt that type of mental stonewall before, and this was different but no less disconcerting.

Shane's fangs broke free the instant Horace started to get more physical with Maya. Shane leaped to his feet, and though he wanted to fly down there and intervene, he resisted. He knew that he had to give her the opportunity to get out of this situation on her own. All bets were off when the situation grew more violent and Horace began to shift into the wolf.

Maya was in way over her head.

Shane flew down like a bullet with her scream filling the predawn sky. He slammed into them, which released Maya from Horace's grasp and sent her curling up into a weeping ball in the corner. Shane wanted to grab her and take her back to the apartments beneath The Coven, but Horace was spoiling for a fight.

He leaped onto Shane's back, snapping his powerful jaws and attempting to bite the vampire, but Shane reached around, grabbed Horace, and tossed him through the glass doors into the living room. A werewolf bite was almost certain death, due to the poisonous effects of the saliva on vampires. That bite could turn a human into a werewolf, but it could kill a vampire.

Seconds later, the remaining glass shattered to the ground like rain, and all five of Horace's pack members appeared in their werewolf forms. Shane barely noticed the human women running out of the suite or the two vamps who flew out the windows because the only sound he could hear was Maya. Her keening wail tore at whatever shred of soul he had and cut him deep in his core. The wolves leaped toward him but skidded to a halt when Shane drew a gun loaded with silver bullets.

All of them froze and one, a wolf with darker, almost black fur, tilted his snout to the air. Their eyes glowed orange, and the smaller brown one on the right took a step forward, but the big one growled a warning. Shane knew the wolves could telepath with each other, and in all likelihood, the big one smelled the silver.

Horace was naked and had shifted back to his human form. He rose to his feet, swiping at the blood that dripped from his forehead and with a wicked smile on his face. His five pack members stood by his side, all of them snarling at Shane.

"Thanks." Horace laughed at Shane's obvious confusion. "Not bad. A sentry for the Presidium attacked a member of the royal family and, in the process, has broken the truce."

"Hardly." Shane kept his voice even and took a step toward Maya, who had passed out. "I was protecting a member of the czars' coven—one of Olivia's progeny—from a wolf attack. I'd say the truce was broken by you."

"I guess it will be your word against ours." Horace gestured wide with both arms. "I'm sure your czars won't be too happy with you or the girl. She comes here, leads me on, plays games with me, and then the bitch tried to suck my blood," he smirked, the lie slipping easily from his mouth. "If anyone used self-defense, it was me. She's a fuckin' tease, and from what Rat tells me, everyone knows it."

Shane gripped the gun tighter, frustration surging through him. Maya's reputation for toying with men and her willingness to break the rules was working against them now. Olivia and Doug would believe Shane's version of events, but what would King Heinrich and the rest of them believe?

"I will make a full report to the czars about exactly what happened here." Shane holstered his gun beneath his jacket but didn't take his eyes off the pack. "Feel free to do the same with your father."

Their growls rolled around him in the air like a herd of elephants, and he knew it was only a moment before they'd attack. The moment that thought went into his mind, the five wolves lunged. Without taking his gaze off Horace, and in a blink of an eye, Shane scooped up Maya and shot into the sky like a bullet. As he flew away, he heard Horace shout, "Welcome to the war."

Shane told them everything.

The dreams, the telepathic contact, bloodmates... everything.

Sitting on the couch in Maya's apartment, Shane rested his elbows on his knees and held his head in his hands. Waiting for Olivia and Doug to say something, he felt battered by shame, anger, and frustration. Maya was passed out in her bed, with Trixie and Sadie keeping watch over her while Shane had rattled off the evening's events to the czars with an unusual edge of emotion.

Normally, when recapping a patrol, he was all business, but with Maya, it was entirely personal.

"What a shit show." Olivia ran her hands over her swollen belly and paced back and forth on the other side of the room. "I knew that little bastard was up to something. He deliberately baited the two of you into a fight, and it sounds like our friend Rat is playing both sides. Why would the prince want to start the war again?"

"I'm not certain," Shane said quietly. "But if I had to venture a guess, I'd say his motives have something to do with the throne. The fact that he came here to New York and started all of this while his father is overseas is far too coincidental. Maybe he wants his father to see him having heir potential, rather than just being the spare?"

"Perhaps." Olivia looked from Doug to Shane. "I find it difficult to believe King Heinrich would support this kind of crap. He even offered to have his oldest son, Killian, come to town to babysit his little brother, and I may just take him up on it."

"The king wants peace, Liv. He's not going to reignite the freaking war because of this little *incident*." Doug rubbed her back reassuringly. "You've told me over and over that he's totally on board with the truce. Wasn't it his ancestor who signed the treaty?"

"Yes." Shane rose from the couch and stood at attention. "And I have risked that peace, due to rash and impulsive actions that are not fitting of a sentry. I will accept whatever punishment you see fit."

"Give it a rest, Shane." Olivia waved him off. She sat in the oversized chair, and Doug took a protective stance beside her. She smiled warmly at her mate. "If anyone understands how upside down the world gets during the bloodmate bonding process, it's us."

"Thank you." Shane bowed his head, but he could not shake the horrible feeling of having failed the Presidium and, even worse, Doug and Olivia. Over the past few months, the two czars had become more like friends than his superiors, and it galled him to think he had let them down. "But that is still no excuse for my behavior…or hers."

"Maya is your bloodmate. I still can't believe it," Doug said with genuine wonder. "Damn, brother. You are gonna have your hands full with that one."

"Hey," Olivia protested. "I know she can kind of be a pain in the ass but—"

"Kind of?" Doug asked incredulously. "*Kind of?* That girl has done nothing but cause trouble from the minute I met her. It's like she's trying to get herself killed. If I didn't know better, I'd say she has a serious death wish." Doug's brows knit together and he ran a hand over his short blond hair. "And I don't get it. I know that the werewolves are strong, stronger than humans certainly, but Maya should have been able to get away from him. Right?"

"Fear," Shane bit out before Olivia could answer Doug. "Maya is still tormented by the attack she suffered on the last night of her human life. She was reliving it every time she slept until I was pulled into her dreamscape and could intervene. Each time she hunts, every human man she feeds on, is a way for Maya to try to reclaim her sense of power. When Horace went after her, Maya was paralyzed by her deep-seated belief that she is powerless—a victim. I suspect that until she faces that fear and stops allowing her past to haunt her, she will keep fighting the ghosts."

"You mean fighting herself," Olivia said quietly with tears in her eyes. "That girl has been fighting since the night I found her in that alley—fighting for her life and her sanity. Something tells me, Shane, that you are going to be the key to Maya finding some peace."

"No." Shane shook his head and removed his jacket before placing it over the arm of the couch. "Maya will have to do that for herself, but I will be there to guide her. She tells me that you killed the human who attacked her that night."

"Yes." A dark cloud flickered over Olivia's face, recalling what she'd done, and she nodded. "I'm not proud of it, but I did."

"Since Maya can no longer confront him in the physical plane, the dreamscape is her only option." He unbuttoned the cuffs of his shirt and rolled up his sleeves as he spoke. "I will continue to go to her in the dreamscape until *she* is the one to save herself. Not me. When we are finished and she has an opportunity to sleep, I plan to go to her again."

"Interesting," Olivia murmured. "Let her save herself in the dream so that she regains her power and feels safe again."

"I'm impressed, Quesada." Doug made a face of approval and nodded. "That's smart, a little new-agey for a guy from the sixteenth century, but smart."

"With nothing but time on our hands, evolution is inevitable." Shane flicked a glance to Olivia's swollen belly. "A concept you're both familiar with."

"You really feel something for her, don't you?" Olivia asked. "It's not just the bloodmate bond, is it?"

"I have felt several things for Maya." Shane smirked. "If and when I'm able to decipher exactly what those emotions are, I'll be sure to let you know."

"I'm not the one you should tell." Olivia smiled.

Silence hung between them momentarily before being interrupted by the shrill chirp of a text message on Doug's cell phone. He snagged it from the pocket of his leather coat and frowned when he read the message scrolled across the screen.

"What is it?" Olivia took his hand in hers. "What's going on?"

"It's Suzie." Doug turned his serious gaze to Shane. "Horace just called the office. It looks like he and his pack are looking for a meeting."

"How diplomatic of him," Olivia said with a roll of her eyes. "I don't want them in the underground offices. Have them meet us in the gardens of The Cloisters, tonight after dark when it's closed to the public. You and I can withstand the sunlight, but we're still stronger at night."

"I will be there as well," Shane added.

"No." Olivia rose to her feet, shook her head, and held up one hand when Shane opened his mouth to protest. "Doug and I can handle it, with a little help from Xavier and some of his weapons. In addition to Sadie and Trixie, we'll have Damien. He is the club's bouncer, after all. I'll even ask Pete to make an appearance. We'll have plenty of backup, loads of firepower, and the home-field advantage. Your presence would only crank up the tension. In fact, given everything you've told us, we think it would be best if you left town for a while."

Shane flinched. It was like a kick in the gut, and he stared at Olivia and Doug with shock.

"Hang on." Doug held up one hand and wrapped his other arm around his mate. "It's not what you're thinking. We're not banishing you or anything."

"Funny, that's exactly how it feels."

"Shane," Olivia began, "you and Maya are now the

second vamp couple to discover that you are bloodmates. In a couple of days, every leader in the supernatural community is meeting in Geneva, Switzerland." The lines in her face deepened and her hands rested protectively on her stomach. "There's already nervousness, uneasiness about what being bloodmates will mean for our race and for the rest of the world. What do you think will happen when they hear about yet *another* pairing? For all we know, Maya could get pregnant too."

Shane must have made a face because Doug laughed out loud before quickly recovering. "Shit, I didn't think you could get any paler, but you looked like you were going to faint for a second."

"I thought it was Doug's angel bloodline that allowed you to get pregnant." Shane folded his arms over his chest and tried to act like he wasn't terrified at the idea of Maya getting pregnant. "As you know, I am not descended from that lineage."

"That's what we *suspect.*" Olivia shrugged. "The truth is that we just don't know. I don't even know when the baby will arrive. I feel like my stomach grew visibly bigger over the past few days, and I can't stop craving human food. We're all flying blind on this. The entire bloodmate thing comes with a giant question mark. One pairing was weird enough, but now with you two..."

"Add that to what happened with Horace," Doug chimed in, "and that uneasiness can get ugly real quick. People, regardless of whatever supernatural whammy they possess, can be panicky assholes. When I was a cop, I saw it all the time. Nobody knows what the long-term ramifications are of being bloodmates, and that unknown element is making people uncomfortable."

"I will leave immediately." Shane nodded grimly because they were absolutely right. "But I'm taking Maya with me."

"Agreed. We'll tell everyone that you and Maya ran off, and as far as we're concerned, you simply vanished." Olivia elbowed Doug who quickly pulled out his phone and began to type something on the keypad with the ease of a human familiar with technology. Shane had a phone so he could communicate when needed, but he hated it. "Doug is going to send you an address for a safe house in Louisiana. Lottie Fogg is an old friend of mine. She's a gypsy woman who lives in the bayou. She's helped me out in the past, and she's good at being *discreet*."

"A gypsy?"

Shane was more than a little surprised. The gypsies existed off the grid of both the human and supernatural worlds and were known for their unwillingness to get involved in any society other than their own. Shane had tangled with a gypsy or two in his time, and he knew they were not individuals to mess with. Their magic was ancient and powerful and capable of bone-chilling darkness.

The bottom line: Don't fuck with a gypsy.

"The gypsies are unreliable nomads who care for nothing other than themselves and their own kind. I find it difficult to believe there is one who would be willing to help us."

"Well, believe it, and if you know what's good for you, you'll keep your opinion about gypsies to yourself. Lottie isn't exactly a fan of the vamps—or any other supernaturals, for that matter—but she is my friend."

"Of course." Shane bowed his head in an apologetic

gesture. "I apologize if I seemed ungrateful, but this is *surprising*."

"Yeah," Olivia said with a laugh. "I'm full of those. Keep in mind it also means it's unlikely that anyone, wolf or vampire, would go looking for you at a gypsy's house. You and Maya can hide out there for a bit while we smooth things over with the wolves. This will also give the two of you time to…work things out."

"There." Doug stuck the phone back in his pocket, and a second later, the one in Shane's pocket buzzed. "I sent Lottie's address to you. While you have Maya's undivided attention down there in the bayou, might I suggest some fight training? Something tells me she's going to need it."

"I was thinking the same thing." Shane nodded. "If it's alright with you, Olivia, I'd like to pay Xavier a visit before we leave and get Maya fitted for some weapons."

"Done." Olivia took Doug's hand and headed toward the door. "You should head out before nightfall. Take the tunnels to the outskirts of the city until sundown, and then if you fly all night, you can make it there before sunrise. Let me know when you get there."

"I will." Shane watched the czars and marveled at their comfort level with one another. They acted like they'd been together for centuries, as opposed to months. "Olivia?"

"Yes?"

"Be careful. I suspect that Rat is more involved with the wolves than he is letting on. In fact, the more I think about it, the more I think this visit wasn't a surprise to him at all. He can't be trusted."

Olivia smiled and laughed.

"What's so funny?" Shane asked, feeling a tad annoyed at the czar's reaction.

"You know that his real name is Fred and that Rat is his nickname, right?"

"Yes."

"Well"—she grinned, showing her bright, white fangs—"I'm the one who gave him the nickname."

Chapter 7

When Maya woke up, still not quite sure that the incident with Horace had been real, her sisters told her she was being sent away. Maya could barely look them in the eyes and wondered if she'd ever be able to again. Trixie and Sadie were helping her pack a duffel bag in silence. Though neither of them had said more than a few words to her, Maya was relatively certain they were telepathing to one another.

Standing in only her bra and panties, she picked up the sentry uniform that Olivia sent over and tears pricked the back of her eyes. The tears fell silently as she rubbed the smooth, protective fabric between her fingers. This was the clothing of a vampire warrior, a sentry, the elite of all vampires. Maya knew she had no business wearing it, so she wasn't sure why Olivia sent it over. Olivia must have been furious with her because she didn't even come to say good-bye.

Not that Maya could blame her.

Maya knew her actions had been stupid, selfish, thoughtless, and childish, and she wouldn't blame Olivia—let alone Shane—if they never spoke to her again. Maya swiped at the tears and turned her back on her sisters, who had averted their eyes. *They must hate me too*, she thought.

They don't hate you, youngling. Shane's voice, gentle but firm, entered her mind like a caress. *Quite the contrary, but please hurry up*.

You're still speaking to me? Maya asked with a sideways glance at her sisters.

It would seem so. Silence lingered for a moment before Shane continued. *We must leave right away. I am waiting for you in the living room...the very pink living room. I do hope that when we acquire a home of our own, after this nonsense has passed, you will not insist on bathing the entire space in shades of bubble gum.*

Maya stilled and nibbled her lower lip. Their own apartment? Together? A home with him? The idea wasn't unpleasant but it was...unexpected. *I'll be out in just a minute*, she responded quietly.

She pulled on the leather-Lycra catsuit and slipped on the knee-high black boots that went with it. She made quick work of slicking her blond hair back into a tight ponytail, and when she turned around to face her sisters, they gaped at her in stunned silence. She adjusted her necklace with the gesture that never failed to reassure her and nestled the stone against her chest.

"What is it?" Maya asked in a barely audible voice. "It looks ridiculous on me, doesn't it? I probably look like Dominatrix Barbie, and I know I don't deserve to wear this but—"

"That's not it," Trixie said with a wide grin. "It actually looks so right on you, it's scary."

"The only one who thinks you're unworthy of this, or anything else, is you." Sadie grabbed the black duffel bag and closed the distance between them. "You're not the first one to fuck up, and you won't be the last."

"I don't know what happened." Maya looked down at her hands clasped tightly in front of her, and shame washed over her. "Horace made that comment about

Shane keeping me on a leash, and then the next thing I knew, I was in the limo with him. But that wasn't the worst part."

"Go on." Sadie tossed the bag on the bed and Trixie moved in next to her, eager to hear the rest. "Keep talking."

"I'm glad Olivia is sending me away." Maya looked at her sisters through wide, frightened eyes. "My body or my gut—something deep inside me—was pulling me to Horace and the rest of the wolves," she whispered. "It scares the hell out of me. My head and my heart were screaming to get away, but…it was like a magnetic pull that I could feel right here." Maya made a fist and held it over her stomach. "When I was in that suite with them, my senses went on overload or something and I passed out."

"Did you tell Shane this yet?" Trixie asked. "Or Olivia?"

Maya shook her head. "She hates me and I don't blame her. That's why she's sending me away. She can't stand the sight of me."

"I never thought you were a dumb blond," Trixie said.

"Trixie," Sadie warned.

"No, seriously. She thinks Olivia hates her?" Trixie swatted Maya playfully on the side of the head. "Hello? Anybody home? Shit, Maya. Olivia is sending you away for your own safety, not just because of the fight with Horace, but also because of the whole bloodmate thing."

"You know?" It was like a punch in the gut. "He told you?"

"Well, we figured it out once we realized you couldn't telepath with us anymore, but then Shane told Olivia and Doug."

"How do you feel about it?" Sadie asked. She picked the bag up off the bed and handed it to Maya. "I know

Olivia's a little worried about how the supernaturals will react to another bloodmate couple. I don't think anyone's bothered to ask you or Shane how you guys feel about it."

Before Maya could answer her, an impatient knock at the door interrupted them. It was just as well because Maya had no idea how she felt about it, other than confused.

"We have to go, Maya." Shane's voice boomed from the other side. "The sun has been up for over an hour, and we still need to go see Xavier."

"She's coming, Quesada," Trixie barked. "Keep your fangs on."

Maya slung the bag over her shoulder just as her sisters gathered her up in a big, weepy hug. Even Trixie shed a tear, but Maya didn't point it out because her sister would only deny it. They each gave her a quick kiss on the cheek, and when she opened the bedroom door, Shane was there, impatiently waiting. Once again dressed in the black, leather sentry gear, he looked like the fiercest warrior she'd ever seen and some of her fear ebbed. If nothing else, Maya knew she was safe with Shane.

He gestured toward the open front door, and staring into those dark, hypnotic eyes, Maya realized her world had changed forever. Walking side by side with Shane, she wondered if she'd be able to change with it.

They flew through the tunnels beneath the city streets as quickly as possible, and even though the dank, smelly conditions in the sewer tunnels grossed her out, she refrained from complaining. How could she possibly complain after everything that had happened? Maya flicked a glance at Shane whisking along beside her, and guilt swamped her. He was being forced to leave the job he loved because of her. He wouldn't even have been in the situation with Horace if she hadn't been such a stubborn ass and gone with the werewolves.

This entire stupid mess was her fault.

His jaw was set and his fiercely intense gaze remained focused on the path ahead of them. Maya fought the urge to cry and turned her attention on the tunnels ahead, vowing to make it better. Somehow, some way she was going to make things right and straighten this mess out. No one had to tell Maya how fucked up she was, and nobody wanted her to get her shit together more than she herself. She was tired of being afraid.

They skidded to a halt at the entrance of the Presidium, and she silently followed Shane through the secret doorway and into the brightly lit hallway. He pressed his thumb to the flat panel by the enormous wooden door and it swung open, immediately allowing them access to the stone hallways of the Presidium's underground facility.

When Maya glanced up at the iron light fixtures that dangled from the ceilings between massive stone archways, she couldn't help but feel like she'd stepped back in time. The intricate network of hallways and rooms that sat beneath The Cloisters and Fort Tryon Park had been there for centuries and made Maya feel small.

She stole a quick glance at Shane when they rounded a corner, and a smile played at her lips. He towered over her by almost a foot, even with the heels on her boots, making her look small standing next to him. Her gaze skimmed over his tall, muscular form and lingered on his profile. He had a strong, square jaw, a perfectly straight nose, and a generous mouth with firm lips that curved into a lopsided smile. Maya's eyes flicked to his, and she gasped when she realized he had caught her ogling him.

"Wait until you see the new setup in the lab," Shane said with nod of his head. "Xavier recently had some new doors installed with a security camera, so chances are he's going to make me buzz into the room."

"I've never been in his lab before." Maya looked away and kept walking, feeling embarrassed for staring at him so blatantly.

"Really?" Shane stopped when they reached a set of shiny steel doors and shot Maya a look of surprise. He clasped his hands in front of himself and looked her up and down. "I didn't realize you haven't visited the armory or the labs before. Looking at you in that sentry uniform, it's no wonder I find it hard to believe… It suits you."

"That's what Trixie and Sadie said." Maya adjusted the duffel bag on her shoulder and shrugged. "But wearing it makes me feel like a fraud."

"Why?" Shane stepped closer and leveled a serious stare at her. "Why does it make you feel like a fraud, Maya?"

"Because I'm no warrior or badass ninja like you or Olivia. Okay?" Her voice rose, reflecting her frustration with her own inadequacies. "I'm just some dumb bartender who's nice to look at. I'm not a fighter."

"Well, you are partially correct."

"Which part?" Maya asked warily.

"You are indeed lovely to look at, but contrary to what you think, that's not the only gift you have to offer.

You suffer from the misguided perception that your value lies only in your appearance, and that could not be further from the truth. You are a fighter, Maya, and buried beneath that gorgeous exterior is a strong, powerful warrior waiting to be released. Although, *there is* one person you beat up every day, and it needs to stop."

"Who?" Maya asked with genuine confusion.

Shane leaned in and whispered, "Yourself."

Holding her stare, he stepped back and rang the buzzer along the side of the stainless steel doors. It was unsettling to have someone see her so clearly, perhaps even more clearly than she saw herself, and it was far more unnerving to have him point it out. She clutched the strap of the bag as though her life depended on it and said nothing. Maya faced the door just before it swished open and revealed Xavier's massive laboratory.

She let out a sound of pure awe and followed Shane into a cavernous space alive with motion, sounds, and lights. The far wall was stainless steel, much like the front doors, and the ceilings had to be fifteen feet high. All kinds of antique weapons dangled from the ceiling, some of which looked positively ancient. There were swords, daggers, muskets, spears, a scythe, and even a few that looked like torture devices.

Several lab tables each held different experiments. Beakers and tubes ran this way and that, and the concoctions inside looked like everything from liquid ultraviolet to some kind of witch's brew. Maya had met Xavier and spoken with him once or twice, but she'd never seen where he worked. The place was out-of-this-world cool and full of moving parts, which made her afraid to touch anything. With her luck, she'd blow the place up.

"Welcome, my friends," Xavier shouted from the stool he stood on. Pushing his reading glasses up the bridge of his nose, he pressed a button on the remote control in his hand and the doors swished shut behind them. "I have been expecting you."

He flew across the room and landed in front of Shane and Maya with an enormous grin. His shock of white hair stood out in about a thousand directions, and the clothes and lab coat he wore were equally disheveled. Xavier was a dwarf with a huge personality, and he always seemed to fill the room with his boundless energy.

"It's been a while since I've seen you, Maya." Xavier reached up and offered his hand, which Maya promptly shook. He looked her up and down with a nod of approval. "Olivia told me you would be coming by to stock up on weapons, but I didn't realize you were training to be a sentry."

"I'm not, not really," Maya said nervously as he released her hand.

"Yes, she is." Shane leaned down and shook Xavier's hand, but he didn't miss the surprised look on Maya's face. "By the time I'm done with Maya, she'll be able to tangle with the best of them. Sentry or not."

"I may not be able to show you how to fight," Xavier said with a wink, "but I can give you some outstanding weapons. I have a new gun that's so easy to use, even a youngling like yourself will feel like a pro in no time."

A fluttering noise from above captured Maya's attention, and she looked up to see where it was coming from. All she could see were the dangling weapons. A few of them wobbled as though something or someone had flown past. Looking toward the ceiling, Xavier chuckled and stuck his hands in the pockets of his lab coat.

"We have guests," Xavier called. "You should come out and say hello."

The fluttering noise echoed through the room, but Maya still couldn't pinpoint the location. Xavier was a bit eccentric, and part of her wondered if he was shouting at nothing at all.

"Come on." He waved them toward the back of the room. "I have some items set aside for you, Shane, but I thought you'd like to select certain things yourself, like the ammo."

"Thank you." Shane followed Xavier and motioned for Maya to do the same. Hands clasped behind his back, Shane glanced briefly at the ceiling before stopping in front of the back wall. "Has Bella been paying you more visits?"

"Who's Bella?" Maya asked, looking warily toward the ceiling.

"She's a friend," Xavier said with a sly smile. "But she's shy. Probably for the best anyway. She only speaks Romanian. I've been working on teaching her English, but so far I can't get her to say much. Usually she just hangs around and smiles at me while I work."

Isabella is a ghost. Shane's voice slid into Maya's mind with welcoming familiarity and instantly put her at ease. *She's haunted the halls of The Cloisters for years but recently took a liking to Xavier. I've never seen her, but he talks about her all the time. Don't worry, I'm sure she's harmless.*

I hope so. Maya eyed the ceiling again. *I've had all the trouble I can handle.*

"Do you know any Romanian?" Xavier asked while fishing the remote out of the pocket of his white lab coat.

"Me?" Maya shook her head. "No. English is my first and only language."

"You?" He nodded toward Shane.

"Sadly, I do not, but if you need Spanish, French, German, or Japanese translations, then I would be of some assistance."

"Wait a minute." Maya stopped dead in her tracks. "You speak all those languages?"

"I have been roaming the planet for four centuries." Shane frowned. "Actually, it's rather appalling that I haven't learned more. Most vampires my age are fluent in many more languages than that."

"Yeah." Maya pursed her lips and nodded. "I was just thinking what a slacker you are."

Shane shot her an annoyed look that quickly faded when he saw the teasing look in her eyes. "Glad to see you're feeling better."

Maya smiled and lifted one shoulder but said nothing because he was right. She was relieved that he didn't appear to hate her after what had happened. Then, her smile faltered as she realized why he was being so forgiving.

He was her bloodmate, and without her, he would never walk in the sun. Did Shane truly care for her, or was he merely following the bloodmate trail?

Xavier pushed another button on his remote, and seconds later the back wall slid away to reveal a massive arsenal—but it didn't stop there. Another wall covered with guns disappeared behind the neighboring panel to reveal a walk-in closet that would make any warrior drool. It was the NYC Presidium's armory.

When Maya looked at Shane, the expression on his face was a combination of excitement and simmering aggression. He reminded her of a tiger, pacing back and forth, and waiting for the right moment to strike. Shane stepped into the cavernous armory and immediately started picking up various guns and slipping them into hidden compartments within his jacket. He handled them with absolute confidence, and while Maya watched him, the word "graceful" actually came to mind.

Shane was most definitely in his element.

Maya, however, was not, and to say she was intimidated by the space would be an understatement.

"Don't be shy." Xavier waved for her to come in. He flew up and stood on top of a stool at the far side of the room. "I have something here that's perfect for you."

Maya went over to him, although she couldn't help but notice that Shane was watching her while he packed various items into his bag, which now had more firepower than clothing. When she finally reached Xavier, he was holding a gun out to her with both hands.

"Here." He smiled warmly. "Give it a try. It's not loaded, so you don't have to worry about any accidents."

Maya licked her lips, which suddenly felt dry. She stared at the shiny stainless-steel weapon. Slipping the bag off her shoulder, Maya placed it on the ground before tentatively taking the gun from Xavier.

She held the weapon in both hands and turned it over, carefully inspecting it. It was lighter than she expected and had a long, thin barrel with what looked like a skinny pole running along the top of it. The handle was smooth, and wrapping her fingers around it, she was surprised at how easily and naturally it fit in her hand.

"How is it?" Shane's voice drifted over her left shoulder, making Maya jump a bit. He'd moved in behind her without a sound and stood just inches away. "Is it too heavy or cumbersome feeling?"

Maya lifted one shoulder and looked at the weapon in her hands. "I have no idea how it's supposed to feel. I've never held a gun before. At least, not since I was turned," she added quickly. "I couldn't tell you what the hell I held or didn't hold when I was human."

"Well, I doubt you ever held anything like this." Xavier pushed his glasses up onto his head and pointed one pudgy finger at the gun. "That gun takes standard silver bullet ammo and *liquid* silver bullets."

"That's new." Shane had moved closer, but Maya did her best to focus on what Xavier was saying instead of the way her body was reacting to Shane.

"And deadly to both vamps and werewolves." Xavier snagged two ammunition magazines from the shelf behind him and held them up. "The black mags contain the solid silver bullets. As you know, they kill only with a shot to the head or heart. The white mags have the liquid silver bullets. Once they hit the target, liquid silver is injected into the bloodstream. Given the amount, it's almost always fatal."

"You're a genius, my friend." Shane reached past Maya and took the ammunition from Xavier. "I'll hold on to these."

"Fine with me." Maya shuddered. "Just being near this stuff is a little intimidating."

"That's not what's frightening," Shane said, zipping up his bag before moving in behind her again.

"Oh really?" She looked over her shoulder at him. "Then what is?"

"Like most creatures, you fear what you don't know."

In a blink, Shane reached out and wrapped both arms around her. Pressing his body against hers, he spun her so that she was facing the stainless steel wall and could see their combined reflections. He slid his hands along her arms until his fingers were wrapped around hers, which were curled around the gun.

"But we can remedy that." He kissed her cheek, a featherlight brush along her flesh, making her stomach do that flip-flop thing again. Holding her stare in the mirror-like finish of the wall, he adjusted her grip on the gun and gingerly slid her finger onto the trigger with his. His flesh covered hers at every possible spot, and he nestled his head alongside hers then gently adjusted her stance.

"The trick is to be gentle." Shane's voice, quiet but strong, filled the room. His hands remained over hers, merely resting there like a caress, guiding her. "You don't need to apply much pressure to make it fire."

Maya nodded and did her best to concentrate on what Shane was talking about. Having him so close, and feeling the hard planes of his body along hers, was highly distracting. The slow burn of desire crackled and simmered through her blood when Shane's hips pressed against her. If he kept this up, a lot more than the gun was going to fire.

"Your stance should be balanced." He grinned and slid one boot-clad foot between hers, gently but insistently nudging her feet apart. "Shoulder width apart. And never, ever take your eye off the target."

He added the tiniest bit of pressure against her finger on the trigger and a bright-red light beam came out of the barrel.

"Laser sighting," Shane murmured. The scruff of his unshaven face rasped enticingly along her cheek as he spoke, creating delicious friction. His voice rumbled in his chest and vibrated through her and around her. "All you have to do is point and shoot."

"You can't miss," Xavier added with a clap of his hands. Maya stiffened in Shane's embrace, having almost forgotten they weren't alone in the room. Xavier flew from the stool back out to the main laboratory. "Hold on, you can't go without some silver throwing weapons."

"Throwing weapons?" Maya asked with trepidation.

"That's later." Shane held her stare, his hands trailing up her arms, and she lowered the gun. "We'll start training in hand-to-hand combat when we arrive in Louisiana."

"Hand-to-hand combat?" Maya squeaked. Shane rested his hands on her shoulders while he peered at her intently. "I—I don't think I can do that."

"Yes, you can." He squeezed her shoulders and kissed the top of her head. "But we'll take it one step at a time. You are capable of more than you know."

"There's something I have to tell you, Shane," Maya whispered. She looked away, too embarrassed to look him in the eyes. "Last night, when we were with the wolves—"

"We don't have to discuss it right now," he interjected. The muscle in his jaw flickered and tension settled in his shoulders. "It's done."

"Yes, we do. Listen, Shane. Something happened to me in that hotel." She grabbed the pendant for reassurance and squeezed her eyes shut, remembering the bizarre sensation of being drawn to the wolves. "I-It was like my senses got totally out of whack and I couldn't see straight. It almost felt like I got drugged."

Before she could finish, the same fluttering sound from earlier whisked into the armory and she felt Shane's body tense. Maya's eyes flicked open and she found herself face-to-face with a young woman who was most definitely a ghost and had to be Isabella.

Bella looked to be no more than eighteen or twenty, and she had large, dark eyes rimmed with sadness. She floated in midair with long, black hair flowing loosely down her back, and she wore a dark-colored dress with a high neck and long sleeves. Her hands were clasped in front of her, and she was entirely transparent.

"Well, well, well," Shane murmured. "You must be Bella."

The girl's eyes flicked to Shane briefly and she looked annoyed, as though his greeting was unwelcome. Bella floated closer, the fluttering sound whispering around her, and Maya leaned back against Shane. The ghost girl flicked her gaze to Maya's necklace and then back to Maya's face, studying her closely. She raised one delicate hand, pointed to the pendant at Maya's throat, and whispered, "*Vanator*."

Maya's hand instinctively grabbed the pendant and held it to her chest, while the girl continued to float in midair and stare at her.

"Here we are." Xavier's excited voice boomed into the room, and Bella vanished like a candle blown out by the breeze. He stopped a few feet away and smiled. "Was that Bella?"

"Yes." Maya handed the gun to Shane and went to Xavier. "What does *vanator* mean?"

"She spoke to you? That's the first time she's spoken to anyone other than me." He handed Shane a black leather bag that undoubtedly contained the throwing weapons. Running a hand through his unruly white hair, Xavier turned and walked back into the lab, waving for them to follow. "What was that word again?"

"*Vanator*," Shane said.

The doors to the armory slid shut behind them, and the smooth stainless-steel wall slid back into place, hiding the stash of weapons.

"Get Maya suited up with those," Xavier said, waving absently at the bag. "I'll look up that word. I bought a Romanian-English dictionary once she started talking to me, but she talks so fast that most of the time it doesn't help. Usually she just hangs around and watches me work."

Shane placed the bag on the counter before pulling on his leather gloves. Maya watched him carefully remove sterling-silver ninja stars and a few daggers from the bag.

"Stand still and hold your arms out to the side."

Maya did as he asked. "Like this?"

"Yes." Shane picked up two sterling-silver ninja stars and must have seen the look of concern on her face. He stepped closer. "Do you trust me?"

The pungent smell of silver filled her head and burned her nostrils, and she could only imagine the pain she would feel if it actually touched her skin. Holding his dark stare, Maya nodded, almost imperceptibly.

"I'll be gentle," he whispered.

Then with the speed and agility of a seasoned sentry, Shane slid each of the weapons into the secret compartments that lined the long, leather duster coat Maya wore. Though it felt heavier, she knew she'd still be able to move around easily and that she was protected from the silver by the layers of leather. She dropped her arms, thinking they were finished, but he shook his head and held up two throwing knives. Each had a leather handle and was about six inches long. They looked like they could cut through a vampire or a werewolf like butter.

"Almost done. Take off the coat." Shane stood only a few inches from Maya and watched while she did as he asked and carefully draped the weapon-laden garment on the table. He leaned closer. "Raise your arms," he whispered, "and no matter what happens…don't move."

His rich, male scent filled her head, a welcome relief from the strong stench of silver. With a dagger in each hand, Shane stood face-to-face with Maya and reached around her with both arms as though he was going to wrap her up in a hug. She felt a slight tugging on the back of her catsuit when he slipped the daggers into some kind of compartments.

She turned her face and her cheek brushed his shoulder while his scent grew stronger and filled her head seductively. Closing her eyes, she allowed herself to simply feel the effect of having him so close to her. His hands slid down her back and stopped along the top of her ass. His body tensed against hers and his fingers gripped her hips while her breasts crushed against the broad, muscular plane of his chest.

"Can I move now?" Maya asked and opened her eyes. She tilted her face to look him in the eye, and a smile played at his lips. "Is it safe?"

"Yes." He took a step back, his fingers trailing along the curve of her hip. "You'll always be safe with me."

"I found it!" Xavier exclaimed.

Maya and Shane looked away from one another, the intensity of the moment broken. She pulled on her coat and gloves, and Xavier flew over with a book in his hands. Shane shouldered his bag, and when Maya went to carry hers, he took it from her and slung it over his other shoulder.

"Get used to flying with the extra weight of the weapons first, and then you can add the bag."

"Thanks." Maya smiled at him and then turned her attention back to Xavier, who was looking at Maya with genuine curiosity. "What does that word mean? I think she was pointing at my necklace."

"Interesting." Xavier snapped the book closed, removed his glasses, and nodded toward Maya's necklace. "Where did you get that?"

"It was in my family." She fiddled with the stone. "I think it was my grandmother's, but to be honest, I really don't remember much. Why, Xavier? What does *vanator* mean?"

"Hunter."

Chapter 8

Shane knew Maya was exhausted, but to her credit, she didn't utter a single complaint, not a peep out of her the entire trip south. They used the intricate network of underground passages to travel the entire day, not taking time for so much as a nap, and they took to the sky when the sun set. She remained alert, focused, and silent. Even when he took out some bottled blood for her to drink and told her that they wouldn't be hunting that evening or anytime soon, she didn't utter a complaint or roll her eyes. She simply thanked him and drank it.

Flying over the swamps of the Louisiana bayou in search of Lottie Fogg's house, Shane sliced a glance in Maya's direction. Her blue eyes, usually smiling and full of life, were flat and rimmed with dark circles, and he could tell she was completely spent—both physically and emotionally.

They were both tired from not having slept during the day, but the events of the past twenty-four hours were what had them both spinning. Maya was clearly unnerved by what Bella had said, and when they left, she zipped her catsuit all the way up to her neck, effectively covering up her necklace. He couldn't blame her for feeling uneasy because Bella's comment about the necklace was all he could think about.

Vanator. Hunter.

What was Bella trying to say? Maya was a hunter?

That didn't make any sense to Shane, but she'd clearly pointed at Maya and her necklace. Maybe Xavier had gotten his translations mixed up and she'd said something totally different. Damn it all. Shane's brow furrowed and a growl rumbled in his chest. She could have been saying "necklace" or "emerald" or something.

The only thing he knew about the necklace was that it was some kind of family heirloom. Maya's inability to recall specifics about her past was beyond frustrating, but Shane hoped that Lottie Fogg would be helpful in more ways than one. Gypsies were known for their psychic abilities, and maybe she would be able to help Maya get in touch with more of her past.

Safe houses for vampires were scattered throughout the United States and most were occupied by human familiars. Olivia selected one owned by a gypsy, and if there was one quality Olivia had, it was deliberateness. She didn't do anything without a crystal-clear purpose. She could have chosen any number of other houses, but she picked the gypsy. He wished he knew why.

When they approached the location of the house, Shane motioned for Maya to follow him. Obviously deep in thought, she blinked rapidly when he interrupted her but nodded her understanding. He descended cautiously, reaching out with his heightened senses to look for any other supernaturals in the area, but he found the air around them clean. He was relieved to see that the house was on several acres of property and in a remote area of the bayou. Other than a few pesky swamp creatures, he should be able to train Maya undisturbed while they waited for word from Olivia.

Shane and Maya landed silently at the end of the

dirt driveway and stood side by side, scanning their surroundings one more time. Their enhanced night vision enabled them to see nocturnal creatures scurrying through the brush, and various sets of eyes staring down at them from the sprawling, moss-covered oak trees. Beneath a canopy of branches, they walked down the long driveway toward the massive Queen Anne style house. Although it had fallen into disrepair, it was still beautiful. Light flickered inside and Shane could tell it came from candles, not electric lights.

They stopped at the foot of the steps, and the front door of the house slowly opened. A woman stood in the doorway with a lantern dangling from her hand. Shane watched her carefully, looking for any sign that she might not be happy to see them, as Olivia suggested, but seconds later, a loud, feminine laugh joined the sound of crickets in the bayou.

"Well, don't just stand there starin' at me like a couple of ghosts." She waved them forward and stepped out to the edge of the steps. Long, black hair, streaked with gray, fell over narrow shoulders, and her slim body was wrapped up in a white cotton bathrobe. If Shane had to guess, he'd say she was around seventy years old. "The sun will be up soon, and unless you two want to get your pasty asses singed, I suggest you get in the house. Come on. Lottie Fogg ain't gonna ask you twice."

Then without another word she went back inside.

"At least she left the door open," Shane murmured with little humor in his voice as he and Maya started toward the stairs. "I hope Olivia knows what she's doing."

"Olivia always knows what she's doing," Maya said quietly.

They climbed the stairs quickly. Closing the door behind them, Shane saw a glimmer of light along the horizon and felt the familiar tug in his gut. They'd made it to their destination with little time to spare. When he looked around, Shane was immediately taken aback by the sparse furnishings of the massive home. The living room to the left had a couch, a chair, a coffee table, a baby grand piano, and an enormous fireplace with an intricately designed wooden mantel. The only other items he spotted were stacks and stacks of magazines that indicated Ms. Fogg was a bit of a hoarder.

Enormous crystal chandeliers hung from the ceiling in that room and in the front hall where he and Maya currently stood. A narrow staircase with a mahogany banister was directly across from the front door, and Shane could see a lit candle on a table in the second-floor hall. To the right was the dining room with a table for eight but only chairs enough for four, and based on the look of them, they weren't safe to sit on. Another glittering chandelier hung above the table, but given the candles lit in both rooms, he doubted the house had working electricity.

Lottie was out of sight, but he could hear her bustling around toward the back of the house. Based on the clinking and clanking, he suspected she was in the kitchen.

Shane was about to call out for the gypsy woman, but a moment later, the swinging door in the dining room opened and Lottie backed into the room, bumping the door open with her hip. When she turned around, she had the lantern in one hand and two bottles of blood in the other. With a big grin, she joined them in the front hall and handed a bottle to each of them.

"Thank you," Maya said before taking a sip.

"You're welcome, Maya. Olivia told me you aren't gonna be huntin' while you're down here, so I've got a bunch of this bottled stuff on hand for you. I heated it a bit." Lottie tilted her head to one side and looked Maya up and down. "You're a little bit of a thing, but I hear you're good at stirring up big trouble."

"Yes, ma'am. I guess I am." Maya took the bottle from her lips and lifted one shoulder, looking away awkwardly. "Thank you for letting us stay with you in your home, and for the food."

"I figured you'd be hungry once y'all finally got here." Lottie put a hand on the small of her back and stretched a bit then slid her inspecting gaze over Shane from head to toe. "Shane, you're one of those vampire soldiers, aren't you? Olivia tells me that you're one I can trust."

"One what?" Shane asked before taking a sip from the bottle.

"Vampire, of course," Lottie said, looking at him like he was the dumbest kid in class.

"I see." Shane's brow furrowed and his back tensed. "You don't like vampires, and yet you open your home to them as a safe house?"

"Not *them*. *You*." Lottie wagged a finger at him and pursed her lips. "Only Olivia has ever used my home for that purpose, and now the two of you. It ain't that I don't like 'em, mind you, but I don't trust 'em. There's a difference. Gypsy blood is rich with generations of magic running through it, and I don't feel like sharing it with any Tom, Dick, or Shane. Got it?"

"Got it." Shane raised the bottle to her.

"Besides, I heard you two are hiding out here because of some mess with a werewolf."

"Yes, ma'am," Maya replied quietly.

"If there's anything I distrust more than a vampire, it's a werewolf." Lottie made a face of disgust. "They're nasty, vicious creatures, and from what I hear, they don't do nothin' but cause trouble."

"I assure you, Ms. Fogg," Shane said with a tilt of his head, "you will be safe with us."

"Ha. Call me Lottie. Ms. Fogg was my grandmama. She was a real proper Southern woman who didn't know she'd married a gypsy man until she caught him and his mama teachin' their three daughters magic. My mama told me that Grandmama chased Granddaddy around the swamp for a week before finally lettin' it go, and then she pretended not to know about it at all. Funny how the mind can choose what it wants to remember and what it wants to forget."

Lottie waved them toward the steps with the lantern dangling from her hand. "Come on now. We best get you two upstairs. I have a couple of rooms set up for you in the attic. I figure the heat won't bother ya, and there were only three small windows for me to cover up."

Shane urged Maya to go first, and he brought up the rear as they ascended the two flights of stairs with Lottie in the lead.

"These rooms used to be servants' quarters back in the day, and there are still a couple of beds up here." She stopped at the top of the staircase and turned to face them, the light of the lantern brightening the dark, narrow attic stairs. "You don't need coffins, do ya? Olivia used a bed but…well…I don't know many vampires. So, do ya?"

"No, ma'am." Shane suppressed a grin and shook his head at yet another myth about his kind that was perpetuated by the movies. "A bed is just fine."

"Good." Lottie turned her attention to Maya and held the lantern near her face so she could see her better. "When were you turned, girl? You seem different from the other vamps I've seen."

"Five years ago," Maya answered quietly, and her hand went involuntarily to the necklace hidden beneath her clothing. "What do you mean, I seem different?"

"Not sure." Lottie pursed her lips and leaned closer, peering in Maya's eyes. "You've got a glimmer or something. See, most vamps are like black spots in the tapestry of psychic energy. Kind of invisible. Maybe it's because technically they aren't alive, but you have a glimmer. It's not constant, though. Kind of like a candle blowing near a drafty window."

"A glimmer?" Maya asked nervously.

"Sorta." Lottie made a sound of frustration and pulled back. "Maybe it's just the light from the lantern. I'll look at ya again later, but it's probably nothin' more than my old eyes playin' tricks on me."

Lottie grasped the crystal doorknob and pushed the creaky attic door open, making particles of dust rain around them like snow. Coughing and waving dust from her face, she stepped into the little hallway and placed the lantern on a tiny table that sat between two more closed doors. She quickly lit another candle off the flame within the lantern and set it on the hall table.

"I'm not a fan of the dark," Lottie said with a strained smile, picking up the lantern and slipping past Maya to open the door on the left. Shane watched her, wondering if the *dark* she referred to was him. "This is your room, young lady, and the one on the other side is yours, Shane."

"Thank you, Lottie." Maya gave the older woman a smile and glanced at Shane briefly. "I know that I've made a big mess and—"

"Hush up." Lottie shook her head and slapped one hand over Maya's mouth. Maya looked almost as startled as Shane was, and her big blue eyes stared at Lottie in shock. "I never met nobody, human or otherwise, who ain't screwed the pooch a time or two. You get me?" Lottie asked, letting her hand fall away from Maya's mouth and nodding. "Good. Because I don't allow no pity parties in my presence. You want to change somethin' about yourself or your life, then it takes actions, not words."

Lottie patted Maya's cheek gently and then went to the door at the top of the stairs. "You two get some sleep and we'll talk some more later. I know you don't need the *facilities* the way us humans do, but if you want to take a shower, I left you both some towels on the dressers in your rooms. Use the bathroom on the second floor if the fancy strikes you. When you wake up, I'll probably be in the living room reading my magazines or making something in the kitchen. Sleep tight."

Without waiting for a response from Shane or Maya, Lottie left and closed the door tightly behind her.

"She's quite a character," Shane murmured, following Maya into her bedroom.

Although it was pitch dark, the two of them could see quite clearly. If a human could look through their eyes, the nighttime world would seem to be painted in brown and silver sepia tones. The room was small, perhaps ten feet square, and the ceilings were angled like the roof. If Shane got too close to the window, he'd have to duck to avoid hitting his head.

To the right was a full-size bed with a white coverlet and two pillows. The headboard and footboard were curved with brass spokes, and on the left side of the room, across from the bed, was a small wooden dresser with an oval mirror. There were two windows, but both had been covered by heavy cloth blankets to prevent rays of sun from streaming in.

Maya walked over to the windows, grasped the edge of the cloth, and stood silently with her back to Shane. He moved closer and placed her bag on the bed. He didn't take his eyes off her because he was terrified she was going to rip off the fabric and fry herself in the sun. She had the same look that she had that morning on the roof of the club, as though she was ready for the light to claim her.

"Maya?" he asked gently. Standing directly behind her and ducking his head so he wouldn't hit the ceiling, he removed his leather gloves and stuck them in his pockets, letting his gaze slip over her long, blond ponytail. He'd been dying to tangle his fingers in her hair the minute she walked out of that bedroom dressed in the sentry uniform, but he kept his hands at his sides. "You should get some sleep."

"I'm so tired, Shane," she whispered, running the edge of the cloth between her fingers. "My body…my soul." She sniffled and he knew she was crying. Unable to stop himself, he ran his hand gently down the length of her ponytail and wrapped the silky ends around his finger while she spoke. "I'm tired of being afraid, and sometimes I think Olivia should have just left me in that alley. Everyone would be a lot better off. Including me."

"I wouldn't," he murmured, reaching around her and placing his hand over hers along the edge of the fabric. She stilled and allowed her body to sag ever so slightly and lean against his, but she didn't let go. He kissed the top of her head gently. "And neither would you. If Olivia hadn't turned you that night, I may never have found you."

"You would be much better off without me in your life." She swiped at her eyes and her frustration rose. "You would be going about your business as a sentry, doing the job you love instead of babysitting a trouble-maker like me and getting into fights with werewolves." Maya let go of the fabric and spun to face him. With her blue eyes flashing angrily, she shoved at him with both hands. "You should leave. I mean it. Get away from me, Shane. Go back to New York."

"No." Shane didn't move. Maya was a vampire and she was strong, but he was older and stronger and knew exactly what she was trying to do. "I will not."

"Don't you get it?" she shouted. "I'm no good, Shane. I was a terrible human being, and now I'm a hot fucking mess of a vampire. I'm defective merchandise."

"Oh really?" Shane folded his arms over his chest and raised one eyebrow at her foolishness. "If I recall correctly, you don't exactly have a clear memory of your human life. So what makes you say that?"

Maya's jaw set and her lips quivered while she fought the tears and struggled to get the words out.

"No one came looking for me," she said in a barely audible whisper. When he gave her a quizzical look, she continued. "After that night in the alley, I vanished from the human world, Shane, and no one came to find me… Nobody cared enough about who I was to even report me missing." Her eyes filled with tears, and when one fat drop fell down her cheek, something inside him crumbled. Weeping, she sat on the edge of the bed looking at her intertwined fingers and murmured, "It's like the world was relieved that I was gone."

Resting her elbows on her knees, she put her face in her hands and sobbed. Shane stared at her for a moment, uncertain of exactly what to do. Watching the woman who was destined to be his bloodmate weeping deep, soul-shredding tears was not something he could slice with silver or wipe out with ultraviolet ammunition.

Viciousness and calculated death-dealing were things he was comfortable with. Crying and emotions were not.

Shane did the only thing he could think of. He dropped the other bag on the floor, then removed his long sentry coat and draped it over the foot of the bed before sitting down next to Maya. Without a word, he wrapped one arm over her shoulder, gently pulled her down onto the bed, and lay back, cradling her body against his. He held her there while she cried, her tears beading off the shirt of his sentry uniform in what seemed like a never-ending ocean.

"Sleep, Maya," he murmured softly. "Sleep, my love, and I promise that I will come looking for you."

It was happening again.

Maya whimpered when her attacker dug his fingers into her bicep and tried to smother her mouth with unwanted kisses. His alcohol-soaked breath filled her head and made her stomach churn in protest. She shook her head and pushed his face away with her hands, but he was too strong. Her knees gave out and she squeezed her eyes shut as he started dragging her toward the frightening darkness of the alley—and that's when she heard Shane.

You have the control, Maya. *Shane's powerful baritone rumbled through the air around her.* He can't hurt you anymore, and you can stop this. *A whisper fluttered in her ear like a caress.* Show him, Maya. *Maya's eyes flicked open, and looking past the shoulder of her attacker, she saw Shane. He stood on the sidewalk, his leather coat flapping in the breeze, looking like the angel of death. He lifted his lip, bared his sharp, white fangs, and growled,* Show him who you are.

Maya gasped the instant her gaze locked with Shane, and every ounce of rage, frustration, and fury simmered through her body and boiled to the surface. Maya's fangs hummed and vibrated. A primal scream built in her chest, and when the sound ripped from her throat, her fangs erupted.

As the brute's hands held her tighter and his thin lips tried to capture hers, he rasped, I own your ass.

NO! *Maya ripped her arms free from his grasp, causing her rapist to stumble back and stare at her with white-hot fear. With fangs bared and unnatural speed, she grabbed him by the shoulders, spun him around, and pinned him up against the brick wall of the club. His thin lips quivered and sweat broke out on his upper lip as he fought to understand what he was looking at.* No more! *Maya shouted.*

Then, as if by magic, her attacker vanished in a swirl of smoke and the world around her grew quiet. Shaking from a feeling of victory, as opposed to fear, a huge smile cracked Maya's face and the sun in the dreamscape began to rise with time-lapse speed. Smiling, she tilted her face toward the brightening sky and a familiar voice wafted over her shoulder.

I told you I'd come looking for you.

Shane. *His name escaped her lips in an almost reverent tone. She spun around and saw him standing on the sidewalk across the street. She started to walk toward him but stopped short and looked down at what she was wearing. For the first time since the nightmare replayed itself, Maya wasn't wearing the outfit on the night she was attacked. Instead, she was clad in the borrowed sentry uniform.* It's over, isn't it? *She looked back at Shane, and holding his stare, she walked over to meet him in the middle of the empty city street.*

Maya squeezed her eyes shut and linked her arms tightly around Shane's neck, hugging him as though she may not get another chance, and to her great delight, he returned the embrace. She buried her face in the crook of his neck and he lifted her off her feet. She smiled as his rich, wild, male scent filled her head in an almost dizzying way. Maya felt utterly and totally safe. You made it stop.

No, youngling. *Shane put her back on her feet, cradled her face in his hands, and brushed his lips over hers with heartbreaking tenderness. He whispered,* You did.

The heavy fog of sleep lifted, and Maya slowly began to register the sensations and sounds seeping into her conscious mind bit by bit. For a moment, she was disoriented and struggled to remember where she was. Shane's familiar scent filled her head, and a smile curved her lips. They were in Lottie Fogg's attic, and he'd held her as she cried herself to sleep.

Her eyes fluttered open. She remembered what had happened in the dreamscape, and her smile grew wider. The last thing she recalled was what Shane had said: "No youngling, you did." Was he right? Had she finally found a way to make the nightmares stop? Was standing up to the memory of what happened the secret to freedom? She sure as hell hoped so, especially if waking up in Shane's arms was part of the deal.

She nestled deeper into his strong embrace and draped one leg over his, her hand resting on his flat, muscular stomach. Her head lay comfortably on his shoulder, his arm curled around her, holding her close. It was the first time she could recall ever sleeping with a man, and as she remained cuddled up against him, Maya thought this was the most intimate moment of her life… and they were still fully clothed.

Just as Maya was about to ask Shane if he was awake, his hand found its way to her thigh and pulled her leg farther over his. He kissed the top of her head. "Good afternoon, youngling."

"Afternoon?" Maya lifted her head and could see glimmers of light behind the makeshift drapes that were keeping out the damaging sunlight. She frowned. "That's weird. I've never woken up before sunset."

"It's at least another hour or so until the sun goes down." Shane's body tightened against hers, and his fingers brushed featherlight strokes along her arm. "You could try to go back to sleep and see if the nightmare has stopped."

"I suppose I could do that," Maya murmured, laying her head back on his shoulder and making tiny circles on his belly with her fingertip. The edge of his shirt had come untucked from his pants and exposed a strip of flesh. Unable to resist, Maya ran her fingers back and forth over his skin, which evoked a groan from Shane. The vibrations rumbled beneath her cheek as she slipped her hand beneath his shirt and rested her palm against the rippled muscles of his abdomen. "Any other suggestions?"

"There's only one that comes to mind," he murmured as his hand, curled in the crook of her knee, pulled her leg up higher. His other hand grasped the elastic of her ponytail and gently took it off before he tangled his strong fingers in her hair and massaged her scalp. "But I'd like to know what you want, Maya."

Maya's eyes fluttered closed while his fingertips whispered over the back of her head, his other hand drifting up the side of her thigh before resting on the swell of her hip. She knew what she wanted. She wanted him, to feel the rush of his skin against hers and to be cradled in his embrace forever.

Intellectually, Maya knew she was safe with Shane and that he would never do anything to hurt her, but she hadn't been with anyone sexually since she'd been turned. Shane placed a tender kiss on her forehead, and though Maya could tell he was aroused, he was patiently waiting for her to take the lead. With courage fueled by desire, Maya lifted her head and shifted her body so she could look him in the eye. He peered at her beneath those thick, dark lashes, and she not only felt his restraint in the tightness of his body but could see it in his eyes.

Maya lifted one quivering hand and brushed the back of her fingers along his stubble-covered jaw before running her thumb over his full lower lip. She gasped as his lips parted and he took her thumb into his mouth and suckled, all while holding her gaze. His tongue ran slow, erotic circles over her fingertip before he gathered her hand in his and trailed butterfly kisses along her palm.

Lust coiled deep in Maya's belly and heat pooled between her legs while she watched him practically make love to her hand. Her entire body quivered with anticipation and she rubbed herself against him. The insistent need to touch him was consuming her like the sun. Exquisite pleasure rippled through her from the attention he was giving her palm, and she wondered how it would feel to have him lavish kisses on the rest of her body.

She tore her fingers from his, pushed herself up, and straddled him before placing both hands on the pillow on either side of his head. A slow smile spread across Shane's face, and he slid his hands up her thighs and settled them on her hips, pulling her against the rock-hard evidence of his desire.

"I've decided what I want," Maya whispered. Her hair fell to one side and she leaned closer so that her lips hovered just above his. She flicked her tongue over his mouth. "It's you, Shane."

Shane's restraint shattered as the words escaped her lips and their mouths collided. He opened to her immediately and teased her tongue with his, his hands gripping her hips tighter and pulling her closer. As she kissed him, Maya's hands gripped the pillow like her life depended on it, and tiny licks of pleasure shot through her while his thick erection pressed against her most sensitive spot. Maya moaned and began to writhe, lust and combustible desire firing through her with every pump of her hips.

Her body felt as though it was on fire, and she wanted nothing more than to be naked and feel her chest press against his. Breaking the kiss, Maya whipped up to a sitting position while Shane watched through a dark, hooded gaze. His fingers gripped her hips, holding her still as she unzipped the top of her catsuit and peeled it off to her waist, revealing her bare breasts. The cool metal of the necklace lay against her skin, and the teardrop-shaped emerald lingered along the curve of her bosom. It was a bold move for Maya to bare herself to Shane, but even as she did it, she knew he'd already seen the most vulnerable parts of her.

"*Bellísima*," Shane whispered reverently as his hands trailed over her bare flesh.

His fingers curled around her waist briefly before he brushed his knuckles lightly beneath the curve of her breasts. Holding her stare, he cupped her breasts in both hands and ran his thumbs over her nipples. Maya gasped as licks of fire flickered through her body from the friction of his flesh rushing along hers. She threw her head back and reveled in the waves of white-hot pleasure that rippled through her body—and then she started to move.

Slowly at first, she rocked her hips, pressing herself against his erection while Shane continued to tease her nipples with his talented fingers. Sounds of pure pleasure escaped Maya's lips as the combination of sensations swamped her and the sweet, tightening coil of the orgasm built. Sensing that she was reaching the edge, Shane sat up and linked his arms around her waist before dipping his head and taking the rosy peak of a breast in his mouth.

Maya cried out and grabbed Shane's hair with both hands, holding him to her as he teased one swollen nipple and then the other. As another wave of searing carnal pleasure shot through her body, Maya's fangs erupted and she knew what she needed.

Blood. But not just anyone's... She needed his.

With the specially tuned instincts of a bloodmate and the intuition of a remarkably tender lover, Shane lifted his head and curled one hand around the back of her neck. Maya linked her legs around his waist, held his stare, and gasped when pressure hit her in just the right spot. Writhing in his embrace, she leaned in and trailed her tongue along his neck, just below his ear. His voice tumbled into her mind on a rush: *Taste me, Maya. Take what is meant only for you.*

Shane's arms tightened around Maya, holding her body firmly against his, her hips pumping and grinding against him. As the sweet, torturous pangs of desire surged, Maya sank her fangs into his neck and the orgasm ripped through her with shattering strength. In that moment, the world fell away and all she could see, feel, or hear was *him*. Shane surrounded her, filled her, and lit her up from the inside out as images of the centuries he'd lived roared through her mind.

Power. Death. Duty. Honor. Loneliness.

When the bone-melting orgasm subsided, Maya licked the wound closed and went limp in Shane's embrace. As she rested her head on his shoulder, her body trembled with sheer exhaustion, and for the first time she could remember, Maya knew what it felt like to be cherished. Shane gave her what she needed but took nothing. He put her happiness and pleasure above his own so that she'd feel safe. Tears stung the back of her eyes, and the magnitude of his generosity settled over her.

Without a word, Shane lay back on the bed and pulled her into the shelter of his body. Her eyes fluttered closed, and Maya thought about all of the images and feelings she absorbed from Shane's blood memories. The one constant in his four-hundred-year existence was his dedication to being a sentry and to the Presidium. He was a soldier. No family. No love. Only duty.

Could this man, this ancient warrior, give her his heart, or was she merely part of his duties? Maya was finally repairing her broken spirit, but she didn't think she could survive a broken heart.

Chapter 9

Shane let Maya sleep, even though the sun had set an hour ago and he knew he should wake her up to start combat training. A grin cracked his face as he stood in the moonlit yard behind the massive house and laid a series of weapons out on the weathered picnic table. Based on what he could sense, Maya wasn't in the dreamscape. He'd watched her while she slept and sensed the deep, leaden sleep of a vampire but absolutely no signs of a nightmare or dream of any kind.

Having changed into a T-shirt and jeans, he felt surprisingly relaxed and was truly looking forward to teaching Maya how to fight. He'd trained plenty of other vampires, but Maya was obviously special. Based on the way she handled herself in the dreamscape, when she finally stood up to her fears, he suspected she'd be one hell of a warrior.

Shane took stock of the various throwing weapons he'd taken from Xavier's place and readied the area for Maya's training. He placed targets on the trunks of three moss-covered oak trees that lined the edge of the spacious backyard. To the left were the calm, moon-dappled waters of the bayou swamp and to the right was a natural landscape of trees, bushes, and low-lying plants. He could hear Lottie banging around in her kitchen, and based on the aroma drifting through the open window, she was making herself dinner.

The vibration of his cell phone interrupted his thoughts, and his gut clenched when he saw that it was Olivia's phone number. He'd texted her once they'd arrived safely, but he hadn't spoken to her yet. Guilt tugged at him when he realized she must have had the meeting with Horace and his pack last night, but he hadn't given it a second thought until this minute. All he could think about was Maya and her well-being. Not exactly the focused calculation of a sentry.

He swore and swiped the touch screen to answer the call.

"Nice to talk to you too." Olivia's teasing tone came through the line loud and clear.

"Sorry." Shane pressed his fingers against his eyes in an effort to squelch his embarrassment. "It wasn't meant for you."

"Then I guess it was meant for Maya? It couldn't be for Lottie, because if you speak to her like that, she'll curse your sorry ass."

"No." Shane cleared his throat and looked out over the moonlit waters. "Did you meet with Horace and his pack?"

"We did," she said on a sigh. "It was one hell of a night, and you would have loved all the tension in the air, but we managed to get through it without any fur or fangs flying. Besides, they were totally outgunned." She let out a short laugh. "I thought Horace would piss himself when he saw the firepower the girls, Pete, and Damien were carrying."

"Did Horace and his pack come to the meeting armed?"

"Of course they did, but they don't have Xavier creating awesome shit all the time—and you were right about

Rat. He's definitely in bed with the wolves, but I'm not sure why."

"Rat was with them?"

"Yes. The slippery son of a bitch escorted them to the meeting and acted like some sort of self-appointed liaison between our races. He's probably in it for some kind of financial gain. Anyway, Horace is willing to let bygones be bygones and overlook your attack on him… if…" Olivia trailed off, hesitating to say the rest.

"If?" Shane asked.

"If we give him Maya."

"What do you mean, 'if we give him Maya'?" Shane bit out, his entire body going rigid with fury. "What the fuck is he talking about? That furry piece of garbage will not lay another hand on her."

"Calm down, Shane." Olivia's voice was calm and clear but firm. "It's a ridiculous demand, and I'm not handing Maya over to him or anyone else. I told the little bastard that I was well aware that he got rough with Maya and refused to let her leave, and that's why you had to intervene. He and his pack denied it vehemently, of course. They said that you started the entire thing and accosted a member of the royal family with no provocation."

"They're lying."

"I know that."

"So what now?" Shane straightened his back and glanced over his shoulder at the house when he heard Maya's voice. She was in the kitchen with Lottie. "Are we to stay down here indefinitely?"

"No. We explained that you and Maya ran off together and that I, of course, have no idea where the two of you went. He started to give me shit and threatened to tattle to his daddy, but when I told him that the king already knew what was going on, he backed down. Big time."

"Interesting," Shane said quietly. "Then he is definitely acting without his father's approval and clearly has his own motives. Why does he want Maya?"

"Are you serious?" Olivia asked incredulously. "Why does any man want Maya?"

"I'm well aware of Maya's beauty," Shane said with waning patience, "but there's something else going on. His behavior is desperate and surprisingly aggressive. It doesn't make sense to me that this is simply about possessing a woman. He wants to reignite the war between our races and he's using Maya to do it, but why?"

"I'm not sure, but Horace and his pack of delinquents are refusing to leave the city until we relinquish Maya."

"Then he's going to be in Manhattan for quite a while," Shane responded flatly.

"I relayed the events to Emperor Zhao directly, and he will be speaking with King Heinrich while they're at the summit. If Horace is still here at the end of the week, then perhaps I can persuade the king to come to the city and deal with his kid. You and Maya should be staying with Lottie for about a week. My guess is that Horace won't leave on his own, and from what I hear, he and his pack had to leave the Plaza after that big mess you all made. Now they're crashing at a hotel here in the Village and spending their waking hours at The Dollhouse getting drunk and banging strippers two at a time."

"Understood." Shane walked over to the water's edge and watched an alligator float by like a log, waiting for some unsuspecting animal to get too close. "We will make good use of our time down here."

"Shane?" Olivia asked tentatively. "How are things going with Maya?"

"They're…progressing. In fact, I'm about to start weapons training and then hand-to-hand combat."

"Right." Olivia laughed. "Well, good luck with that. Sit tight, and I'll be in touch by the end of the week or sooner."

Shane hung up the phone and slipped it in the front pocket of his jeans. A moment later, the screen door from the kitchen creaked open and Maya's scent drifted over him on the breeze. A smile curved his lips, and when he turned around, he saw her standing at the table, inspecting the weapons he'd laid out a few minutes ago. She was clad in the sentry catsuit and once again had her hair tied back in a tight ponytail.

"I see you are ready for training." Shane closed the distance between them and walked around to the opposite side of the table. He glanced over to the kitchen window and noticed that there were actually lights on in the house. Apparently Lottie used her electricity sparingly, but this eccentricity only made her more endearing to him. "What is our friend Lottie up to?

"She's fixing herself something to eat, but then she said she's going into the city for a while. I guess she works as a fortune-teller at a few bars in the French Quarter," Maya answered, holding out a mug for him and taking a sip from the one in her other hand. "But she had something ready for us too."

"I see." Shane took the mug and looked at her intently. "I thought for certain you'd be trying to talk me into letting you go hunting."

"Not really." Maya lifted one shoulder and peered at him over the edge of her mug beneath a row of thick, long lashes. "I'm feeling rather satisfied at the moment."

"At the moment?" Shane smirked before emptying his mug in one big gulp.

"Yes. But you never know when a girl will be hungry for more," she murmured coyly. Maya placed her mug on the table and her smile faltered when she eyed the array of weapons. "Any word from Olivia yet?"

"Yes." Shane put his mug down next to Maya's and paused for a moment. He didn't want her distracted from her training and decided on a less-is-more approach. "Things are quiet, and we're to stay down here and train for a week. Olivia feels that we can return once the summit has finished and King Heinrich is free to deal with Horace himself."

"That's it?" Her brows knit together and she paused for a few seconds, studying him intently. "I didn't cause a new war?"

"No." Shane shook his head and folded his arms over his chest. "But things are still touchy, so until the summit is over and the king is free to be directly involved, we will stay here and you will train. The war with the wolves may not be imminent, but you should know how to defend yourself. Based on what I saw in the dreamscape, you have the makings of a great warrior, Maya."

"Me?" Maya asked with obvious disbelief. "A warrior? Like you and Olivia?"

"Bella did call you a hunter."

"Right." Maya rolled her eyes. "At this point, I'd just like to stop being a liability."

"Good." Passing her a pair of leather gloves, Shane

noticed that her necklace was no longer around her neck. "Maya, where is your necklace?"

"I took it off." Her hand went instinctively to the spot where it usually rested. "I didn't know what to expect, and since it's the only item I have left from whatever family I had, I didn't want to lose it while we practiced."

"Fine." He watched her pull on the gloves. "Then let's begin."

Over the next two hours, Shane worked with Maya on her throwing skills, and to his great surprise, she had remarkably good aim. He showed her how to use her sonar-like senses to focus on disturbances in the atmosphere so she could hit a target without even looking at it. He tossed several objects in the air, and after only three or four attempts, she'd managed to hit almost every one. Her aim with the guns was equally good, and based on the way the targets were shredded, she'd do just fine in a gun battle.

Shane did wonder what would happen once the targets were live and fighting back. It was anybody's guess how she'd handle that.

"Would you like a break before we begin the hand-to-hand combat?" Shane asked, removing the targets from the trees. Lottie was kind enough to let them train, so he didn't want to leave any litter in her backyard. "Take a few minutes to regroup?"

"No." Maya's jaw set with determination, and she stood in the middle of the yard in what could only be considered a battle-ready stance. With feet shoulder-width apart and hands curled into fists at her sides, she looked prepared to take whatever he could dish out. And sexy. The woman looked dead fucking sexy. "Let's do it."

"As you wish."

Shane walked past Maya to toss what was left of the targets into a large trash can by the kitchen door. Then, without any warning, he whisked back to Maya, linked one arm around her waist, pinning her arms at her sides, and brought his other hand up beneath her chin. If he were in battle, he could easily break the neck of his opponent, and though he had no intention of harming her, he wanted to see if Maya would try to defend herself. She froze.

Shane kissed her cheek tenderly and released her from his grasp.

"Why didn't you try to defend yourself?" he asked as she turned to face him.

"I—I wasn't ready for it," she said quickly. "Besides, I knew it was you and not some werewolf."

"Do you expect there to be a formal announcement before they come after you? Because I can assure you there won't be."

"No." Maya's eyes flashed with anger. "I'm not stupid."

"I know that." Shane's tone softened. "You were a quick study with the weapons, Maya, but you can't rely on that. More often than not, we are dragged into physical one-on-one fighting, especially with the wolves. We will begin with self-defense techniques." He stepped back and made a motion for her to turn around. "We'll do it again, but this time I'll walk you through what to do."

"If I just shoot them, then I won't need to worry about this," Maya murmured. She turned around and put her hands on her hips. "Okay, Mr. Miyagi."

Shane paused and his brow furrowed, confusion washing over him. "Who is Mr. Miyagi?"

"Never mind." Maya laughed loudly. "Let's go, old man."

"Fine." Shane stilled and stood about two feet behind her. "You need to focus on and tune in to the changes in the air around you at all times, much as you did with the targets. When you sense the ripples in the air getting stronger, your opponent is getting closer. The more you focus on the changes, the quicker it will become second nature. If you concentrate, you can anticipate your attacker's movements. To defend yourself, it's best to be face-to-face."

"Then why did you have me turn around?" she asked far too sweetly.

"Close your eyes." Shane grinned. "Focus on the sound waves in the air. What do you hear?"

"Frogs." Maya's voice was quiet, barely above a whisper. "Something moving in the water. An owl to the right." Eyes still closed, she lifted her arm and pointed to the right. "He's in a tree about twenty feet away and maybe fifteen feet off the ground."

Good. Shane's voice touched her mind gently and he remained motionless. *Now keep your eyes closed and tell me what you feel*.

Maya's head tilted to the left. *An animal is moving along the edge of the water. It's small, probably a possum or something*.

Good. He took one step forward. *What else*.

You. Her body tensed. *You moved closer*.

How can you tell? Shane's voice remained even and he tried to focus on their training, instead of how enticingly sexy her ass looked in the sentry catsuit. He took two more steps toward her. *Tell me what you feel*.

There it is again. Her voice was laced with excitement, but her body stayed tense and ready to spring into action. *It reminds me of being in the ocean when the waves rise suddenly after being calm. Kind of like what happens when another person swims by*.

Excellent. Shane held his ground. *Now I'm going to come after you again, like I did a few minutes ago, and I want you to see if you can avoid getting caught*.

Maya nodded but didn't respond.

Shane held off and he could feel the tension rising in the air while she patiently waited for him to make his move. Then with no warning he exploded toward her, but to his great delight, Maya spun around, anticipating his move. He'd hoped she'd fly off, but instead she jumped up into his embrace and linked her arms and legs around him before placing a big kiss on his cheek. Grinning like she'd won the lottery, she clung to him while he gripped her leather-clad ass with both hands.

"How was that?" Maya asked playfully.

"That is not exactly what I had in mind," Shane said, struggling to squelch the smile that played at his lips. No matter how charmed he was, he could not let her turn this training session into some kind of game. "You did manage to sense my approach."

"Would it be safe to say that I bested my opponent?" Maya whispered, brushing his lips with hers and squeezing him tighter, seductively wiggling in his embrace. "Perhaps I distracted you?"

"No." Shane gripped Maya around her waist and placed her on her feet before stepping back and increasing the distance between them. Hurt flickered over her features, and even though his gut instinct was to gather in his arms and protect her, he knew that would be a mistake. There was no time for childish nonsense with both of their lives hanging in the balance. "This is not a game, Maya. If you don't learn how to defend yourself, you'll never make it past your first century, and let's not forget that your games landed us down here in the first place."

"Fine." A wounded look flickered over her features, and her mouth set in a tight line. "But I wasn't the only one who screwed up, Shane. So don't try and act like you're not partially to blame for us being sent away."

Shane leveled a stern gaze her way, but he knew that what she said was spot-on. He'd lost his fucking senses because he had let his emotions cloud his judgment, but that would not happen again. Bloodmate legend be damned.

Even as he told himself that, he knew it was utter bullshit. He was in love with Maya and had been for months. The bloodmate legend was…incidental.

"You're correct." He stepped back and kept his voice free of emotion. "I allowed my personal feelings to get in the way of my duty, and as you've pointed out, it cost us dearly. I can assure you that situation will not be repeated."

"That makes two of us." Maya folded her arms over her chest and glared at him with a cold, detached look that was like a kick in the gut. "So what's next?"

As if on cue, the engine of a car starting and the sound of tires crunching along the dirt and gravel driveway rumbled through the wild quiet of the rural Louisiana night.

"Lottie must be leaving for work," Shane said tightly. "Good. Then we can continue our training undisturbed. We have much to do."

"So stop talking," Maya said. She placed her hands on her hips and sent him a challenging look. "And start doing."

Maya never thought she'd enjoy fighting. In fact, the idea of any physical violence used to make her sick to her stomach. But when Shane took her through yet another round of sparring, she couldn't wipe the exhilarated grin off her face. For the first time since she could remember, Maya felt empowered—strong and unstoppable.

She was able to deflect every punch Shane threw. Each time he tried to grab her and pin her arms to her sides, she was able to spin out and throw a defensive heel thrust to the chin. However, her favorite move had to be the roundhouse kick because almost every ounce of anger and frustration could be expelled in the process.

He came at her again, flying through the night like the deadly warrior he was. Eyes wild, he whipped toward her, but instead of attempting to throw a kick or a punch, Shane rolled right into Maya's legs and knocked her feet out from under her. Before she could counter or right herself, Shane straddled her and had her pinned to the ground with her arms held above her head.

"Not every attack will come in the way you are trained for, youngling." Shane's dark eyes peered down at her, and a smile played at his lips. "You have to be prepared for the unexpected."

"Lesson learned." Lying trapped beneath his body, Maya kept her sights on Shane and let her body relax. "I won't make that mistake again."

"We shall see," Shane murmured. He released her

arms and rested his hands on his thighs while he continued to stare down at her. "It's always a different experience in the heat of a battle."

"You know what they say?" Maya murmured seductively, trailing her fingertips up his bare arms. She traced the lines of his muscles and they flexed beneath her touch. "Don't you, Shane?"

"No," Shane murmured. His gaze skittered over her face and his body tensed. "What do they say?"

With every ounce of strength she had and using the leverage technique he taught her, Maya grabbed Shane's shoulders, pushed her body up, and flipped him onto his back, totally turning the tables on him. Straddling him and pinning his wrists over his head, she didn't miss the sly smile on his face or the look of approval in his eyes.

"All's fair in love and war," Maya whispered.

Shane's grin widened as he remained held within her grasp, and she felt his body harden beneath hers. His smile faltered when her grip on his wrists relaxed and she laced her fingers in his. Still he didn't attempt to get out from under her. Memories of their tryst from earlier came roaring to the forefront of her mind, but she also remembered what he said about the seriousness of their situation.

Shane was right. This was not the time for games.

Maya went to pull her hands from his so they could get up and resume their training but Shane wouldn't release her. His thumbs brushed along the underside of her wrists, sending tiny zings of lightning up her arms with each pass. Maya trembled, staring into the dark, limitless depths of his eyes.

I don't want to be at war with you, Maya. Shane's

deep voice whispered seductively into her mind, sending flickers of desire through her blood. He sat up slowly, still holding her hands in his and keeping that intense gaze locked with hers. With their hands intertwined and pressed between their bodies, Maya sat in his lap, fitting there perfectly as though her body had been made just for his. *I am equally resistant to love. For love is also a dangerous prospect that can wound or maim as deeply as any weapon.* Shane placed a kiss at the corner of her mouth and trailed kisses down her throat, which added to the seductive sensations of the telepathic contact.

Maya let her head fall back, allowing him clear access to the sensitive skin of her neck. She knew that what he was saying was true and that taking the leap into love was as dangerous as going to war, but with his lips brushing her flesh and his voice touching her mind, all she could do was feel. Even when he tried to rationalize why they shouldn't do what they were doing, his fingers were dragging down the zipper of her catsuit and peeling the fabric from her torso.

Moaning with desire and sheer anticipation, Maya sat up, grabbed Shane's face, and kissed him. There was urgency between them, a stark, driving need to touch and be touched. Maya suckled his lower lip and grinned, then gripped the edge of his T-shirt and helped him pull it off. Shane tossed the offending garment aside, and Maya gasped, taking in the sight of his well-muscled chest covered with a dusting of dark hair. She trailed her fingers along his collarbone and down the center of his torso as he covered his mouth with hers.

Maya groaned and pressed herself harder against him, reveling in the erotic sensation of his bare chest brushing against her nipples. Kissing her, he pulled her hair free from the confines of the ponytail and sighed into her mouth, running his fingers through her long locks. They both needed more.

"Stand up," Shane murmured as he broke the kiss. "I want to look at you in the moonlight."

Maya rose from his lap, taking in the sight of him as she went. His broad-shouldered torso was perfectly sculpted, and it was plainly evident that every single inch of him was rock hard. Her eyes widened briefly and panic welled when she saw that his erection was barely contained by the faded jeans, but once she looked back into his eyes, any fear she might have felt abated.

Shane went to his knees and, with incredible tenderness, lifted her left foot before carefully removing her tall boot, tossing it aside, and placing a featherlight kiss on the tip of her toes. Maya lost her balance switching feet and laughed nervously. Shane captured her hand and pressed it to his lips before placing it on his shoulder so she could regain her balance. Desire surged as the muscles of his shoulder flexed beneath her fingers, and she watched him remove her other boot and set it aside. Shivering with anticipation, she stood barefoot in the grass as Shane rose higher on his knees and grasped her hips with his hands.

Maya threaded her fingers through his hair while he rained butterfly kisses over her lower stomach and flicked his tongue in her belly button with wickedly seductive strokes. His tongue trailed a line over the curve of her hip, and he peeled the rest of the catsuit down her legs, kissing and nibbling his way to the crook of her knee before helping her step out of the suit, leaving her totally nude in the light of the moon.

Quivering with gut-clenching desire, Maya ran her knuckles down the sides of his beard-stubbled face while he looked up at her with pure, unadulterated lust. The look in his eyes was savage and tender at the same time, and he reminded her once again of a tiger ready to pounce. On his knees with his gaze locked on hers, Shane let his fingers drift up her thighs, and his thumbs brushed lightly along the inner curve of her legs.

"You're beautiful, Maya," he murmured. Rising to his feet, he linked one arm around her waist and tugged her against him while his other hand drifted in between her legs, slipped between her slick folds, and began to stroke. "And you'll look even more beautiful when I make you come," he growled before capturing her lips with his.

Maya kissed him and clung to his shoulders desperately while his talented fingers rubbed her clit in slow, seductive strokes, delivering knee-bending waves of pleasure with every pass. She lifted one leg and draped it over his hip, allowing him full access to her hot, wet center, and cried out as he slipped one finger and then two inside of her. He gathered her hair in his hands, tilting her head back so he could devour her mouth with deep, penetrating kisses while she rode his hand and the orgasm started to crest. Somewhere through the thick haze of desire, she knew she wanted and needed more. She wasn't ready for it to end.

Maya broke the kiss and pushed Shane's hand aside before quickly unbuttoning the fly of his jeans and pushing them down his narrow hips. Maya licked Shane's lip, grinned, and wrapped her fingers around the hard, steely length of him. He groaned, a low rumbling sound of pleasure, as she massaged him in her hand and ran her thumb over the velvety tip. Maya moved faster, sliding her hand over him in quick, hard strokes while he licked and suckled her lips urgently.

"I have to be inside of you," he rasped. Shane lifted his head and linked his fingers around her wrist, gently pulling her hand away as he stepped out of his jeans. Cradling her face with one hand and circling his other arm around her waist, he pulled her against him, pinning his thick erection between their bellies. "Are you ready, Maya? Will you give yourself to me?"

Staring into his intensely handsome face, she realized she'd known the answer before he even asked, and it was the most beautiful moment of the entire experience. Shane was asking for permission to take the one thing she hadn't given to another man in years. He didn't take what he so clearly wanted, but *asked*, even with the chance that her answer might be no. Her blood surged and every cell lit up like a live wire with his flesh rubbing against hers. One word thundered through her head.

Yes, she whispered into his mind.

"Thank God," Shane groaned before covering her mouth with his.

Kissing her, Shane lifted Maya off the ground as she wrapped her legs around his waist with his cock still pressed between their bodies. She thought he would take her right then, but he didn't. Paying thorough attention to her lips, and with her body wrapped tightly around his, Shane flew Maya up to the roof of the giant house. She shrieked her delight when he landed on the flat section along the back of the house, just above the kitchen.

Shane lay down and pulled Maya with him so she was on her knees straddling him. She leaned forward, bracing her hands on either side of his head, her blond hair spilling around them. His erection, hot and full, was pressed beneath her in just the right spot, and his large, strong hands rested on her hips.

Maya ran her tongue along the seam of his lips and rocked her hips, sliding her hot center along the rigid length of his cock. Kissing him deeply, she moved faster, sliding her slick, swollen flesh over his in long, hard strokes. She rode him with total abandon and brought them both to a fever pitch. Maya whimpered as the orgasm coiled tight and deep. Knowing she was ready, Shane reached between their bodies and slipped himself inside her.

Maya cried his name as the steely length of him filled her. She sat up, taking all of him in, and he gripped her hips tightly, encouraging her to move. Slowly and with deliberate motion, Maya tilted her hips, keeping her gaze locked with Shane's. She put her hands above her head, feeling wild and free, riding him faster while delicious friction sent white-hot pleasure whipping through her body.

As wave after wave of the pounding orgasm tore through them in unison, Maya's fangs erupted and the surge of a familiar primal need took hold. Still buried deep inside her, Shane sat up on a growl with his razor-sharp fangs bared. He tangled his hands in her hair while she rode him, and Maya let out a gasp of sheer pleasure when his mind melded with hers and he growled, "Bloodmate."

Shane sank his fangs into Maya's shoulder, and another orgasm slammed into her with toe-curling force. Maya shrieked her pleasure into the dark Louisiana night before dropping her head and sinking her fangs into the strip of flesh along his neck.

He tasted wild and spicy, and ripple after ripple of bone-melting ecstasy soared through her body. Maya's eyes fluttered closed, the orgasm subsided, and a subtle but insistent sound rumbled through them like a bass beat at the club.

A heartbeat.

Once. Twice. Again.

The pounding continued while they clung to one another and the tiny aftershocks of the orgasm fluttered through them. Licking the wounds closed, they remained wrapped up in each other's arms, neither one wanting this moment to end. Even after they stopped the blood exchange, the heartbeat continued for several more minutes. They were alive. Even if it only lasted for those few brief moments, for that instant in time, Shane and Maya were *alive*.

Chapter 10

Maya lifted her head and the expression of wonder on her face was one of the best sights he'd ever seen. Shane cradled her cheeks with both hands and gingerly brushed his thumb over her flawless skin. A wistful smile played at his lips, and he held her gaze while their synchronized heartbeats slowed beat by beat until finally stopping and leaving them quiet once again.

"Did you feel that?" Maya asked in barely audible tones. "We…we had heartbeats. Both of us."

"I did." A sly grin cracked his handsome face, and he kissed the corner of her mouth. "But it may only have been a fluke. Perhaps something that happens only once between bloodmates."

"Once? Hmm." Maya linked her arms around his neck and flicked his mouth with her tongue. "Then I guess we better do it again. You know, to prove it wasn't just a fluke."

"Your wish is my command, youngling."

Shane made love to her again on the rooftop, beneath the black velvet blanket of the star-dappled sky, and proved that the presence of a heartbeat during a blood exchange was not merely a fluke. Once again when they joined in every way possible, a heartbeat thundered between them loud and strong. Afterward, while they lay next to one another, naked as jaybirds and with their fingers intertwined, Maya struggled with whether or not to ask Shane the question that lingered in her mind.

"What is it, youngling?" Shane turned onto his side. Propping himself up on his elbow, he played with a long strand of her hair. "Something is bothering you."

"Are you a mind reader?" Maya playfully smacked his arm with the back of her hand.

"Not exactly." Shane went back to playing with her hair but kept his eyes on hers. "But I can sense there's something troubling you."

"We're bloodmates." Maya made the statement with some uncertainty. "Right?"

"Yes." Shane rested his hand over her lower belly and stroked the soft flesh gently. "If I had any doubts, they were eliminated during the blood exchange. I haven't had a heartbeat in four centuries. It took a minute even to figure out what was happening, but it was the most erotic, intimate moment of my existence."

"I saw your memories." Maya smiled and stared into the night sky. "The battles, the sadness when your maker left you, and the loyalty you feel for the Presidium. I saw it all."

"Yes. That is part of the process, of giving myself to you."

"Were you able to read my blood memories?" she asked quietly. "I know that you should be able to but… I'm kind of defective or something. I know Olivia couldn't really read them, either."

"Not all of them." Shane's mouth set in grim line, and he tipped her chin toward him with one finger, forcing her to look at him. "There is nothing wrong with you, Maya."

"Yes, there is. Did you know that my turn took five days?" Maya took his hand in hers and sat up, pulling her knees to her chest, suddenly aware of her nakedness and feeling remarkably vulnerable. "*Five days*! It's like I ride the short bus of vampires."

"No." Shane's brow furrowed. "I was unaware that your conversion took so long. A traditional turn is two days, although Doug's was only twelve hours."

"Yeah," Maya scoffed. "But he's got angel blood. If we're bloodmates, then I should be able to share all of myself with you but I can't."

"That's it." Shane's tone was quiet but serious. He studied her closely and nodded. "Your bloodline must carry some kind of unique trait. It could explain why your blood memories are shrouded and why your turn took so long. You're not Fae or Amoveo. I've tasted that type of blood before and I'd recognize it. And since you haven't sprouted fur, it's a safe bet you're not a werewolf," he said with a wink. "It's not angel or demon either, because you don't exhibit any of the traits that Doug and Pete have as vampires. It's something else. That has to be the reason."

"Will you help me, Shane?" Maya rested her cheek on her knees and looked at him pleadingly.

"Ask and it's yours," he whispered. He brushed the hair from her forehead. "Anything."

"Help me find out who I am. How can I commit myself to you, to this whole bloodmate idea, if I don't even know who I am?"

"Like I said"—Shane gathered her into his arms and held her, brushing the top of her head with a kiss—"I'll always come and find you."

The sound of Lottie's car coming down the driveway prompted Maya to get dressed in record time. Shane offered to pack up the weapons and suggested Maya go inside to see if Lottie required anything of them. Maya picked some grass out of her hair before opening the creaky screen door and stepping into the brightly lit kitchen. Turning to close the door behind her, she caught a glimpse of Shane and couldn't help but stop and stare.

He still hadn't put on his shirt, and the clear, moonlit night was giving her a beautiful view of his broad, well-muscled back. Maya leaned against the doorway and watched him organize the weaponry with the same focused intensity that he did everything else, including lovemaking. A smile played at her lips, recalling the way his hands ran over her naked body and the heartbreaking tenderness that lingered in his kisses. Her hand went to her mouth, which tingled at the memory of rasping along his stubble-covered jaw.

"I smell sex."

Maya yelped and spun around, immediately going into a defensive stance, and found herself face-to-face with Lottie, who was laughing so hard, tears were streaming down her face. Feeling totally embarrassed, Maya dropped her hands as Shane appeared behind her with his gun drawn. He immediately tucked it into the waist of his jeans when he saw Lottie guffawing and leaning on the back of a chair for support.

"Yup." Swiping at her wet cheeks, Lottie shook her head and plopped her leather messenger bag on the table. "It's in the air, and it's thick like the fog on the bayou. Damn." She winked at Maya. "I may need a cigarette just from standing near you two."

Maya folded her arms over her breasts, at a total loss for words. Mor-ti-fied.

"If you'll excuse me." Shane slipped past Maya and glanced at Lottie with a look on his face that resembled embarrassment. "I should put this bag away properly so everything is ready for tomorrow's training. Maya, I'll be taking a shower and then heading to bed. The sun will be up soon, and you will need your rest for tomorrow. We'll be adding weapons to the hand-to-hand combat, and you'll be learning to access them from the sentry coat."

"How romantic," Lottie said with a roll of her eyes.

"Okay." Maya glanced at Lottie, who had opened the refrigerator and was cracking open a can of beer. "I'll be up in a few minutes."

"Good night, Lottie." Shane tilted his head. "Thank you again for hosting us."

"You bet." When he walked past her, Lottie smacked him on the ass. "If she needs sleep, then you better make it a cold shower."

Shane paused for a moment before silently exiting the kitchen through the swinging door. Maya fought to keep from laughing.

"How was work? Are you always out this late?" Maya asked, desperately trying to change the subject.

"Shit." Lottie shook her head. "You kidding me? We got ten different conventions in New Orleans this week, which means things are hoppin' down there on Bourbon."

"What is it that you do, exactly?"

"I'm a fortune-teller. I work at a few little pubs in the Quarter. I used to have a table in Jackson Square, but the weather can be a bitch, so I picked up some indoor gigs." Lottie removed the colorful scarf she had tied around her head and draped it over the bag. Obviously stiff from sitting for a long time, she stretched her back.

"I do what it sounds like. I can read the future, but it's nothin' that special. Most gypsies are taught the magic when they're children and pass it on to theirs. I never did have kids." She made a face. "Couldn't find a man I could tolerate for more than a roll or two in the sack. Coulda done it on my own, I suppose, but it just wasn't in the cards for me. Too bad, though."

"Why?"

"My magic will die with me. I don't have any kin, so our gypsy line will go the way of the dinosaur. Serves us gypsies right, I suppose. We are all so damn secretive, you know. The clans don't share their magic with other clans, so when one clan dies out…that's it for their family's magic."

"There are different kinds of gypsy magic?" Maya asked with genuine curiosity.

"Sure." Lottie belched after taking another swig of beer. "There used to be a few hundred clans, but who knows how many are left? Not me. For all I know, I could be the last. Up until a couple of centuries ago, the clans used to gather, but after a lot of bickering and petty crap, that stopped. Us gypsies have powerful magic, but damn if we aren't a stubborn lot. Anyway, like I said, my clan's magic is about seeing the future."

"Can you read the past?" Maya asked tentatively.

"Not usually, but sometimes I can." Lottie took a big sip of beer and looked Maya up and down. "Why?"

"I don't remember much about my human life, and it didn't really bother me until recently."

"Recently, huh?" Lottie jutted her thumb toward the ceiling. "Your sudden desire to uncover your past wouldn't have anything to do with the six-foot, four-inch hunk of man upstairs, would it?"

"Some, yes." Maya lifted one shoulder. "But it's not just because of Shane. How can I move forward if I can't let go of the past? It haunts me, Lottie. Not knowing where I come from haunts me."

"Well, you do still have that glimmer thing going on. It wasn't my eyes playin' tricks on me. Nope."

"Shane thinks that I might have—"

"Stop right there." Lottie held up one hand. "Not another word. I don't like to have any preconceived notions because it can mess with the reading." Lottie grabbed her bag and gestured toward the door. "Come on."

"Where?"

"The living room." She bumped the door open with her butt, making the charms on her skirt jingle. "I like to work in there when I'm at home."

"Work?" Maya looked at her quizzically.

"Let's see what we can see." Lottie drained the rest of her beer, and disappearing through the door, she shouted, "Come on, baby girl. You ain't got much time. That sun won't wait just 'cause you've got questions you want answered, and I'm tired."

Maya steeled her courage. The possibility of learning more about her past was actually rather frightening now that she was faced with it. But hadn't she just been asking Shane to help her?

"Jeez, Maya," she muttered to herself. "Stop being such a baby and get out there."

Shane. Maya tentatively reached out and touched his

mind with hers. *Lottie is going to try and use her gypsy magic to read my past. I—I know you're tired but—*

Before she could finish her sentence, Shane was pushing open the door to the kitchen and gesturing for her to come with him. "No time to waste. The sun will be up soon."

Smiling and blinking back tears, Maya ran to him, wrapped her arms around his waist, and hugged him quickly before popping up on her toes and brushing his lips with hers. "Thank you."

They walked into the living room hand in hand to find Lottie seated on the far end of the couch and tying her long hair back into a bun. She smiled and patted the empty cushion next to her before rubbing her hands together briskly as though warming them up. Shane gave Maya's hand a reassuring squeeze before she sat down, and she shifted her body so that she and Lottie were face-to-face.

Shane stepped aside and stood on the other side of the coffee table with his hands at his sides. Maya couldn't help but notice that he always looked ready for battle. The man was never off duty. She wondered if he'd ever actually been a little boy, or if he'd come out of the womb looking like that.

"Now," Lottie began with a look of caution to both Maya and Shane, "like I was sayin' before, I usually can only see the future of a person, and I've never tried readin' a vampire before. So this could get us a whole lot of nothin'. Everyone understand?"

"Yes." Maya nodded and straightened her back.

"Okay, girl." Lottie clapped her wrinkled hands and extended them, palms facing up, toward Maya. "Give me your hands."

Maya placed her hands in Lottie's. The gypsy's eyes widened with surprise, and she gripped Maya's fingers tightly. "I'll never get over it." Lottie laughed.

"What?" Maya glanced at Shane for reassurance.

"I always expect your kind to be as cold as ice but you aren't." Lottie pursed her lips and shrugged. "A little cooler than a regular person, but you aren't walking icicles like they say ya are in the movies."

"That whole garlic thing is a myth too," Maya said in a conspiratorial whisper. "I do think it smells terrible, though."

"Me too." Lottie winked and settled Maya's hands over her knees. The smile faded from her lips. "I need you to sit quietly and close your eyes. Concentrate on your past or whatever you can remember. A person or a place, maybe?"

"My grandmother." Maya's eyes fluttered closed, and the image of her grandmother filled her mind. Long, silver hair swept up in a graceful bun framing a heart-shaped face soft with age, smiling blue eyes just like Maya's, and the emerald necklace dangling around her neck. "I can see her smiling."

"Good girl." Lottie's voice was quiet and barely above a whisper. "Keep that image in your mind and be still."

The seconds of silence extended into minutes, Maya was beginning to think this was going to be a big waste of time. But she shut down the voice of doubt and kept her eyes closed and her mind focused.

"You have magic in you," Lottie murmured in a barely audible voice. "Powerful magic."

Lottie's voice drifted over Maya, and the faded image

of her grandmother grew stronger and more colorful. The emerald in the necklace glowed brightly and blurred the vision of her grandmother, giving way to a flurry of images, like a slide show of Maya's past. Tears rolled down her cheeks.

She saw herself playing in snowy mountains, running along a beach and jumping in the waves, and sitting next to a tiny Christmas tree opening presents. A warm glow burned in Maya's chest that could only be described as love. Pure, unadulterated, unconditional love, and it all came from her grandmother.

The sound of a woman crying wafted into her mind, and Maya saw herself standing in front of a plain pinewood casket on the same mountainside where she played as a child. She placed a single rose on the coffin before the image faded from her mind and reality came spinning back.

"Dark magic," Lottie whispered as her soft, wrinkled hands squeezed Maya's hands briefly before releasing them.

Maya's eyes flicked open, and she swiped at the tears on her cheeks as she regained her bearings.

"That was totally crazy…and wonderful," Maya said in a shaky voice. Shane looked concerned, but the expression on Lottie's face was one of wonder. Maya glanced from Lottie to Shane and rubbed her palms on her thighs nervously before asking a question she almost didn't want the answer to. "What is it, Lottie? What do you mean that I have dark magic in me? Is it because I'm a vampire?"

"No." Lottie shook her head slowly and stared at Maya through wide eyes as a smile slowly cracked her face. "You, my dear girl, have gypsy magic."

"Gypsy?" Maya's eyebrows flew up. She wouldn't have been more surprised if Lottie said she was part chicken. She let out a nervous laugh and looked up at Shane, who had moved in beside her. "I'm a gypsy like you?"

"Not exactly." Lottie waved her finger and rose from the couch, wringing her hands nervously. Walking toward the large bay window, she kept her back to them. "Like I said earlier, there are different clans with varying types of magic, and most of the clans kept their magic to themselves. But not all." Lottie turned around slowly to face them. "I've seen that necklace before," she said somberly. "The one your grandmother was wearing in that vision."

Maya opened her mouth to tell Lottie it was upstairs, but Shane shot her a look of warning. *Wait, youngling.*

"Where?" Maya asked, tearing her gaze from Shane and back to Lottie. "Did you know my grandmother?"

"No." Lottie sat on the edge of the windowsill and folded her hands in her lap. "My grandfather showed me a picture once when he was spinning tales about the gypsy clans, and it was the same story his father told him. Like I said before, all of the clans had rivalries and grudges against one another, but one clan was feared above all others."

Lottie got a faraway look in her eye, and Maya instinctively reached out and took Shane's hand in hers. "He told us that we should stay away from that clan in particular because they would bring bad luck and a curse upon our clan." Lottie looked at Maya with wonder. "Amazing...I thought they were all gone."

"Great." Maya swallowed hard and tried not to show how unsettled she was by what Lottie was saying. "Like I don't have enough problems. What do you mean a curse?"

"Remember how I told you all of the gypsies used to gather their clans together but stopped a couple hundred years ago?"

"Yes."

"Well, it was because of this clan I'm telling you about. According to the story my grandfather told me, the dark magic used by this clan brought the wrath of the werewolves down onto all of the gypsies. There were random wolf attacks on our people off and on for years, and that was when the gatherings of the clans stopped. After that, everyone kept to themselves and the dark magic clan was considered cursed because its members had encouraged the wrath of the wolves."

"Well, I guess I've lived up to that part of the family reputation," Maya said with no humor. She sent a sidelong look at Shane, whose expression had grown increasingly concerned.

"He showed us a photograph of a young gypsy woman." She waved her hand in the air absently. "It was one of those old sepia-tone tintypes, but I can still remember it as clear as day. The woman in the picture was wearing the same necklace as the one your grandmother was wearing, and come to think of it, you look a bit like her." Lottie pointed at Maya. "You, young lady, are descended from the dark-magic gypsy clan."

"Can I see the picture?" Maya asked hopefully.

"No, sorry." Lottie shook her head and looked at Maya sadly. "There was a flood many years back, and I lost almost everything on the first floor." She looked around and sighed. "I never really did get it back in top shape around here."

"What was the name of this clan?" Shane asked quietly.

"Vanator," Lottie murmured.

Maya's gut clenched, and Shane's grip on her hand tightened. "That's what Bella called me," Maya whispered and looked up at Shane through wide eyes.

"Who's Bella?" Lottie asked, folding her arms over her breasts.

"A ghost who haunts the Presidium's offices in New York." Shane sat on the arm of the sofa and rubbed Maya's back reassuringly. "She only speaks Romanian, and according to our friend Xavier, it means—"

"Hunter," Lottie said. "I know."

"You speak Romanian?" Maya asked.

"Nope. But my grandfather did, so I know a few words." Lottie scoffed. "Mostly swear words."

"What significance does the necklace have?" Shane asked. Maya held his hand tighter and waited for Lottie to answer.

"Not sure." Lottie looked from Shane to Maya. "But at the very least, it represents the Vanator clan."

"I was wearing it that night." Maya's hand fluttered to her throat where the heirloom usually lay, and she turned her eyes to Shane, the pieces coming together. "That night at the club when everything happened with Horace and his pack."

"Son of a bitch," Shane seethed. "That's got to be why Horace is so intent on getting his hands on you."

"I'm not going to go near him or any other werewolf ever again," Maya said firmly. However, the look on Shane's face gave her pause. "Shane? What is it? There's something else that you're not telling me."

"Remember how I told you that Horace still hadn't left the city?"

"Yes."

"Well, he's refusing to leave until Olivia and Doug turn you over to them."

"He must have recognized the necklace," Maya said quietly. Dread settled in her chest because she knew what she had to do. "We have to go back, Shane. I'll give them the necklace. I don't want to cause any more trouble for Olivia or anyone else."

"No. Aside from the fact that I'm not letting those wolves near you, we're not going anywhere until we find out what the hell this necklace does and why the wolves hate the Vanator gypsy clan so much that they're willing to start the war all over again." Shane turned to Lottie. "What exactly did the Vanator clan do that incurred the wrath of the werewolves?"

"I got no clue." Lottie narrowed her eyes and wagged a finger at Maya. "You're full of surprises, young lady, and I have a sinking suspicion that you have even more to reveal."

"The necklace hasn't ever done anything magical, though." Maya's brows knit together and frustration crawled up her back. "How the hell are we going to figure out what kind of magic this necklace can do anyway?"

"In my experience, most objects don't do the magic. The person who holds the object does. Chances are that the necklace is just a family heirloom passed down through the Vanator gypsy line. Based on what you're saying about this Horace character, the wolves must have been keeping an eye out for the necklace and the Vanator gypsies."

Lottie held up her left hand and wiggled her middle finger, which was adorned with a gold band with an oval ruby at the center. "This was passed down through the generations of my clan, and like your necklace, my ring is a symbol for the Fogg gypsy clan." She let out a curt laugh and shook her head. "I'll be damned. Not only do I have two wayward vampires stayin' in my house, but one of 'em is a Vanator. My grandfather is probably rollin' in his grave."

"I'm sorry, Lottie." Maya stilled and held Lottie's stare. "Do…do you want us to leave?"

"My grandfather always was a crazy old bastard." Lottie shrugged. "I'm a shitty gypsy woman. I don't speak Romanian. I didn't get married or make babies, and I use my magic to make money but have no one to teach it to. Believe me, he's been rollin' for so long, he's probably been around the world twice."

Lottie rose to her feet and padded across the room quietly, her sandal-clad feet whispering over the faded oriental rug before she came to a halt at the edge of the coffee table. She looked from Maya to Shane and then back to Maya before a huge smile cracked her face and she gently patted Maya's cheek. "I don't want you to leave. In fact, I'm as curious as you are to find out more about your kin and the dark magic that has the wolves so worked up."

"I don't think I have any kin left." Maya's brows knit together again. "My grandmother died. When you were doing the reading, it opened up more memories and I saw a funeral, but I'm pretty sure I was the only one there."

"Yes." Lottie nodded and let out a sigh. "Is that why you don't think you have any other kin?"

"Well, after I became a vampire and my human life ended, no one came looking for me. It's like I just disappeared and no one cared. There was no missing person's report filed anywhere."

"Well, of course not." Lottie made a sound of derision. "You're a gypsy. We live off the grid, girlie. Hell, I don't have a social security number and there isn't even a record of my birth. I was born out here, like the generations before me. In fact, my clan was considered freakish because we stayed in this house. Most gypsies are nomads and don't stay in one place for long. Report a missing person to the cops? Ha! Gypsies take care of their own business."

Maya had about a hundred more questions, but before she could ask them, a strong cramp flared in her chest. She grimaced and squeezed Shane's hand tightly. "What the hell is going on?"

It's the pull of the sun, Maya. Shane's mind touched hers like a soothing caress. *The blood exchange must have heightened and accelerated your abilities.*

"Holy crap, that took me by surprise." Maya gave him a weak smile. "This is not what I would consider one of the perks." *I guess that whole daywalking part takes a while to kick in?*

For all we know, Maya, that may not happen for us. Our bloodmate bond may have different side effects than Olivia and Doug's.

Maya didn't respond but nodded her understanding and rubbed absently at her chest. Disappointment tugged at her briefly. It would be nice to be able to walk in the sun again, but when Shane's fingers brushed over hers, a smile curved her lips and she reveled in the sweet feel of his mind touching hers. Nothing could be better than that, not even a day in the sun.

"Are you alright?" Lottie asked with genuine concern.

"She'll be fine, but we should go to our room because the sun is rising." Shane tilted his head toward the brightening sky. "Thank you, once again, for your hospitality."

"Sure thing, but I don't know how much sleep I'm gonna get. My mind is gonna be racing about all this, that's for damn sure." Lottie walked out of the living room with them and led the way up the stairs. When they reached the second floor, she stopped at her bedroom door. "I have an idea of how you might be able to find out more about yourself. I know someone else who might be able to help you."

"Can't you do another reading?" Maya asked hopefully.

"No." Lottie yawned loudly. "We hit a wall tonight. Trust me. I saw all I'm gonna see out of you, but I have a friend who can probably see a bit more than I can. She's a psychic human—palm reader."

"I don't know," Maya said hesitantly and leaned into Shane's comforting embrace. "I'm not sure if I should go around talking about this with just anyone."

"She ain't just anyone," Lottie snapped. "Lillian is a damn powerful psychic and she's married to an Amoveo man, one of them shifters. Anyway, Lillian and Boris own one of the bars I work in, and they know all about your kind. You can trust her the same as you can trust me."

"Lottie's right." Shane gave Maya a reassuring look. "I haven't met them, but I've heard Pete speak highly of both of them. His mate is an Amoveo from the Bear Clan, and as you know, Pete's a liaison between the Amoveo and the vampires."

"Maybe one night this week, you two could take a little break from…whatever you been doin'," Lottie said, waggling her eyebrows, "and take a trip over to The Den. That's their bar. It's at the edge of the Quarter."

"Could we?" Maya looked up at Shane, excitement lacing her voice. "I never have been to New Orleans, and we wouldn't have to stay long. It would be a nice break from training."

Shane paused as though he was weighing all of his options. After what felt like an eternity, he finally nodded his agreement. "Perhaps we could make a quick visit, but it would be a good idea to speak with the czars about it first."

"Thank you." Maya kissed his cheek and hugged him. "And thank you, Lottie. For everything."

"Yes, well…I'll see you after we all get some sleep," Lottie said, before disappearing into her room.

Maya went to go upstairs, but Shane grabbed her hand, stopping her. He stared down at her with his trademark serious and intense gaze.

"Shane?" Maya teased. "What's the matter? Can't handle having a gypsy-vampire girl for a bloodmate?"

Shane's hand cradled her face gently, and though she could tell there was something he wanted to say, he didn't. He placed a kiss on her forehead just before he carried her up the stairs and tossed her onto the bed with a wicked grin. They removed their clothes in a blur of movement, and an instant later, Shane's nude body covered hers. Wrapping her up in his arms, he trailed kisses over her shoulder and his deeply seductive voice floated into her mind. *Gypsy or vampire…you are mine, and I would die to protect you.*

Chapter 11

Shane stood in the front yard of the grand old house and stared out over the moonlight-dappled water, waiting for Olivia to pick up her phone. He and Maya had spent the past four nights training and making love, and he wasn't surprised that Maya was excellent at both. A smile curved his lips as he recalled her willingness to please him and her increased bravery with each sexual interlude. The woman was a spitfire in the bedroom, and he knew his sex life with Maya would never be boring.

Nothing about Maya was bland or ordinary. Her fighting abilities improved with remarkable speed, and he was eager for the rest of the coven to see the formidable warrior she was becoming. While her skills on the battlefield would be for others to see, Maya's talents in the bedroom would be only for him.

A sudden and dark surge of jealously gripped him at the mere thought of another man touching her, but he shoved it down quickly. Not only did he believe Maya had genuine feelings for him, but they were bloodmates and had performed the blood exchange multiple times. His brow furrowed when he recalled how strong the pull of the sun still was for both of them. Perhaps they would not become daywalkers like Olivia and Doug. Maybe the czar's ability to daywalk was linked to Doug's angel bloodline more than anyone believed.

The string of unanswered questions that rumbled

through Shane's head was interrupted when Olivia's voice mail picked up. Shane made a sound of frustration and hung up before quickly dialing Doug's number. It was unlike the czar not to answer her phone, and he wanted to speak with her before he and Maya went to see Boris and Lillian. They'd been training nonstop for several days, and Maya had been asking to visit with the New Orleans couple to try to learn more about her past. As much as he wanted to help her, Shane still felt some reservations about making the trip.

They'd managed to remain at Lottie's home without being detected, but if they weren't careful, a trip into the French Quarter could change that. New Orleans was a hotbed of supernatural activity and considered one of the few neutral zones in North America. While some supernaturals made it their home, no single supernatural group ran the city the way the vampires did in New York.

"Hello?" Tight with tension, Doug's voice rang through phone, interrupting Shane's thoughts.

"It's Shane." A tickle of warning flickered up his back. "What's happened? Why didn't Olivia pick up her phone?"

"She's having the baby." Doug sounded terrified and frustrated. "So she's kind of busy."

"Olivia?"

"No, the Virgin Mary," Doug said sarcastically. "Yes, Olivia. Right now. She's in there screaming in pain, and they can't even give her pain meds."

"No," Shane said somberly. "Our bodies don't respond to any type of pain medication."

"Yeah, well, Suzie, Xavier, and that fucking ghost

girl kicked me out of the room—out of my own fucking apartment—and I'm standing out here in the hallway like a schmuck talking to you. I can't even telepath with her because she cut me off, and I feel useless like tits on a bull."

"I-I'm sorry." Shane felt like a jackass. He had no idea what to say or do because he was relatively certain Olivia was in an enormous amount of pain, and from the sound of it, so was Doug. Childbirth and handling a nervous father in the proverbial waiting room were definitely not his forte. "What can I do?"

"Just keep your girlfriend out of trouble." Doug spoke quickly, and Shane could hear him pacing back and forth, his footsteps echoing through the stone hallways of the Presidium. "That powwow of bigwigs will be finished in two days, and when Emperor Zhao hears that Olivia's having the baby, my bet is that he's going to get his old ass to the city in about two clicks. King Heinrich was already planning on coming because that little shit Horace is still whoring around Manhattan with his pack of degenerates."

Shane had planned on telling Olivia and Doug about the necklace and why the wolves were so intent on having Maya turned over to them, but given the current situation, he opted against it. Better to wait until there was more specific information to share because right now Shane had more questions than he did answers. The last thing the czars needed was an additional bunch of unanswered questions.

"I had hoped Horace would give up and go back to where he came from."

"No such luck," Doug said tightly. "He's got a serious

hard-on for Maya and is hell-bent on getting his paws on her as some kind of repayment. What a dick."

"Who is patrolling the city?" Shane asked. He felt like he was shirking his responsibilities.

"Pete's back on duty, and Emperor Zhao sent in a new recruit from Texas."

"A trainee?" Shane pressed his fingers against his eyes, attempting to contain his frustration. "With a pack of werewolves in the city?"

"Oh, don't get your panties in a bunch. Apparently the guy was military when he was human, so he's already had plenty of training and he's not that new. He was turned back in the '50s."

"The 1850s?"

"Oh for shit's sake." Doug growled. "The 1950s. Maya's right. You are an old man."

"Perhaps, but that is still quite young to be a sentry in one of the largest and most populated territories in the world."

"Yeah, well, I guess a bunch of the old, experienced guys like you are working security at the summit with the Emperor. So we take what we can get."

"What's his name? Perhaps I know him."

"Dakota." Doug made a sound of frustration. "What's taking them so long in there?"

"I don't recall a sentry by that name." Shane rested one hand on his hip and glanced over his shoulder at the dimly lit house. Maya was upstairs getting ready for their one night out, and Lottie had already left for work. "I realize that it might be wise for us to return to the city now, but—"

"No way. You two stay there until we give you the

all clear." Doug let out a short laugh. "I'm not throwing that curveball to Olivia right now. She's kind of busy making a person, and something tells me that distracting her isn't real smart. Why did you call anyway? Wait… hold on."

Silence filled the line for a moment, and Shane was about to apologize when he heard Xavier's excited voice in the background. "It's a girl, and Olivia is fine."

"Holy shit," Doug shouted, letting out a loud laugh. "I have a daughter. I'm a father." Shane smiled because Doug's voice drifted from excited to almost reverent tones. "I'm a daddy. Oh man…I gotta go. Just sit tight, and we'll call you later."

The line went silent and a funny feeling settled in Shane's chest. It wriggled around inside him with irritating persistence, and he realized it was envy. Shane never even entertained the notion of having a child, and until just this second, he didn't think he wanted to be a father, not to mention that until recently he never thought it was possible. Hearing the joyful and awe-inspired tone in Doug's voice made Shane realize that everything he'd accepted about himself over the past four centuries was being called into question.

Allowing himself to love again, to love Maya, was terrifying enough, but a child? Shane couldn't begin to imagine the weight of that responsibility. He hadn't even had the nerve to tell Maya that he loved her because the prospect of it was so unsettling. Being bloodmates and bonding with her was one thing, but baring his soul to her was quite another. Shane cursed at himself and shoved the phone into the back pocket of his jeans. He had more important matters at hand than thinking about his feelings—like finding out what magic Maya was capable of and why the wolves were so desperate to get it.

The sound of the front door slamming shut interrupted his thoughts. A smile played at his lips when he heard Maya humming a tune as she trotted down the steps to meet him. Since they'd arrived at Lottie's house and Maya began her training, she seemed less encumbered. Of course, a part of him hoped that their mating contributed to her free spirit too.

Shane turned to greet her, but whatever he'd planned on saying went out of his head the moment he laid eyes on her.

The woman was spellbindingly beautiful.

Clad in sandals, a simple white sundress that came to just above the knee, and a sweater that matched the blue of her eyes, Maya looked every bit the beauty queen. Her long, blond hair flowed over her shoulder in loose waves, just the way Shane liked it, and she wore very little makeup. If a summer breeze could be embodied in a woman, it would look the way Maya did at this moment.

Smiling, she tucked her hair behind her ear and closed the distance between them with her hands clasped behind her back. Stopping only a few inches from Shane, she popped up on her tiptoes and pressed her lips to his.

"Ready to go?" she asked before kissing him one more time.

"You look positively fetching." Shane slid his hands down both her arms and tangled his fingers with hers, holding her arms out to the side so he could look her up and down. He had asked her to be sure she brought at least one weapon with her, but he was unable to detect where she'd put it. "Where on earth did you hide—"

Before Shane could finish asking her where she'd hidden the leather-handled throwing knives, Maya pressed one finger to his lips and shook her head.

"Ye of little faith," she whispered. "I've got it covered."

Maya spun around and pulled her sweater partway down her back to reveal a slim harness with the two knives discreetly tucked inside and easily accessible for her. Shane nodded his approval as Maya turned around, shifted her sweater back into place, and put her hands on her hips.

"Not bad." Shane's eyes wandered over her from head to toe, and his body immediately responded. "As always, Maya, you are full of surprises."

Maya laughed and playfully avoided his grasp when he tried to pull her into his arms.

"Nope." She wagged a finger at him and placed both hands on his chest, holding him at arm's length, which only made him want her more. "If we start *that*, then we'll never get out of here before sunrise. But if you behave yourself now, then I promise I'll make it up to you later."

"How?" Shane growled.

"You'll see," she sang. "But first I have to talk to Lillian, and in case you were wondering, I have the necklace in my skirt pocket so she can look at it." Maya grinned, but then her smile faltered. "Hey, did you talk to Olivia?"

"I did." Shane linked one arm around Maya's waist and yanked her against him while his other hand found its way to the top of her ass. He didn't do it to instigate sex; he simply loved the feel of her, and it made him happy to touch her whenever he could.

Shane kissed the tip of her nose. "But you distracted me with your beauty."

"Well?" Maya giggled when Shane nuzzled her neck. Nibbling her lip, she linked her arms around his waist. "What did she say when you told her about the whole gypsy thing?"

Shane stilled and lifted his head because he realized he'd totally forgotten about the conversation with Doug, which was highly unlike him. His feelings for Maya were cluttering up all of his senses. "I didn't."

"What?" Maya's body tensed. "Why not?"

"Olivia had the baby."

"Oh my God!" Maya squealed her delight and hugged him ferociously. Tangling her fingers in his hair, she peered back up at him with wide blue eyes. "What did she have? I mean Suzie kept saying it was a girl. Are they okay?"

"Doug said they are both doing well, and she had a baby girl." Shane adored watching Maya's joyous reaction and doubted that anything could make him happier than watching his mate smile. "Given the circumstances, I thought we should wait until we have more information."

"I guess you're right." Maya's smile faltered and she started fiddling with the buttons on his shirt.

Shane leaned back and tilted her chin, forcing her to look him in the eye again. "What's wrong, Maya?"

"I miss them," she whispered and let out a soft laugh. "Even Trixie."

"You'll see them again soon. Contrary to the way it feels, we won't be down here forever."

"No." She shook her head and paused, struggling for

the right words. "It's not that…I miss hearing them, and it's still strange not being able to talk to them anytime I want. It was hard enough when Olivia stopped telepathing with us and could only speak that way with Doug, but now…" She trailed off and looked away.

"Now you can only speak that way with me," Shane said quietly.

"Yes." She flicked her eyes back to him and grabbed his arms with both hands. "Please don't be offended. It's not that I don't love…being able to talk to you like that," she added quickly. "It's just going to take some getting used to, that's all."

Shane froze for a moment when she uttered the word "love" because he thought she was going to say she loved him, but she didn't. To his great surprise, he was disappointed. But what did he expect? Up until a few days ago, she could barely tolerate his presence. Now, because they'd slept together a few times and the universe deemed them bloodmates, should he simply expect her to fall in love with him?

With Maya staring up at him expectantly, waiting for him to respond, he realized that was *exactly* what he expected—and he felt like an idiot.

"Shane?" Maya's brows knit together. "Are you upset with me?"

"No, youngling." He stepped back and glanced toward the sky in an effort to shut down his feelings of stupidity. "We should leave if we want to have ample time for you to meet with Lillian. I don't want to risk getting caught in the city after sunrise."

"I hope she can help me remember more." Her voice wavered. "Even if this magic I can do is the blackest of all magic, I still want to know. The truth can't possibly be worse than not knowing."

Looking back at Maya, Shane noticed the concerned expression etched into her features. He extended his hand and wrapped her fingers in his. When their flesh met, the line between her eyes smoothed and her lips curved into a smile.

"Agreed." Shane brought her fingers to his mouth and kissed them lightly. "Just remember, Maya. All creatures are capable of darkness, but not all choose to succumb to it."

As they leaped into the sky and flew through the night swiftly and silently, Shane couldn't stop thinking about something Lottie said the night they arrived. *Funny how the mind can choose what it wants to remember and what it wants to forget*. Perhaps, he thought while they raced toward the city, some things would be best left forgotten.

They landed silently in a dark alley at the edge of the French Quarter, but even along the outskirts, the lights and sounds of the bustling district could be heard. Shane linked Maya's hand with his and walked down the quiet, dimly lit cobblestone street toward the corner of Ursuline and Dauphine. Holding her hand seemed the most natural thing to do. Though far smaller and more delicate than his, her hand fit in his like it had been made only for him.

A pungent, familiar scent filled his nostrils and brought the reality of their situation crashing back in on him. *Werewolf*. The distinctly woodsy aroma slammed into him just before they reached the intersection where The Den was located. Maya stilled and her body tensed next to his. When he glanced at her, he was pleasantly surprised to see a ferocious, battle-ready look on her face.

I smell it too. Maya's voice touched his mind curtly. *And I'm getting that weird feeling again, but it's even stronger this time. Like an invisible rope pulling me toward them. There's more than one, and they're to the left, maybe a block or two away.*

There's a pub not far from here that's run by a pair of wolves. Shane nodded his agreement and scanned the area, attempting to pinpoint the wolf's location more clearly. His search was interrupted when Maya's hand squeezed his almost to the point of pain. *The scent I'm picking up is coming from that direction.*

Shane. Her voice whispered into his mind on a rush. *Look at my pocket…it's glowing.*

He looked down to see that Maya was absolutely correct. The left side of her white dress now had an almost ghostly green glow emanating from the pocket where the necklace was. With shaking fingers, she pulled the necklace out and held it up between them. The large stone that dangled from the bottom of the gold chain was glowing as though lit from within.

They looked from the stone to each other, and Maya's expression was nothing short of amazement.

"I don't recall it lighting up like that at the club," Shane said, looking more closely at the unique jewel. "Although I was admittedly…distracted."

"No. I've never seen it do this before." Maya shook her head and laid the necklace in her hand, but once the stone touched her flesh, the light dimmed. "Whoa. That felt weird. It's vibrating."

"Come here." Shane took Maya's arm and brought her into an alley across the tiny street, away from anyone who might pass by. Human or werewolf. He stopped and looked around before turning his attention back to Maya. "Let go of the stone." Maya did as he asked, and they watched the stone begin to glow again. "Now, lay it in your hand."

Once the stone touched her flesh, the light dimmed.

"It may not be glowing anymore, but it's humming or vibrating or something." Maya's eyes lit up with excitement. "I bet I know why it's doing this. It's warning me that there are wolves in the area. I should put it on."

"No." Shane grasped her forearm and shook his head. "Maya, we know there's a werewolf in the area and that the wolves have it in for you because of this necklace or whatever they think it stands for."

"*And* we know that this necklace has magic or, at the very least, it's connected to some magic that I'm supposed to have." Maya's chin tilted. Her eyes flashed and she pushed his hand away. "I've worn this necklace every day for as long as I can remember, and I feel naked without it—unprotected or something. Look, I can't explain why, but I do."

"You're being stubborn." Shane folded his arms over his chest.

"And this is news?" Maya asked playfully, putting the necklace around her neck and nestling the stone at the top of her cleavage. "See. It's not glowing anymore, but I do feel that vibration. It's really subtle, though, and like I told you before, when I was in that suite with all the wolves, my senses were going haywire. That's probably why I didn't notice it then. And I probably didn't feel it when we were at The Dollhouse because that place is total sensory overload."

Shane's mouth set in a tight line. He grasped the smooth stone between his fingers then frowned as he released it. "I don't feel vibrations."

"Really? Maybe that's because you're not a gypsy person or whatever." Maya pressed it to her chest and looked at him. "I can feel it, and I'm still getting that tugging feeling in my gut, which is actually really unpleasant. Can we just go see Lillian now? Please?" She buttoned up the cardigan sweater so that most of the necklace was covered. "Look. Now you can't even see it. Okay?"

"Fine." Shane grabbed her hand and walked with her toward the corner. He flicked a serious gaze in her direction. "Keep your senses alert, and do not leave my sight for one second. Are we clear? We are to keep our visit here quiet, and we don't want to attract any attention to ourselves."

"Fine." Maya bumped her hip into his and laughed. "You really don't get it, do you?"

"What?" Shane asked tightly. He stopped at the corner and noted the oval wooden sign with a snarling tiger on it that read, The Den. Glancing around at the busier street, which was open only to pedestrian traffic, he was relieved to note that the scent of the wolf had diminished. "What don't I get?"

"You." She laughed. Shane looked at her with genuine confusion, which only made her laugh harder. "You are a six-foot, four-inch hunk of drool-worthy hotness.

Believe me, you attract attention, whether you like it or not. See?" She leaned into his embrace and nodded toward two human girls who were giggling and staring at Shane while they stumbled away. "You're a hottie and the ladies love you, but don't go getting any ideas." Maya tugged his hand and pulled him toward the doorway of The Den. "I don't like to share."

"Good," Shane murmured, following her into the bar. "Neither do I."

When Shane crossed the threshold into the bar, the clear and distinct scent of an Amoveo shifter hit him. Unlike with the werewolves, the Amoveo scent didn't evoke feelings of danger or unpleasantness. The bar was sparsely populated and dimly lit, but Shane could see everything clearly. Keeping his arm around Maya protectively, he surveyed the pub with its pirate-ship theme. There were a series of tables and chairs to the left, a long beat-up wooden bar to the right, and a staircase along the back wall that led to balcony seating on the second floor. All of the patrons were human, and other than the Amoveo man behind the bar, he and Maya were the only supernaturals in the place.

"Welcome." The bartender's voice boomed through the small pub, and Shane immediately knew it was Boris Zankoff, an Amoveo from the Tiger Clan. He was about Shane's height with shoulder-length black hair and the eyes of a warrior. From what Shane heard, Boris was one hell of a fighter. "You must be Shane and Maya. Lottie said we might be seeing you two." He extended his hand over the bar and welcomed them both with a broad smile. "I'm Boris and I'd introduce you to my mate, but she's—"

"She's right here," said a bright, bubbly blond woman from the second-floor railing. With long, windblown hair, a peasant blouse, and a flowing skirt, she looked more like a gypsy than Maya did. Lillian Zankoff leaned over the railing and waved at them. "Hey! Come on up, I was just setting a table for us up here so we could have some privacy."

"That's Lillian," Boris said with obvious pride. He leaned closer, with both hands on the bar so the old man at the end of the bar wouldn't hear him. "She's really excited to meet you both and has been talking about doing your reading, Maya, ever since Lottie told her about you."

"Me too," Maya said with a nervous smile.

"Boris," Shane began, careful to keep his voice low. "Have you had any other *unique* patrons this evening?"

"You mean wolves?" A slow smile cracked Boris's face, and he pushed his long hair off his forehead. "No. They usually steer clear of my place. Two weres own a bar called Full Moon Café at the end of Royal, a couple of blocks from here. When wolves come to town, they tend to spend time there. You know how it is in neutral-zone cities like New Orleans. Everyone tends to stick to their own kind. It's safer that way."

"Thank you." Shane shook Boris's hand again and felt some relief. "That's reassuring."

Climbing the stairs to the second level, Shane extended his senses in search of any signs of a wolf—or other vampires, for that matter—and, to his relief, found none. Maya sensed his apprehension, and when they reached the top of the stairs, she turned around and gave him a quick kiss on the cheek. *It's all going to be fine.*

"I'm so excited to meet you both," Lillian's voice interrupted. She scooped Maya up in a hug and held her by both arms, giving Maya the once-over. "Damn, man. You've got some groovy vibes."

"Thanks." Maya smiled sheepishly and shrugged. "I think."

"And you have some dark, spooky vibes, dude," Lillian said, waving at Shane from a distance. "You're hot and everything, but whoa. You're like *way* spooky."

"You should see him when he's dressed in his sentry uniform," Maya said with a wink to Shane. "Super spooky *and* super hot."

Shane clasped his hands in front of himself and stood at attention because he didn't know what else to do. Being scrutinized like this was highly unusual and not something he wanted to get used to. He was comfortable flying under the radar and slipping in between shadows, and right now he was experiencing the exact opposite of that.

"Sorry." Lillian laughed and made the peace sign with both hands. "You'll have to forgive me. The only other vamp that I've really met is Pete. I've seen plenty of 'em here in the city, but I haven't actually met them." She gestured for them to follow her to the back wall where a candlelit table and chairs were waiting. "You see, until a year ago when I found Boris, I thought my ability to read palms made me a total freak. Now that I know about all the different supernatural species, well, I feel almost normal."

Lillian and Maya sat at the table, and Shane stood by the wall where he could have a clear view of the two of them and the stairs. The last problem they needed was for someone to slip up here undetected. He took a mental inventory of the weapons he had with him and thought perhaps he should have brought more, but the silver throwing weapons were difficult to use without the protective leather of his sentry uniform. He had the special-issue sentry dagger, the one with "Eternity" engraved down the center, in a harness strapped to his back and a gun tucked in an ankle holster. Even though he was armed, he couldn't escape a sense of worry, but when his gaze landed on Maya's gorgeous face, he realized why he felt so out of sorts.

It was her. More specifically, his feelings for her.

A weight settled in his chest, and the gravity of his situation came roaring into focus. If he allowed himself to love her, he would never feel truly prepared or be one hundred percent convinced of his power, because for the first time in four centuries, he was afraid. Shane was terrified of losing her. Be it at the claws of a werewolf, the skin-searing rays of the sun, or Maya herself telling him to take a flying leap—the thought of losing her was paralyzing.

How could Shane protect Maya, or anyone else, if he was weakened by fear?

Chapter 12

THE NECKLACE STOPPED VIBRATING BY THE TIME THEY went into The Den. That weird pulling feeling in Maya's gut had gone away too, but now she couldn't stop shaking. Her nerves were on edge and the anticipation of being so close to finding out more about the necklace and her family legacy was torture. The only reason she hadn't totally freaked out was because of Shane. The man was a rock, an immovable force that Maya knew she could count on, no matter what.

"Are you ready?" Lillian asked. Her eyes widened and she clapped her hands together. "Oh wait. Lottie said you have a necklace too. It's a family heirloom or something."

"Yes." Maya flicked her eyes to Shane, who was watching her like a hawk from his spot against the wall. A wry smile played at her lips. He stood there still as a statue, yet ready to spring into action at any moment. She hated to admit it, but Shane's protective nature was one of his most attractive qualities. Maya turned her attention back to Lillian and started to unhook the necklace. "Do you need to hold it?"

"Maybe." Lillian pushed a mass of wavy, dark blond hair off her face and smiled, laying her hands, palm up, on the table. "First I want to do a straight-up palm reading and see what I get. Okay?"

"Alright." Maya dropped her hands and placed them

in Lillian's, forcing herself to remain calm. "How do we do this?"

"Well, before I found Boris, I could only get images from the lines in a person's palm, but once I hooked up with him, I started to pick up readings from objects too. It's pretty wild."

"So you just hold my hand, and you'll see things?" Maya asked.

"Not exactly. I usually get an image when I run my index finger along the deep lines of a person's palm." Lillian gently turned Maya's left hand over, cradling it in one hand while the other hovered just above without touching. "But I've never done a reading for a vampire before, so I have no idea what I might see or not see."

Maya could feel the heat of Lillian's human body and heard her strong, steady pulse as thick, warm blood coursed through her veins. A pang of hunger struck Maya, but she bit it back. There would be time to feed later; right now she needed answers.

"Why the lines and not just touching someone?" Maya cleared her throat and steeled herself against the surge of hunger. Asking questions was helping her focus on the task at hand.

Are you alright, youngling? Shane's voice touched her mind gently.

Yes. Maya closed her eyes and fought to clear her head. *I know Olivia doesn't want us hunting while we're here, and that live feeds get us all hopped up, but I think I miss it. I don't know...maybe I'm just nervous about what she's going to see.*

We cannot hunt, but if you truly want to have a live feed, I will take you somewhere safe so that you can satisfy that desire. Shane's voice was edged with seductive promise. *But you must finish this first*.

"Hey?" Lillian snapped her fingers in front of Maya's face. "Are you okay?"

"Sorry." Maya shook her head. Laughing nervously, she glanced at Shane. "I was distracted."

"Right." Lillian looked over her shoulder at Shane before giving Maya a wink. "Boris does that to me too. Like I was saying, those lines in your palm are the ones that were formed when you grew in your mother's womb, when you clenched and unclenched your tiny hands. They are as deeply connected to you as I can get." Lillian's hand hovered over Maya's, and she looked at her intently. "I want you to close your eyes and stay real still, okay?"

Maya nodded and let her eyes flutter closed. Doing as Lillian requested, she cleared her mind. But the instant Lillian's fingertip touched Maya's palm, lights danced behind her eyes and a flurry of images came roaring to life.

Summertime in the mountains. Blue skies blanketed the heavens, and Maya lay on a blanket in dandelion-covered grass with a young woman's face hovering over her. Long blond hair spilled over slim shoulders and a pair of familiar blue eyes smiled down at Maya, but the woman wasn't alone. A man with shaggy brown hair and pale green eyes sat next to the woman with his arm around her, looking at Maya lovingly.

"My parents," Maya whispered. Her voice sounded far away, and for a second she wasn't sure if she'd said it out loud. Tears spilled down her cheeks and the comforting warmth of love filled her chest, washing over her like the sun. "I can see them, Shane."

The howl of a wolf shattered the golden moment, and the red haze of fear curled inside of Maya like a fire. Her father's voice ripped through the fear and he screamed, Run, Elizabeth! *Maya's mother picked her up, running with Maya cradled to her chest. Her heartbeat thundered through Maya's body, and her labored breathing surrounded Maya like a shroud.*

Maya was covered in darkness, and the sounds of her mother's crying filled her head. Snarls. Growling. A man's scream. Silence. She could hear her mother whimpering while she cradled Maya's small body to her shaking chest. Soon the darkness gave way to light and her mother laid her on a pile of blankets in a closet. I love you, Maya, *she whispered before she closed the door and left Maya in the dark alone.* I won't let them find you.

Silence.

Darkness.

The scream of a woman amid the snarling and growling of wolves rumbled around Maya. The sharp sound of furniture breaking and then the triumphant howls of wolves filled the dark. The howl faded and the aching sound of silence filled the darkness...but only for a moment.

"They're out there," Maya whimpered. "I can hear them sniffing around. The wolves are looking for me."

The terrifying sound of claws scratching at the door grated through Maya's head, and just when she thought they'd break through the door and tear her to pieces, a door slammed and the wailing whine of a wolf in pain pierced the air. More growling preceded a high-pitched wail and then—silence.

Maya's body shook with fear and anticipation. The door of the closet opened, temporarily blinding her. When her vision cleared, she saw her grandmother. She was younger than Maya remembered, but the necklace was draped around her neck as it always was. She cooed softly and picked Maya up, whispering gentle, soothing words.

Her grandmother carried her out of the cabin, and Maya peered over her shoulder at the wreckage of a battle. Broken furniture was strewn about the cabin, and in the middle of it, two men lay naked and bleeding. The last image Maya saw as her grandmother carried her outside was her mother's lifeless hand covered in blood.

The memory blurred and spun. Lights flickered behind her eyes, and when Lillian released Maya's hand, the past vanished and the present came roaring to life. Shaking, with Shane squatting next to her and rubbing her back with one hand in a sweet, reassuring gesture, Maya pressed her fingers to her eyes and wiped away the tears.

"They died for you," Lillian said in a quiet voice. She sat back in her chair and folded her hands in her lap, looking from Maya to Shane. "Your parents were killed by werewolves, but your grandmother took the wolves to task. If it wasn't for her, you wouldn't be here right now."

Maya nodded but couldn't make any words come out.

"That necklace you're wearing is the one your grandmother was wearing in the vision." Lillian pulled her hair back and rested her hands on top of her head. "I don't know exactly what she did or how she did it, but she kicked their hairy asses."

"She killed the wolves?" Shane asked with genuine

surprise. "How is that possible? Gypsies are human, and no human could possibly overpower a werewolf."

"I dunno." Lillian shrugged and pointed at Maya's necklace. "But that necklace must harness the gypsy magic somehow. Maya's mother and father were obviously no match for the wolves, but her grandmother, the one wearing the necklace, was."

"The wolves don't want me, Shane." Maya grasped his hand and settled her other hand over the necklace. "They want the necklace, and I guess I can't really blame them. How would the vampires feel if the werewolves had one item that could destroy vampires as easily as this necklace killed those two werewolves? My grandmother, an older human woman, killed those two wolves without even getting her hair messed up, and it had to be because she was wearing this necklace."

"Thank you for your assistance, Lillian," Shane said, rising to his feet. "I will be sure to inform the czars of your generosity and your willingness to help."

"Cool." Lillian stood up, stretched her arms over her head, and let out a sound of relief. "Man, that took it out of me and my muscles are way stiff." She dropped her hands to her hips and jutted her chin at Maya. "I know that I've never read a vampire before, so I really don't have anything to accurately measure it against, but you have a really funky energy. It's different from a human and an Amoveo. It's thick and sticky."

"Sticky?" Maya said and laughed, rising to her feet on surprisingly steady legs.

"Yeah." Lillian shrugged and headed toward the stairs. "Pushing into your memories was kind of like swimming through cotton candy. I don't know if it's because you're a vamp or a gypsy…or both."

"I agree." Shane's voice drifted over Maya's shoulder. "Maya's blood memories were next to impossible for me to read. I only get glimpses, bits and pieces. Granted, they have come more easily over the past few days, but they're still not visible to me the way they should be."

"Must be the gypsy in you, then." Lillian headed down the stairs. "Lottie did say that the gypsies are a secretive group."

"Well, it looks like the secret's out now," Maya said, following Lillian down to the bar. "I'm from some long line of werewolf assassins or something."

"You may remember more as the night wears on." Lillian slipped behind the bar and poured herself a shot of bourbon. "When we were done, that weird, sticky veil that I had to push through in the beginning was gone. Maybe we cracked the seal on whatever was bottling up your memories."

Shane slipped his arm around Maya's waist and watched Lillian throw back the shot of brown liquor. She squeezed her eyes shut and let out a slow breath before slamming the shot glass onto the bar.

"Sorry." Lillian swiped at her mouth with the back of her hand, and Boris sidled up next to her, kissing the top of her head reassuringly. "Sometimes I need to take the edge off after a vivid reading, and yours was way freakin' vivid. I don't think I'll ever look at the weres the same again."

Maya nodded her agreement. "I know what you mean."

"Can I get either of you something to drink?" Boris

asked, raising one eyebrow. "I do keep your drink of choice on hand, just in case."

"No." Shane shook his head and tilted his head in deference. He slanted a sly glance at Maya, the one that made her stomach flutter. "I have made arrangements for us this evening, and we've taken up enough of your time."

"Thank you, Lillian." Maya extended her hand over the bar, but Lillian gave her a doubtful look.

"A handshake? Please." Lillian laughed and came around from behind the bar before gathering Maya up in a warm embrace. "We're practically family now. I have been inside your head, and we dug up all kinds of information. I think we're well past handshakes and have moved right to hugging."

"True." Maya giggled and hugged her new friend tightly. She pulled back and smiled. "I mean it. Thank you, Lillian. You gave me more than information. You gave me back my parents and allowed me to feel their love again. I—I don't know if I can ever repay you for that."

"No repayment required." Lillian winked. "I know what it's like to feel lost."

"Me too," Maya whispered, glancing at Shane. "But not anymore."

Shane and Maya waved good-bye to their new friends and stepped out onto the sparsely populated street. Smiling, he took his hand in hers.

"I have to give the necklace to the wolves," Maya said, with Shane leading her down the street. She wasn't sure where they were going, but he certainly seemed to have a destination in mind. "I think that's the right thing to do. Besides, they're not going to stop until they get it, Shane."

"Agreed." Shane nodded but kept his sights on the street ahead as they wove their way through the growing crowd of humans. "I will call the czars tomorrow night and let them know what we've discovered, but right now we have something else that needs to be addressed."

"What's that?" Maya asked. The fluttering of the human heartbeats swarmed around her, making her hunger surge.

She gripped his hand tighter, holding on to him for strength, when a group of four drunken humans stumbled by and bumped into her. The physical contact had her fangs humming and begging to be released. Until this second, she hadn't realized how much she'd missed having a live feed, and walking down Bourbon Street, the most populated street in the French Quarter, wasn't helping.

I know you want to satisfy your urge for a live feed. Shane's seductive voice slid enticingly into her mind as he turned down a side street and pulled her away from the throng of humans. *I know going hunting is not permitted at the moment, but we do have another option. There's a vampire-run establishment not far from here, and it will provide you with exactly the relief you need. I even called ahead to get us the best table in the place.* He cast that sexy grin in her direction. *After all of your hard work and the intensity of the past week, I thought you could use a break.*

As long as it's not a break from you. Smiling and eager with anticipation, Maya went with him willingly. Shane was absolutely right. After the craziness of the past week and all of the revelations, she was desperate for a break.

They turned down a few side streets until they came to a small brick building on a dimly lit corner. It had an intricately designed wooden arch with images of various creatures of the night carved into it, and it framed a massive, shiny black door. Above the arch hung a painted sign that read, "Bayou Escape," in bright red letters that looked as though they'd been written in blood.

Shane pulled the door open and, as always, allowed Maya to go first. She had to admit it was one of his old-fashioned gestures that she appreciated. As the heavy door closed behind them, Maya noted the lighting was dim, much like the nightclubs in Manhattan, but instead of stepping right into the venue, they were standing at the beginning of a long hallway that looked like it led into a formal dining room. Based on the fluttering of heartbeats, she could tell that it was packed with humans who were eating dinner.

Sitting at the hostess station was a human girl, and not a vampire like Maya was expecting. She had long, red hair and was dressed in a simple black dress with a single strand of pearls draped around her neck. Neither the girl nor the restaurant was what she was expecting. Maya thought Bayou Escape was going to be a nightclub like The Coven, but it was the exact opposite.

"Good evening," Shane said in his most gallant voice. He slipped his arm around Maya's waist as he spoke, and she didn't miss the look of disappointment on the hostess's face when it was clear that Shane was taken. "I called ahead and requested a reservation for a private room in the wine cellar. The name is Quesada."

"Of course, Mr. Quesada." The girl's green eyes widened and a look of recognition flickered over her features. "Diego and Sebastian asked me to let them know when you arrived." She picked up the phone as her voice rose with excitement. "Please have a seat," she said with a gesture to the red velvet bench along the wall. "They'll be up in a moment."

Feeling far too anxious to sit, Maya tangled her fingers with Shane's and perused the various photographs along the wall. Two men appeared in all of the pictures, either separately or together, and in each photograph they were with someone famous. Actors, writers, and politicians from various points in time like Sophia Loren, Alfred Hitchcock, Bill Clinton, and Jennifer Lopez. Though the images clearly spanned several decades, the two men in the pictures were ageless.

"I take it these two guys are Diego and Sebastian?" Maya asked quietly, with a glance to the hostess. "It's kind of risky to post pictures of themselves like this, isn't it?"

"Not at all." Shane pointed to the photo of Sophia Loren. "As far as anyone else is concerned those men are their uncles, to whom Diego and Sebastian happen to bear a striking resemblance."

Maya nodded, but the blatant display still made her uncomfortable. These two vampires seemed to be flaunting their immortality and daring the world to discover them. "I can't imagine the Emperor would approve," she murmured as her gaze skittered over the pictures.

"Are you kidding?" An unfamiliar male voice boomed through the corridor. "Zhao has been coming here at least once a year since we opened the place."

Maya squeezed her eyes shut, embarrassment flooding her as she realized she'd been overheard. Some of her uneasiness eased back when Shane laughed, that low, sexy sound that curling around her like a blanket.

Maya turned to face the two vampires and was surprised to see they looked more like they belonged on Wall Street than at a club in New Orleans. They were tall, blond, gorgeous, and dressed impeccably in fine gray suits, with perfectly pressed French cuff shirts and matching bright orange ties.

"Good to see you, old friends," Shane said as he shook hands with the two men. "Sebastian and Diego, this is my…Maya." Shane stiffened for a moment, but his arm remained around her waist possessively. "She's been training with me for the past several days, and as always, when it was time for a respite, your fine establishment came to mind."

Maya smiled politely and went along with Shane's story about her training to be a sentry. She hadn't expected him to introduce her as his bloodmate or to go into the nonsense with the werewolves, especially given the uneasiness that could evoke, but he could have called her his girlfriend or something. Maya wasn't sure why, but it bothered her that he sidestepped that aspect of their relationship.

"It's lovely to meet you, Maya." A tall, slim man with blond hair took her hand delicately in his and kissed it regally. "I am Sebastian, and this far less handsome fellow is my brother, Diego."

"Charmed." Diego bowed with the old-fashioned flair she recognized from being around Shane. His hair was as blond as Sebastian's, but it was longer and brushed his shoulders as he kissed her hand. "Leave it to Quesada to find the most beautiful youngling I've seen in centuries and train her to be a sentry." He made a face and shook his head. "I can think of far more pleasant experiences than policing rowdy vampires in New York City."

"It's very nice to meet you both," Maya said, leaning into Shane's embrace and giving him a coquettish look. "But I can assure you that my experiences with Shane have been quite pleasurable."

"I'm sure this evening will be no different." Sebastian sent Shane a knowing look and then snapped his fingers at the hostess. "Maryanne, please make sure the wine-cellar staff is notified that our guests have arrived."

"Yes, sir," Maryanne responded.

"This way," Sebastian said with a sweeping gesture. "As you can tell, the main floor of the building is a restaurant for our human clientele."

"Yes." Maya's hand fluttered to the necklace hidden beneath her sweater, hunger swamping her along with the swarm of heartbeats. "It looks like you have a booming business."

"True." Sebastian winked at her over his shoulder. "But it's nothing compared to our facility downstairs."

Maya linked her hand with Shane's as they walked down the hallway behind their hosts, and she snuck a glimpse at him. His strong, masculine profile contrasted starkly with Diego and Sebastian's more metrosexual flair. Shane was all man and sexy from head to toe. Suddenly, the idea of feasting on a human seemed far less appealing to Maya, and all she could think about was feasting on Shane.

The wallpaper was black with a gold scrolled design, and the ornate crystal light fixtures hanging from the ceiling cast a glittering light over the hallway. The black carpet whispered beneath her sandals, and she ran one hand over the skirt of her sundress, wishing she'd worn something else. She looked past Sebastian and Diego and could easily see the lavish dining room ahead that was filled with human patrons and bustling with elegantly dressed waitstaff.

As they got closer, Maya's necklace began to hum against her chest and that tugging sensation filled her gut, making it glaringly clear there were more than just humans enjoying the ambience of Bayou Escape. She tightened her grip on Shane's hand and touched her mind to his. *There's a werewolf in there, Shane. My necklace is doing that buzzing thing.*

I know. His voice was tight and edged with tension, but looking at him, no one would suspect how he was feeling. *I picked up the scent, and it's getting stronger as we get closer to the dining room.*

"It seems your restaurant has become popular with all kinds of people, Sebastian." Shane's voice was light and his tone was casual, but Maya knew better. "But I suppose that's to be expected in a neutral zone like New Orleans."

"Yes." Sebastian nodded. He waved to a bearded man seated toward the front of the dining room but kept his voice down. "We get all kinds in here, and my business wouldn't have lasted this long without *tolerance*. I can assure you there will be no trouble in our establishment, Shane."

"Of course," Shane murmured. "I'd expect nothing less."

Maya inched closer to the shelter of Shane's body, and

though she tried not to look, she couldn't stop herself. She scanned the room and within seconds found herself locking gazes with the bearded man that Sebastian had gestured at. A slow smile cracked his face, and he raised his glass to Shane and Maya.

"Who is that?" Maya asked as they stopped by the dining-room entrance. Her necklace hummed beneath her sweater with more force as her hand drifted over it. "That man with the beard?"

"You have sharp instincts for a youngling," Sebastian murmured. "No wonder they're training you to be a sentry. That's Otto. He's one of our regulars, and before you ask, yes, he's a werewolf. He's a loner, and from what we hear, he doesn't have a pack, which is one of the reasons I don't mind having him as a guest."

"Besides," Diego added, "he's loaded, and it's fine by us if he wants to spend his money here on whatever human girl he's bedding at the moment."

"So, he's not connected with the werewolf royalty?" Shane asked evenly.

"Not that I'm aware of." Sebastian's brow furrowed and he looked at them curiously. "Why do you ask?"

"I may not be on duty at the moment," Shane said with a smile, "but I still represent the Presidium. You know that our relationship with the wolves is delicate, and I'm sure the czars would want me to pay my respects if a member of the royal family or their entourage was here."

"Of course," Diego murmured. "Fear not, old friend. Otto is of no importance, at least not as far as politics are concerned. He's merely a wealthy wolf with an insatiable appetite."

Maybe we should leave. Maya touched Shane's mind as she squeezed his hand in hers. *What if he knows who I am?*

I don't believe he's of any concern. Sebastian and Diego would know if Otto was connected to the royal family, and believe me, they'd tell us.

Maya tried to relax and take Shane's common-sense approach, but that memory of the wolf attack was still vivid. To Maya's great relief, Sebastian turned to the right and opened a black lacquered door which, to her surprise, led into an elevator. Diego tugged open a brass gate and stepped into the tiny elevator ahead of them. When they slipped inside, Sebastian closed the gate and remained in the hall.

"I must bid you farewell at this point, but Diego will take you the rest of the way." Sebastian grinned and quickly flashed his fangs. "Enjoy."

A chill ran up Maya's spine and relief flooded her when the door closed and Sebastian's grinning face vanished, along with the scent of the werewolf. As the vibrating of her necklace subsided, Shane wrapped his arm around her waist, once again sensing exactly what she needed. The hum of the elevator filled the space, and she watched the cement wall whisk by through the gate before the car finally came to an abrupt halt.

"Apologies for the bumpy landing," Diego said with a smile. "The elevator can be quite *temperamental*."

"That's okay." Maya laughed. "So can I."

"I like to think of you as spirited," Shane said, kissing the top of her head. "It's what will make you a great sentry."

"Are you enjoying the sentry training?" Diego asked, tugging open the gate. "I've heard it's quite strenuous."

"It's been…interesting." Maya lifted one shoulder and struggled with exactly how much she should reveal. "Shane is a wonderful teacher."

"A teacher is only as good as his student," Shane interjected with a sly look.

"Yes." Diego stepped out and held the door open for them. A moment later, sexy jazz music filled the air. "Well, Quesada may be a great sentry, but Sebastian and I have cornered the market on knowing how to service our customers. I do hope you'll enjoy your time here."

Maya was about to answer him but was rendered speechless when she saw what was waiting for them. With her hand linked firmly with Shane's, she looked around in awe as the elevator door shut tightly behind them and a whole new world was revealed.

Chapter 13

Below the Bayou Escape restaurant was a thriving vampire jazz club, complete with a staff of human familiars who were clearly there to serve the vamps as needed. The main club space looked to be about the same size as The Coven, but instead of a DJ, there was a jazz band along the far wall. The coolest part was that the walls were covered in video screens that depicted New Orleans on a bright sunny day.

The screens on the left depicted a massive steamboat drifting on the Mississippi River beneath a crystal clear, blue sky, while the screens on the right showed the hustle and bustle of the French Quarter. The crowning achievement was the ceiling. At least twelve feet high, it was painted to resemble a gorgeous blue sky dotted with a few drifting clouds. Even the sun was shown shining brightly, and the whole ceiling seamlessly connected with the screens on the walls.

If Maya didn't know better, she'd think she was standing outside on a beautiful summer day and not two stories underground.

At the center of the club was a series of tables that looked much like the outdoor café tables Maya saw at several eateries in the French Quarter. Instead of feasting on beignets and gumbo, the vamps were partaking of the humans, who were clearly enjoying it. It was the largest gathering of vampires she had ever seen in one place, and every one of them was out and proud.

"This is amazing," Maya whispered as Shane's arm slipped around her. She looked around in awe but didn't miss the look of pride on Diego's face. "I-It's absolutely incredible. Everyone is...well...they're not hiding."

"No." Diego clasped his hands behind his back and surveyed the bustling club as he spoke. "Sebastian and I opened this place because we wanted our kind to have somewhere they could relax and socialize without fear of discovery."

"The humans that work here," Maya said quietly. "They're familiars?"

"Of course." Diego swept his arms wide as they walked toward the wrought-iron railing, stopping short of the three steps that led into the main dining area. "All of my human employees are here because they want to be. No humans are allowed to be forced or glamoured into feedings at Bayou Escape. Diego and I live in apartments down here that are directly linked to the club, so the last thing we want are any bad vibes."

"There are so many of them." Maya nodded her understanding as a pretty, young human girl slipped by them and down the steps. She was dressed in a tiny red dress, but Maya noticed that the other humans weren't all adorned in the same outfits. Some of the human men were scantily clad but others wore business suits. "I've never seen anything like this."

"Thank you, Maya." Diego smiled, and his fangs flashed briefly. "We recently opened two other clubs here in the United States, one in Miami and the other in San Francisco. Both cities are neutral zones, as you know, and if Sebastian has anything to say about it, we'll be opening one in Geneva as well."

Maya tensed at the mention of Geneva because it brought the summit, the werewolves, and everything else back to the forefront of her mind. She grimaced and flicked her gaze to Shane who, based on the look of concern on his face, had noticed her sudden change in demeanor.

"How are things in New York?" Diego asked quietly. "Any word on the birth of this immortal child? The whole event is…strange."

"Oh really?" Maya tensed and her defenses went up at the way he spoke about Olivia and the baby. "What exactly are you trying to say?"

"Apologies." Diego's expression went from curious to concerned in a split second as he clasped his hands in front of himself and bowed his head. "Sometimes I forget myself. Olivia is your maker, is she not?"

"Yes." Maya wrestled with her urge to punch Diego in the mouth. "She is. Which means that her daughter will be a part of my family too."

"I meant no disrespect." Diego flicked his gaze to Shane briefly before looking at Maya again. "But you can't tell me that you're surprised by the community's reaction to this whole bloodmate revelation, can you? I mean, honestly, daywalking vampires and immortal children are not exactly a common occurrence. I'm sure that you can understand why some vampires might be nervous."

"I don't see why it's anybody else's business," Maya said all too sweetly. "Olivia and Doug having the ability to daywalk. That is about them—not us or anyone else."

She glanced briefly at Shane. "It's nobody's business but theirs."

"Of course, youngling. Diego was merely expressing a natural curiosity," Shane said evenly. His arm tightened around Maya's waist, and his fingers brushed her hip in gentle, reassuring strokes. "I'm sure that once Olivia and Doug introduce their child to our community, everyone's nerves will be calmed."

"Perhaps." Diego let out a sigh. "The truth is, unless there is some kind of outbreak of bloodmates, the only daywalking most vampires will ever be able to do is in one of our clubs. Be honest, this is as close to a sunny day as any of us will see. Am I right?"

"Your club is second to none," Shane said as he shot a glance in Maya's direction. "Isn't it, Maya?"

"It is the first all-vampire club I've been in, but I can't imagine one that would be any more perfect." Maya smiled sweetly at Diego and kept her tone even. As nice a host as Diego might be, she didn't like the tone he took when he spoke about Olivia and Doug being bloodmates, but she knew it was best to keep her feelings to herself. "Perhaps you should speak with the czars about opening a club in New York."

"Oh no." Diego made a face and shook his head. "We will only operate our clubs in neutral zones because they're really the only places where the clubs are needed. Our clubs provide a safe haven for vampires in cities where no single government is in power. Besides, Sebastian and I quite like being the go-to club for the vamp set. There's a certain exclusivity that we enjoy."

"Speaking of which, is our private dining room ready?" Shane asked.

"Of course." Diego clapped his hands and gestured for them to follow him. "What am I doing talking politics anyway? We have much more fun matters to address, like your special evening. Right this way."

They turned down a hallway to the left that was lined with a series of mahogany doors, each of them identified with brass numbers. They reached the door at the end of the hallway, marked number thirteen, and Diego promptly opened the door and ushered them into the room.

The space was about ten feet square and was entirely black, from the ceiling to the ebony tiled floor. Dim lighting emanated from glittering chandeliers in the ceiling, giving the space a seductive feel. Along the back wall of the room was an elegant table with a pristine white tablecloth and a lit candle flickering brightly at the center. Instead of chairs there was a curved, cushioned red bench encircling the table that could easily seat four or five people. "Are you alright, dear?" Diego asked Maya with a knowing glance at Shane. "You seem surprised."

"Well…" Maya stepped out of Shane's embrace and walked toward the center of the room, looking around with curiosity. "It's not exactly what I expected. I guess I thought it would look like daytime the way the main dining room does."

"Patience, my dear," Diego said with mild amusement. "Don't have private spaces like this at The Coven, do you?"

"Private rooms?" Maya arched one eyebrow and waved one hand. "No. Nothing like this. The only other room in the club, aside from the main dance floor, is Olivia's office."

"Well, this room is all yours for the evening." Diego winked at Maya and punched a button next to the door. An instant later, the curved walls and ceiling flickered to life, making her squint at the sudden brightness of the space. Maya let out a gasp when she found herself bathed in sunlight and surrounded by the banks of the Mississippi River.

"Oh my gosh," Maya whispered. Shane's fingers tightened over hers almost imperceptibly when she smiled at him. "This is beautiful. It looks like we're actually outside and sitting by the river."

"Then my goal has been achieved." Diego bowed gallantly. "Some of the familiars will arrive shortly so you can feed. I wasn't sure what your preferences are, so I'm sending in an assortment of choices. Other than that, you will be uninterrupted." He gave Shane a knowing smile. "If you'd like to remain undisturbed, simply flip the lock above the handle and a Do Not Disturb light will go on outside, alerting my staff to your…*desires*."

"Thank you, Diego." Shane crossed the room and shook hands with their host. "Your service is second to none."

The door clicked shut, leaving them alone in the beautiful space. Maya suddenly felt nervous because she was totally uncertain about what was going to happen. She'd never had a human brought to her willingly, and the idea made her oddly uncomfortable. She folded her arms over her chest and began to fiddle with her necklace through the sweater.

"So, the humans will just come in here and let me feed on them?" Maya asked in a far shakier voice than she expected. "That's kind of weird."

"Come here." A slow smile spread across Shane's face as he extended one hand and waved her closer. Maya's stomach fluttered as that sexy, smoldering gaze of his wandered over her body in such a way that she could swear she practically felt his hands on her. "I promise that tonight we will satisfy all of your appetites."

Maya closed the distance between them and placed her quivering fingers in the steady grip of his hand. His flesh encompassed hers, making any nervousness she felt drift away like smoke. Staring into his exquisitely handsome face, she knew, without a shadow of a doubt, that this man would never hurt her. He wouldn't strike her or force her into something she wasn't comfortable with.

Holding her stare, his lips whispered over her knuckles and everything fell into place.

She loved him. God help her. She was totally, completely, and irrevocably in love with Shane. The realization was both terrifying and exhilarating, but not as much as the idea that he might not feel the same way. Even though she wanted to tell him, to shout it to the world, she didn't. Instead she whispered, "I—I trust you."

"I would hope so," Shane murmured before standing to his full height and escorting her to the table. He kissed her hand, allowed her to sit on the bench and then slipped onto it next to her. Draping his arm behind her, he played with a long strand of her hair and pointed to the scene scrolling across the wall. "I chose the river scene because I thought it was the most lively. If I close my eyes, I can practically smell the water."

"It's gorgeous, Shane." Maya snuggled into his embrace and rested her head on his shoulder while they watched the steamboat drift lazily by on the river. "If I didn't know better, I'd say that I could actually feel the sun on my skin."

"Heat lamps." Shane pointed to the ceiling. "Clever, isn't it? Diego and Sebastian are making a fortune with these places because where else can a vampire feed openly? I brought you here, Maya, because I wanted to give you the opportunity to have a live feed. It's important to you, and you can do it here without breaking Olivia's no-hunting rule."

Oddly enough, Maya's hunger had taken a backseat to her other feelings. A knock at the door interrupted them, and Maya's stomach tightened with anticipation. She scooted even closer to Shane and rested her hand on his thigh, the muscles flickering beneath her touch. He gave her a sideways glance and shouted, "Come in."

A parade of ten humans, five men and five women, strolled into the room and lined up in front of Shane and Maya's table. Diego had told them he was sending in several choices, and he wasn't kidding. Not only were the humans of different races and varying ages, but they were also dressed in an assortment of styles. The man wearing the suit looked much like a human she would have selected in the past, yet choosing a man seemed wrong.

"Do any of them appeal to you?" Shane asked, his fingers trailing tiny circles over her shoulder. "See anything you *want*?"

"I usually fed on men," she said quietly. Shane's body tensed against her, and though he didn't say it, she knew he didn't want her feeding on a man. Maya smiled and squeezed his thigh beneath the table. "Perhaps it's time for a change."

"Perhaps," Shane murmured. Without taking his eyes off Maya, he said in a firm tone, "The men can leave."

Taking a deep breath, Maya turned her attention to the five women, all of whom were staring at Shane. The tall brunette dressed in a blue evening gown with a curvy, lush figure was licking her lower lip and practically screaming, *Fuck me*. Maya looked at Shane who, to her great delight, was looking at Maya, not the busty brunette.

"What's your name?" Maya asked the petite redhead. The girl, who looked about Maya's age, was dressed in a pair of shorts and a T-shirt.

"Rita," she replied quietly. She fiddled with the frayed edge of her cutoff jeans. "Rita Sue."

"I'd like Rita to stay," Maya said. She didn't miss the look of disappointment on the brunette's face. "The rest of you can go. Thank you."

"What about you?" the brunette asked Shane. Hands on her hips, she watched the other three women leave and then turned her attention back to Shane. "A big fella like you must be hungry."

A pang of jealously swamped Maya, and she wanted to fly over the table to rip the broad's long hair right off her head. She didn't want Shane feasting on another woman, human or vampire, any more than he wanted her near another man. Luckily, Shane spoke up before fangs started to fly.

"While I appreciate your offer, I will politely decline." Shane looked at Maya lovingly. "I have all I desire right here. You are dismissed."

The brunette flounced out of the room, giving Maya a withering look on the way out. Rita moved in silently and sat next to Maya. Giving her a shy smile, Rita shrugged and said, "Where would you prefer to feed?"

"I'm sorry?" Maya blinked with surprise and shifted her body so she could look the girl in the eye. With her back nestled against Shane's strong form, she found it difficult to concentrate, and feeding was no longer high on her list of priorities. "What do you mean?"

"Neck?" Rita pointed to her throat. "Wrist?" she asked before extending her arm onto the table, palm up. "Just tell me what you like."

"Oh." Maya tucked her hair behind her ear and sat up, feeling silly for not understanding what Rita was asking. "Wrist, I guess."

"Okay." Rita leaned back against the seat, getting comfortable, and held her arm out for Maya. "I'm ready whenever you are."

Her fangs bared, Maya took the woman's hand in hers. She ran her thumb over the pulse that beat strong and steady in the girl's wrist, but as tempting as the woman's blood was…Maya hesitated.

"What's wrong, youngling?" Shane asked quietly. He kissed her head and ran his fingertips along her arm. "I thought you wanted to have a live feed."

"I—I did." Her hands quivering, Maya released the girl's arm and folded her hands in her lap. "But…I'll get her blood memories." Maya looked at Rita and then turned her wide eyes to Shane's, allowing the weight of what that really meant to sink in. "And I don't want them."

"Did I do something wrong?" Rita asked in a shaking voice.

"No," Maya added quickly. She took Rita's hands in

hers and looked her square in the eyes. "I promise you didn't do anything wrong. It's me. We'll be sure to tell Diego and Sebastian how lovely you are."

"Agreed." Shane's brow furrowed with confusion. "Thank you, Rita. You are dismissed."

"O-okay." Rita slipped out of the booth and scurried out the door without looking back.

"You've had plenty of live feeds before, Maya." Shane followed Rita to the door and locked it behind her. Folding his arms over his chest, he studied Maya closely. "Why the sudden change of heart?"

"Ever since I was turned, I loved the hunt." Maya slid out of the booth and sat on the edge of the seat, watching the river scene as she spoke. "I fed on men that I knew were bad, and their blood memories always confirmed what I suspected. I saw the pain they inflicted on other people, and toying with them allowed me to feel some satisfaction in revenge. But now…everything's changed," she said quietly.

"Maya," Shane whispered. Closing the distance between them, he took her hands in his and pulled her to her feet, urging her to look at him. "Tell me, youngling. What has changed?"

"Me," she whispered. Tears filled her eyes as she looked up at him. "I don't want anyone else's pain or memories. Maybe getting blood memories from others helped fill that void that I had, but now that my own memories are coming back, I don't want anything to get in the way." She swiped at the tears with the back of her hand and laughed. "If Olivia could see me now, she'd be so proud. She always hated that I liked live feeds and would lecture me about the dangers. I didn't really understand why she felt that way until right this minute."

"Bottle feeds would not give you others' blood memories. Would you be satisfied with only bottle feeds from now on?" Shane asked with a hint of doubt. "Your appetite is sated?"

"Well," Maya purred, stepping closer to Shane so that their bodies brushed against one another, "maybe not *all* of my appetites."

A slow grin spread across Shane's face as Maya's hands found their way up to the buttons of his shirt and began to undo them one at a time.

"In fact, I doubt I'll ever get enough, at least as far as you and I are concerned, but I have one problem right now."

"What's that?" Shane asked on a growl. His body hummed with tension, and his hands settled over the curve of her hips. "Tell me."

Maya popped up on her toes and murmured against his lips, "You're wearing too many clothes."

With the scene of the river flickering around them, Maya ripped Shane's shirt open and exposed his broad chest as she captured his lips with hers. She sighed contentedly as their tongues tangled and grinned when his strong hands slipped beneath her skirt before skimming up her thighs. They divested each other of the rest of their clothing, and Maya tangled her fingers in his hair as he gathered her nude body against his.

Shane's mouth paid thorough attention to hers, and when his arms encircled her possessively, Maya knew she was no longer lost. With every touch, kiss, and caress, he discovered her and branded her as his. This must be what love feels like, Maya thought, with Shane trailing kisses down her throat.

But was it? Was this love she felt in his touch, or was it merely desire and lust?

Maya tangled her fingers in his smooth locks and stared up at the sunny sky.

The sky that wasn't really there.

"Is all of this a mirage?" she whispered in a quivering voice. Shane lifted his head and his dark, passion-filled gaze settled over her, his fingers drifting lightly over her sensitized flesh. Her body shook with anticipation and the genuine fear that perhaps what Shane felt for her was as false as the river scene that surrounded them. "Is any of this real, Shane?"

"It feels quite real to me." A wicked grin cracked his handsome face. Shane's hand slid over the damp flesh of her hip, and his other arm tightened around her waist, holding her tightly to him. He kissed the corner of her mouth. "This feels real."

"Yes." Maya gasped when Shane's hand drifted down and cupped the hot, swollen juncture between her legs.

"And this," he rasped. She gripped his shoulders and held his heavy-lidded stare as one finger slipped into her slick folds and stroked the tiny nub gently. "Tell me, Maya. Tell me what you feel."

Maya wanted to answer him, to scream how right it all felt. When another ripple of pleasure surged and stole her breath, talking was out of the question. Clinging to him, she held his gaze and cried out from the orgasm that started to coil deep inside.

"Not yet," he growled. Shane hoisted Maya up and placed her on the table. Kissing her deeply, his strong hands running up and down the length of her thighs, he spread her wide and tugged her hips against his. The thick, hot length of his cock pressed between them, and it would have been so easy to help him slip inside. Maya reached in between to satisfy the throbbing ache between her legs, but Shane linked his hands around her wrist, preventing her from going further.

"If you put me inside of you, this will be over far too quickly." Shane suckled her lower lip and brought her hands to his mouth. "First, I want to taste you."

He stood between her legs in all his gorgeous, naked glory. Maya shivered and wrapped her legs around his waist, pulling him closer. Heat pressed enticingly against heat, and all she could think about was having him inside her. The muscles in his chest flexed and he grinned before releasing her wrists. Shane ran his hands over her thighs, stepped back, and spread her legs wider before dragging her bottom to the edge of the table.

Maya reached behind herself and grabbed the edge of the table, staring up at the blue sky flickering across the ceiling. Her body was taut with desire and anticipation.

Shane leaned down, placed both hands on either side of her shivering body, and flicked one of her nipples with his tongue, sending a wicked lick of fire over her flesh. The tip of his erection brushed over her swollen entrance, teasing and tempting her. She arched her back and wrapped her legs around his waist, urging him closer still.

Not yet, youngling. His mind touched hers with an erotic whisper while he kissed and licked his way down her belly. Shane dropped to his knees and wrapped his strong arms around her thighs, opening her to him even further. He kissed the tender flesh of her inner thigh. *It seems you need more convincing, and I don't want to leave any doubt in your mind about how real this is.*

Maya was about to respond when Shane's talented tongue found her most sensitive spot and stroked. He licked and suckled her clit, sending wave after wave of carnal heat thundering through her body, making Maya scream. His arms clamped over her legs, holding her there while he continued his wickedly erotic assault. The tension of the orgasm crested brightly, and just when she thought she'd explode, Shane rose to his feet and buried himself deep inside her.

Maya's fangs erupted with the surge of primal need. Sitting up, she wrapped her arms around him as he pounded into her time and again. Tilting her head to gain access to her neck, Shane pierced her flesh, and while his hips pumped furiously, another toe-curling orgasm rippled through Maya. Locking her ankles behind his back, she held him to her, never wanting him to stop.

With his scent surrounding her, there was only one more thing Maya needed. Nuzzling his shoulder, she sank her fangs into his flesh, A deep guttural groan rumbled through him, and tightening his hold, he thrust even faster. Riding the final wave of pleasure, they could feel the now familiar beat of their hearts beginning to pound in unison, and Maya surrendered to it all. As their unified heartbeat thundered through their entwined bodies, she whispered into his mind, *I love you, Shane.*

Chapter 14

SHANE AND MAYA HAD USED EVERY PRECIOUS MINUTE of their two hours in the private room, and when they left, two bottles of warmed blood were waiting for them in the hallway. Sebastian and Diego had provided the perfect experience, which didn't surprise Shane. His friends had more than lived up to their reputation as the best hosts in the industry.

Flying through the dark Louisiana night with Maya at his side, Shane could barely contain the grin he'd had on his face since their tryst at Bayou Escape. Maya told him that she loved him. He didn't think just a few small words could sound so sweet, but they did, and he doubted that he'd ever forget the surge of joy that bloomed in his heart when she whispered them.

Making the approach to Lottie's house, Shane felt his smile fade when he saw the defeated look on Maya's face. Instead of looking happy and joyful like he expected, she seemed pensive and lost in her own thoughts. Shane reached out and tangled his hand with hers, which evoked a small smile but not a convincing one.

They landed side by side in Lottie's backyard, and Shane couldn't help but notice that Maya was looking everywhere but at him.

"The sun will be up soon," she whispered, looking out over the moonlit waters of the bayou. "We should go inside but be quiet so we don't wake up Lottie. I saw her car in the driveway."

Shane grabbed Maya's hand, preventing her from leaving, and waited for her to face him. Her back was to him and her shoulders shook as her blond hair fell over her face. Shane realized she was crying. Panic and pure fear shot through him. He flew around and stood in front of her before placing both hands on her arms and urging her to look at him.

"Maya?" Shane asked urgently. "What's wrong?"

"Nothing," she sniffed and stepped back, out of his embrace. She folded her arms over her breasts and walked toward the water. "It's nothing."

"You're crying. Am I supposed to believe that nothing is bothering you?" Shane stayed where he was and tried to keep frustration and anger out of his voice. "After all that we have been through and everything that we've shared? Why won't you tell me what's upset you so much?"

"I think I've told you plenty tonight, Shane," Maya said tightly. She looked over her shoulder at him and rolled her eyes when she saw the confused look on his face. "Right," she said through a curt laugh while swiping at the tears with the back of her hand. Spinning on her heels, Maya glared at him before stalking past him toward the house. "Just forget it."

"I will do no such thing." Shane moved quickly and stood in front of her, blocking her path. "Why are you acting this way?"

"You really don't get it, do you?" Maya placed her hands on her hips and looked at him as though he were the dumbest vampire on the planet. "You probably think it's stupid that I'm upset, and you know what? Maybe it is." Her voice rose and she poked him in the chest with one angry finger. "Maybe I'm a dumb, silly girl with a ridiculously modern notion, but if you ask me, when a woman says she loves you, Shane, you should have some kind of response. *Something*." Her blue eyes, rimmed with pain, stared up at him. "But you didn't. You just left me hanging out there."

Her chin tilted defiantly, and the words fell from her lips in a rush. "I know you were sent down here by Olivia to keep an eye on me and I know that we're bloodmates, but there is still a choice. You don't have to stay with me, Shane. If you don't love me, I don't want you to be with me out of duty or obligation. When we get back to New York, we can go our separate ways."

Shane blinked, and before he could stop himself, a laugh bubbled up, making his shoulders shake. He grabbed Maya's furious-looking face with both hands and tossed his head back as he laughed loudly before firmly kissing her lips. Her brow furrowed and the line between her eyes deepened while she continued to look at him as though he'd lost his mind.

"I'm the one who is stupid." Shane brushed a kiss on the corner of her mouth and rested his forehead against hers. Squeezing his eyes shut, he rasped his thumb over the silky, soft skin of her cheek and whispered, "You'll have to forgive a foolish old vampire for getting wrapped up in his own thoughts. I've been alone for so long, Maya." He lifted his head and looked her in the eyes, holding her close. "I suppose it will take some time for me to remember that I am no longer a solitary creature."

"What are you saying?" Maya looked at him through wide violet-blue eyes.

"I am saying that I am a fool—a fool who is desperately and hopelessly in love with you, and like a foolish man, I assumed that you knew. How could you not? I've loved you for so long, it seems, that I can no longer recall a time when the thought of you wasn't buried deep in my soul or when your voice wasn't drifting through my mind like a siren song, willing me closer at every turn."

Shane dipped his head, placed a gentle kiss on her lips, and reached out to her with his mind. *I love you, Maya.*

Maya smiled and kissed him back, wrapping her arms around his neck and holding him tight. Shane's joy was short-lived when her body tensed in his grasp and she started to shake. Her fingers curled along the back of his neck and she whispered, *Werewolves.*

An instant later, the pungent scent of a werewolf filled Shane's head. Growls rumbled in the air around them, and a pair of bright orange eyes glared at him from the brush just before a massive brown wolf charged across the lawn.

"Fly, Maya," Shane screamed. He flung her out of the path of the charging, snarling beast. "Get out of here."

Two wolves slammed into him, knocking him to the ground before he could react. Amid the struggle, he caught a glimpse of Maya. In a battle-ready stance and with her fangs bared, he watched her shoot into the air. She was safe. Maya was safe. That was all that mattered.

Jaws snapping and claws tearing, the two beasts forced him to his knees while their razor-sharp teeth tore into the flesh of his shoulder. Shane's fangs unsheathed and he hissed with rage while they continued their assault. Barely registering the pain, he ripped one wolf off his back before tossing it aside. It yelped and struck a tree, but Shane watched it scramble to its feet before stalking back toward him. The other tackled him to the ground before he could get to his feet, and an unfamiliar weakness plagued him. A burning sensation fired through his body, and though he'd never felt it before, Shane knew what it was the effects of the werewolf's saliva.

He was going to die.

Weakened by a substantial loss of blood and the poisonous bite, Shane held the snapping, drooling muzzle of the wolf just inches from his own face. His body burned, and he could feel the potent, poisonous werewolf saliva searing through his blood. With what little strength Shane had left, his other hand reached for the gun in his ankle holster. His fingertips grazed the butt of the gun right before the other wounded wolf came back from the treeline and latched its powerful jaws around his leg.

The beast's teeth scraped against bone, and Shane screamed with rage. A split second later, the wolf whined in pain when a sterling silver dagger whizzed through the air and lodged deeply in its neck. *You didn't really think I'd leave you here alone, did you?* Maya's teasing voice touched his mind as the wolf released Shane and stumbled away before crumpling in a heap.

He set eyes on his mate, her blond hair wild and flowing, and the deadly gleam of a warrior in her eyes. Shane held the wolf's muzzle with both hands with his waning strength and moved it away from him. A high-pitched sound pierced the air, and Maya's second sterling dagger hit the wolf with streamlined precision.

Weak and shaking from the significant loss of blood and the poisonous effects of the wolf's saliva, Shane fell back onto the grass as Maya ran toward him. She slipped her arm beneath his head and moved his bloody shirt to inspect his wounds. He didn't need to look at the injuries to know how grave they were because the horrified look on Maya's face said it all.

His body felt heavy and cumbersome, much like the feeling all vampires had when drifting into their deep sleep during the daylight hours. Maya wept and held his head in her lap. She pierced her wrist with the sharp points of her fangs and offered him her blood.

"Drink, Shane." Her voice was shaking. Still weeping, she held her wrist against his lips. "Please. You have to drink so you can heal."

He took what she offered, knowing it would not be enough. His hand clasped loosely over her wrist and pulled it away gently while staring into her frightened eyes. "There are some things, youngling," he bit out between clenched teeth, "that even our bodies cannot heal from."

"*No!*" Maya screamed. She glanced frantically at the dead werewolves who had shifted back to their human form. "What about their blood? That will help, won't it?"

"They must be alive for their blood to help neutralize the effects of the saliva," Shane said haltingly.

"Drink my blood, Shane. Right now," Maya yelled. She pushed his hand away and pressed her wrist to his mouth once again. "You will not leave me here alone, Shane. Do you—"

Maya's eyes widened briefly and her body tensed before pure, unadulterated rage etched into her features. In a blur she released Shane, rose to her feet, and spun around just as a third wolf leaped from the treeline. Weak and barely able to keep his eyes open, Shane turned his head and watched Maya deliver a roundhouse kick to the wolf's face. She reached back for her daggers, but remembered they were no longer there and flew toward the bodies of the fallen werewolves. The other wolf leaped onto her back, knocking her to the ground before she could reach the dead wolves.

Shane watched in helpless horror while the snarling beast loomed over her. Maya's gaze locked with Shane's. The beast reared its head back to deliver what was sure to be a fatal blow, and her face twisted into a mask of fury.

"*No!*" Maya screamed and placed both hands on the chest of the wolf.

Blinding light surged from the necklace, flickered up Maya's arms, and slammed into the wolf with a blast of power. The beast was tossed through the air and shifted back into its human form before landing in a heap by the base of a tree.

As the darkness threatened to swallow him, one thought ran through Shane's mind. His feelings for Maya had blinded him to the arrival of the wolves, and due to his carelessness, he almost got her killed. Maya sat up, shaking and stunned, and Shane watched her cautiously approached her attacker. Shane realized Maya survived only because *her* instincts had alerted them to the presence of the wolves. Before he passed out, Shane realized that if he survived, there was only one choice he could make.

His feelings were irrelevant. Shane knew he would have to let Maya go.

"He's still alive," Maya whispered. "But his scent is different. He doesn't smell like a werewolf...he smells *human*."

Scrambling to her feet, Maya moved toward the naked man with caution. Her body hummed from the bizarre surge of power that shot through her arms and made her toss the wolf away like he weighed nothing. Her skin tingled like she'd suffered some kind of electric shock, and when she got closer to the naked man, it became glaringly clear that two things were true.

The man was still alive, and he was no longer a werewolf. Maya looked from the man to her shaking hands before grasping the stone of her necklace.

"What in the devil is going on out here? Y'all are gonna wake the dead, but you woke me up first and that's bad enough." As Lottie emerged through the kitchen door, her voice cut through the night. Her hair was braided, and clad in her plain, white cotton robe, she padded barefoot across the lawn toward Maya. She lifted her lantern and surveyed the three naked men strewn on her back lawn. "Holy shit. You sure do live up to your reputation. They all dead?" Lottie leaned over Shane with the lantern. "Well, looks like Shane got his ass kicked sideways."

"The two that I got with the silver daggers are dead. That one," Maya said, pointing to the man by the tree, "is alive but he's...changed." Maya glanced at Lottie who knelt beside Shane and began to inspect the wound on his neck. "We need to try and use his blood to help heal Shane. Werewolf saliva is poisonous to vampires, and the only thing that might counteract it is blood from a living werewolf."

"Bring him over here." Lottie placed the lantern next to her and pulled Shane into her lap. She waved toward the other man but didn't take her eyes off Shane. "Go on. What are ya waitin' for?"

Maya tried not to think about how bad Shane looked while she ran over and grabbed the unconscious man by the arm. She dragged him across the grass and placed him next to Shane, but seconds later, the man's eyes fluttered open and he woke up. He let out a yelp when he saw Maya and tried to scramble away from her, but she was too quick for him. In a blink, Maya was kneeling on the ground in front of him, holding him in a sitting position by both of his arms.

"If you want to survive this," Maya seethed, "then you will do exactly what I tell you. Do you understand? I have plenty more silver weapons, and given your unwarranted attack, I'd be more than happy to decorate your pathetic carcass with them. Got me?"

He shook his head and continued to try to get away. Maya knew she couldn't glamour a werewolf, but this man no longer seemed to possess any hint of being one. The voice of doubt and fear fired through her when she realized his blood may not help. Do or die—it was their only hope. She had to try. Maya gripped his arms tighter, locked gazes, and pushed into his mind. To her surprise, it was like running a knife through butter.

"Give me your right arm," she murmured. The man nodded. His body relaxed and his jaw went slack while he extended his arm to her. "You won't move or fight, and this will not hurt. Do you understand?"

Maya took his arm and pierced the flesh with her fangs. Lottie held Shane's head in her lap, lifting it slightly so Maya could press the man's wrist to Shane's lips. While blood flowed into Shane's mouth, Lottie chanted something under her breath and rocked slowly. Maya threw a prayer to the universe, to whatever god or goddess might be listening, and begged for her lover's life to be spared. Shane remained motionless and her hopes began to fade. Just when she thought she'd scream with frustration, Shane's body twitched.

"It's working," she whispered.

Maya pushed the blood-soaked fabric of Shane's shirt aside, and tears of relief spilled down her cheeks when she watched the wound begin to close. Laughing, she swiped at the tears, allowing Shane to drink for a few more minutes. When the man's heart began to beat erratically, Maya knew they had to stop. It wasn't that she cared whether or not their assassin died—he had information they needed.

Pulling the man's arm from Shane's lips, Maya licked the wound on his wrist closed. Shane's body was healing, and though he hadn't woken up yet, she felt confident that within a few more hours he would fully recover. Lottie continued to chant and stroked Shane's head the way a mother would with a sick child.

The naked man's eyes fluttered and Maya thought he was going to pass out. So she smacked his face a bit and brought him back to reality. She wanted to kill him. To tear his throat out and eviscerate him for the way he and the others had attacked her and Shane, but she needed answers more than she needed revenge.

"Wh-what did you do to me?" The man whimpered through wide, frightened eyes. Trying to get out of her grasp, his hands clenched and unclenched. "I…can't shift. Th-the Vanator legend is true. Otto said all we had to do was get the necklace."

"What's your name?" Maya shook the man, hoping it would shake some sense into him.

"Greg," he said in a barely audible voice.

"Otto? He's the one who sent you here?"

"Yes." Greg, who didn't look to be more than twenty years old, nodded furiously.

"Is Otto working for the royal family? Are they the ones who sent you here, Greg?"

"I don't know. I swear. All I know is that he told us we had to wait for you here and get the necklace." His muscles tensed when he saw the bodies of his dead pack members. "You killed Mario and David…why?" His brow furrowed and his voice remained small. "You have the necklace. You could have taken their wolf, like you did with me. You didn't have to kill them."

"What are you saying?" Maya asked warily. She loosened her hold on his arms and stared at him through frightened eyes. "What do you mean, I could have taken their wolf?"

"You're Vanator," he whispered. Greg's eyes flicked to her necklace and then locked on to her face once again. His thin lips quivered with fear, and he barely got the words out. "You really did what they said you could do. You took my wolf."

"Took your wolf?" Maya repeated the words again, hoping they would make more sense, but they didn't. "I don't understand what you're talking about."

"You made me have to live as a human," he whispered.

"Well, there it is," Lottie murmured. Pursing her lips together, she looked Maya up and down. "I'll be a son of a bitch. No wonder the wolves want that necklace so damn bad."

Maya's body went numb and she sat back, releasing Greg from her grasp. She lifted her quivering hands and stared at them before looking back at Greg, who was inching farther away from her. He looked at her like she was a monster. Maya's gaze skittered over the two dead men on the lawn, and she started to feel like one.

With lightning-fast reflexes Maya grabbed Greg by the arms and stood up, dragging him to his feet. Shaking with absolute terror, he whimpered, "Please don't kill me."

Maya pushed into his mind, dropped her voice to a low tone, and glamoured him. "You're going to run," she whispered in a shaky voice. Maya turned to Shane, who looked almost as surprised as Lottie. "You'll have no memory of me or of what happened here tonight. You and your friends got drunk on tequila, and you woke up naked and alone."

"Naked and alone." Greg's eyes had a faraway look while he nodded his understanding. "Too much tequila."

"Forget me and this place." Maya leaned close and whispered, "Now run."

When she let go of his arms, Greg ran past her into the wild of the bayou with the stumbling gait of a drunk. As his naked ass disappeared into the darkness, Maya turned around to find Shane standing behind her.

She let out a cry of relief and wrapped her arms around him, burying her face in the crook of his neck.

Instead of returning her affection, he linked his arms around her wrist and pulled her off him.

"What's wrong?" Maya looked at him with confusion and immediately felt stupid for jumping all over a man who'd just been horribly wounded. "Oh my God! I'm so sorry, Shane. Did I hurt you? I probably shouldn't have jumped your bones like that, but I'm so relieved you're okay. I wasn't sure if Greg's blood would work but it did. Here, let me see how you're doing."

Her hands flew to his shirt and she attempted to look at his wounds. Shane pushed her hands away and shook his head. Recognizing the serious, flat look in his eyes, she felt a heavy sense of dread creep up her back and something inside her ached. Maya knew that look. It was the same cold, calculated, emotionless expression he used to have.

"No. I'm fine." Shane winced and took a step back. "It will heal completely once I've had an opportunity to sleep." His expression darkened. "Did I hear that correctly? Did you turn the boy into a human with the power from that necklace?"

"Yes." Maya nodded excitedly and grinned, but based on the look on Shane's face, he didn't share her excitement. "Why do you look so unhappy? I mean, I know it's kind of weird and everything but…"

"It's a death sentence for you, Maya." Shane stared at her through furious eyes. "Don't you understand? Are you such a child that you don't fathom what this will mean?"

"I am not a child." As she glared at Shane, anger flickered up her back. "I'll just go back to New York and give the stupid wolves the stupid fucking necklace, and then everyone will be happy."

"Somehow I doubt that," Shane murmured quietly.

"Oh please," Lottie scoffed. "Can you two zip it for five minutes? I've got two dead werewolves in my yard, and I'd like to get 'em cleaned up so I can go back to bed. I don't know what kind of crazy shit y'all do up there in New York City, but this ain't exactly my usual Saturday night."

Before Maya could ask Lottie just what she planned on doing, the old woman raised her palms to the sky and started chanting again. It was a language Maya had never heard before, and as her chanting grew louder, the ring on Lottie's hand glowed brightly. Shouting one final chant, Lottie leaned forward and swept her hands, palms down, above the bodies of the two dead werewolves.

The energy from Lottie's ring flickered and shot out in a circular burst of light and heat, which made Maya squint. When she finally opened her eyes and looked, the bodies were gone. A perfect circle of scorched grass covered almost the entire lawn, and all that was left of the two dead werewolves were the leather-handled daggers. Maya, Shane, and Lottie stood at the center of the burnt circle, and Maya let out a low whistle before picking up the daggers. Lottie wavered on her feet, clearly drained by using her magic. Shane caught her by the arm before she fell over.

"I thought your family magic was only about reading the future," Maya said with a raised eyebrow. "Looks like I'm not the only one who's full of surprises."

"Don't ya know by now?" Lottie said with a laugh and a wink to Maya. "Us gypsies are a secretive bunch, and we only share our magic on a need-to-know basis.

Speaking of which, you should take that advice to heart. I don't think anyone *needs* to know about your little gift."

"Well, I have to tell Olivia and Doug, and they're going to have to tell the Emperor, which means all the vamps will probably find out about it." Maya stilled, her gaze meeting Shane's while they walked toward the house. Shane seemed to be doing his best to avoid looking at her. "I'm sure they're going to want me to turn the necklace over to the wolves, and honestly, I'm fine with that. If they don't get it, then they'll never stop coming after me."

"Perhaps," Lottie murmured. "But like I said, I think the magic is more about the gypsy than the jewels."

Shane remained quiet, and nodding his agreement, he helped Lottie into the house. Once she was settled in her bed, the two of them made their way up to the third floor, and though there was still an hour until sunrise, Maya was more than ready to sleep. Shane moved slowly up the steps in front of her, and Maya sensed he was far weaker than he wanted her to know. She desired nothing more than to curl up beside him in bed and soothe his pain.

When they reached the landing of the attic, instead of going into the bedroom they'd shared when they arrived, Shane turned to the right and opened the other door. Maya stared at him in shock. He had no intention of staying in bed with her.

"You fought well tonight, Maya," Shane said tightly. He stood tall, his body tense and stiff, but the cold, detached look in his eye sent a chill down her spine. "If it weren't for your sharp instincts and your incredibly brave actions, I would be dead. You will make an excellent sentry, and I will be sure to inform the czars of my findings when we return to New York."

"Shane?" Maya took a step toward him but stopped when he moved away from her. "I don't want to be a sentry or some kind of werewolf hunter. I just want to be with you."

"Sometimes, youngling, what we want and what is best are contrary to one another," he said in a barely audible voice. The muscle of his jaw flickered and his mouth set in a tight line while he stared at her intently.

"But…you said you loved me."

"My feelings are irrelevant." Shane cocked his head and folded his hands in front of himself casually.

"What the fuck do you mean, your feelings are irrelevant?" The hallway started to spin and Maya thought for a moment she was going to pass out. "What are you saying?"

"I almost got you killed tonight, Maya." Shane looked at her with something that resembled shame. "I was so distracted by you, so totally and completely enamored with you, that I didn't detect the wolves. You could have been killed, and it would have been entirely my fault." His features hardened and his eyes narrowed, silence stretching out between them. "I'm sorry. I can't do this."

"Can't do what?" She folded her arms over her breasts and stared at him with utter disbelief, unwilling to accept what he was saying. "Tell me."

"Love you," he shouted. Maya stepped back because his words hit her almost as hard as a physical blow. "I can't let myself love you, Maya. I am a sentry, a soldier, and I did what I was sent here to do." His voice, edged with frustration, dropped to a whisper. "You are now more than capable of taking care of yourself and the members of your coven. You have your memories and are no longer wondering about your past or tormented by nightmares. You gained everything we hoped you would. Our mission has been accomplished, and my *feelings* are irrelevant."

"Mission?" Maya could not believe what she was hearing. The sweet, tender, loving man he'd been was gone, replaced by a cold, unfeeling soldier with nothing but duty on his mind. "You fucking coward. I don't need you to protect me, Shane. Wasn't that the reason you taught me to stand up to that bastard in my dream? Why you've been showing me how to fight? Did it ever occur to you that instead of fighting *for* me, you could fight with me? I don't need a protector, Shane. I need a partner."

"I will call the czars tomorrow and inform them of what we've uncovered," he continued, as though he hadn't heard a word she said. "If all has gone as planned, then we should be able to return to the city shortly, and with any luck, we can give that necklace to the wolves without any more bloodshed. However, for now, I must sleep and so should you."

He started to close the door, but Maya pushed her hand on the wooden surface, preventing him from shutting her out.

"I have one more question for you." Maya inched closer and lowered her voice seductively. "What about the fact that you and I are bloodmates?"

"I was mistaken to have allowed the mystique and allure of the bloodmate legend to distract me from my sentry duties." Shane stilled but kept his unwavering stare on hers. "Once we settle this business with the werewolves back in New York and give them the necklace, I will request that the czars transfer me to the Presidium's European facility. I think it would be safer for everyone if you and I go our separate ways. Good night, Maya."

The door closed, leaving Maya alone in the dark hallway with an aching void of loneliness filling her chest. Her hands flew to her mouth to muffle the sob that threatened to escape her lips. Stumbling into her bedroom, she shut the door tightly behind her. With her back pressed against the door, Maya hung her head and wept silently as the magnitude of losing Shane overwhelmed her.

She didn't know why Shane was acting this way, but she was sick and tired of her life being in the hands of fate. Sadness was soon replaced by fury. She may not be able to control Shane or her past, but she could damn well take control of her future.

One hand fluttered to the heavy necklace, and her fingers curled around the stone. Maya glanced at the rumpled, unmade bed. Had it been just yesterday that she'd lain in those soft covers with his strong, gorgeous body curled perfectly around hers? With the cool stone whispering between her fingers, she scanned the room and her gaze stopped at the open bag of weapons that sat on the dresser. The sentry uniform, the one she'd been training in all week, was draped over the chair, looking like a ghost of her past.

"Time to face the past and the future." Maya looked at the two daggers in her left hand. "No more running and no more hiding."

The sterling-silver throwing weapons glinted at her like a beacon calling her home, and Maya knew what she had to do. She had to prove to Shane, and to herself, that she could indeed take care of herself.

She stripped her sundress off and tossed it aside before making quick work of pulling on the sentry uniform. Zipping it up over her necklace, Maya did exactly what Shane had shown her. She tugged on the gloves and lined the leather coat with a slew of weaponry before putting on the belt, heavy with two semiautomatic guns and the liquid silver ammunition from Xavier. The final touch was slipping the daggers into the compartments on the back of her sentry suit.

Maya pulled her hair back into a tight ponytail and donned the weapon-laden coat. Glancing out the window, she saw that she had very little time until the sun would rise. It was just enough to get her where she needed to go.

Chapter 15

MAYA LANDED SILENTLY IN THE ALLEY NEXT TO Bayou Escape while an orange glow began to burn along the horizon. She rubbed absently at her chest. The dull ache throbbed, warning her of the impending sunrise. Peering around the corner of the building, she noted that the ache was weaker than it had been in the past.

A smile played at her lips. Perhaps that meant she and Shane would become daywalkers after all. Stepping out onto the sidewalk, she glanced at the brightening horizon, knowing that being able to walk in the sun would be meaningless without Shane by her side.

He was pushing her away because he was scared of losing her. For a moment, Maya allowed herself to entertain one other possibility.

Perhaps Shane really wasn't in love with her.

"That's bullshit," Maya growled with frustration.

She knew he loved her and that he was pushing her away because of some stupid macho notion. Maya decided that if she could fix this mess with the werewolves on her own, then she could show Shane, Olivia, and everyone else that she wasn't just some silly, flirty airhead. Maybe if she could make it right, then Shane would see her as an equal and perhaps the idea of being her bloodmate wouldn't seem so wrong.

Sebastian and Diego had been living in New Orleans for years, and she knew they would be able to direct her to the underground tunnels that led out of the city. She had to get a head start back to New York so she could deal with Horace herself. The last thing Maya wanted was for anyone else she loved to get hurt. Olivia and Doug would want to be involved, but they were parents now and that baby girl needed them.

The early morning streets of the Quarter were quiet, but she could still hear the subtle fluttering heartbeats of humans in the buildings nearby. Maya moved swiftly along the sidewalk, keeping her senses alert for any sign of wolves or other vampires, but so far she seemed to be alone. She trotted up the steps and grasped the doorknob to the club, letting out a sigh of relief when it turned easily in her hand.

Pushing the door open without a sound, Maya slipped inside and reached out with her senses. Eyes closed, she picked up the distinct vibration of movement toward the back of the club. Steeling her courage and with her hands clenched in tight fists at her sides, Maya strode down the long hallway toward the source. Before she could reach the end, Sebastian and Diego appeared in the hall so quickly that they seemed to have materialized out of thin air.

Fangs bared and eyes wild, they looked poised and ready to attack, but once they recognized Maya, they retracted their fangs and grinned. Sebastian stepped ahead of his brother and greeted Maya with a kiss on the cheek before leaning back and looking her up and down.

"That's quite a different ensemble from the delightful sundress you were wearing earlier, Ms. Maya," Sebastian cooed. "Speaking of sun, aren't you up past a good little vampire's bedtime? We were just about to retire ourselves."

"You are more than welcome to bunk in with us," Diego added before kissing Maya's hand gallantly.

"Thank you but I have some important business to attend to," Maya said, looking from one brother to the other. "I'm sorry to bother you at this hour but it really couldn't wait."

"Where's Quesada?" Sebastian asked, looking past Maya.

"Shane is recuperating and needs to sleep." Maya straightened her back. "I'll be heading up north ahead of him and handling this mission on my own."

"Recuperating?" Sebastian asked with concern. "What on earth from? He seemed fine when the two of you left earlier."

"Shane and I were attacked by a pack of werewolves tonight."

Maya kept her attention on the two vampires, curious to see what their reaction would be. To her relief, both seemed genuinely surprised and appalled. She worried that they might be involved, though given their friendship with Shane, it was unlikely.

"What?" Diego's fangs erupted and his voice was tight with anger. "When?"

"Right after we got back to Lottie's house." Maya fought to keep her voice even. "There were three of them and Shane was bitten, but we were able to use their blood to help him heal."

"Why on earth would you and Quesada be attacked by a pack of werewolves?" Sebastian folded his arms over his chest and looked Maya up and down. "And two sentries for the Presidium, no less. What would make them break the truce and risk all-out war?"

"Well," Diego scoffed, "I hope you had the decency to kill them."

"They're no longer a threat," Maya said with a tight smile. While she wanted to be truthful with her new friends, she'd be keeping information about the anti-werewolf whammy to herself. Besides, once she returned the necklace to the wolves, it would be a moot point and she'd be a regular vampire again. "They've been *neutralized*."

"Maya?" Sebastian narrowed his eyes and waggled a finger at her. "You are a crafty little girl and artfully avoided answering my question. Why did they come after you?"

"I have something they want."

"Honey, you have something a lot of men want." Diego waggled his blond brows at her playfully. "Like Shane, for example."

"Yes, well, I can't get into specifics." Maya's hand fluttered to her throat. "But I can tell you that Otto is the one who sent them after us."

"Otto?" Diego said furiously. "That furry fucker is involved in this? I should drain him dry. I'll tell you this much, at the very least he's never eating here again. I don't care how much money he has."

"Thank you." Maya's brow furrowed. "I'm still not sure how they figured out where we were staying, but that's really beside the point."

"Honey, this is New Orleans." Sebastian flashed his fangs and grinned. "There are eyes everywhere, but if you do figure out who spilled the beans, please let us know. If there's a traitor in our midst, they will be dealt with promptly."

"If you came here looking for Otto, I hate to disappoint you because he's long gone." Diego rolled his eyes. "He's probably at home sleeping off the booze."

"It's urgent that I speak with him." Maya nodded her head adamantly. "Otto is only a middleman, and I'm well aware of who he's working for. I need to speak with him so that he can pass along a message for me. Do you know how I can reach him?"

"Who is he working for?" Sebastian asked.

Maya stilled and looked back and forth between the two men. She wasn't sure how much to tell them and decided that the less information they had, the better off they'd be. She just hoped like hell they would accept no for an answer.

"I'm sorry but it's best if I don't share that with you. It's for your own safety," she added quickly. "Can you help me get in touch with Otto?"

"Can we *help* you?" Sebastian asked incredulously as he elbowed his brother. "That is our business, baby."

"My brother is correct." Diego slipped a cell phone out of his pocket and touched the screen a few times. "We keep our regular clients on speed dial, and up until today, Otto was a regular." His eyes narrowed when handed the phone to Maya. "But not anymore."

"Thank you," Maya whispered. She took the phone and pressed it to her ear. It rang five times, and for a second she thought it would go to voice mail, but on the sixth ring, a sleepy and irritated man answered the phone.

"What the fuck do you want?" Otto growled. "It's five thirty in the fucking morning and I'm still drunk."

"Well," Maya purred, "isn't that a charming way

to answer the phone? My, my, my, aren't you a cranky wolf."

Silence filled the line and Maya's confidence grew. She winked at Sebastian and Diego, a smile covering her face.

"Who the hell is this?" Otto barked. Maya could hear the sleepy voice of a woman in the background. "Shut up, Tiffany. Go back to sleep." He lowered his voice to a rough whisper. "Answer me. Who is this?"

"I'm sure you're surprised to hear from me," she sang, putting on her most playful, seductive voice. "And I can't say that I blame you, Otto. I guess your wolf boys weren't up to the task, and sadly, they will no longer be able to run your errands for you—or do anything else, for that matter."

"I—I don't know what you're talking about, lady," he sputtered nervously. "Wait a minute. I know this number."

"Yes, you do. Sebastian and Diego are rather upset by your behavior, so I think it's safe to say that you should find somewhere else to hang out," Maya hissed. Her fangs erupted as she fought to keep her anger under control. "I know we weren't formally introduced earlier but my name is Maya, and if I'm not mistaken, I have something that you want."

"I don't want it. It's not me," he sputtered. "It's that crazy little bastard Horace. Look, I didn't want to have any part of it, okay? He's blackmailing me, and unless I wanted my dirty laundry aired in public, I had to help him. He could destroy my entire business. Get it? He's the one you want, okay? He believes that stupid story about some gypsy necklace, and the little shit thinks it's going to give him absolute power. I think he wants to overthrow his old man. He's nuts."

"Yeah, I figured as much." Maya's eyebrows flew up with surprise to hear Otto throw Horace right under the proverbial bus. She didn't think he'd roll over that easily, but she was relieved to have her suspicions confirmed. At least she knew exactly who she was dealing with. "I want you to give your boss a message for me."

"He's not my boss," Otto hissed.

"Maybe not, but you're his bitch." Maya rolled her eyes. She turned her back on the brothers and walked away, keeping her voice low. "Tell Horace to meet me at midnight on the Gapstow Bridge in Central Park. I'll give him what he's after."

"Gapstow Bridge at midnight. Got it."

"And tell him to come alone," Maya added quickly.

Turning around, she ended the call and passed the phone back to Diego. She was relatively sure that Horace wouldn't show up alone, but then again, he wasn't expecting her to be armed to the fangs, either. As far as Horace was concerned, Maya was just a silly little girl who flirted too much, not a sentry-trained vampire with a werewolf whammy.

"Not bad." Sebastian nodded his approval. "You're a feisty little youngling, aren't you? No wonder Quesada chose you."

"He's trained a bunch of vampires," Maya said. Suddenly feeling self-conscious, she adjusted her ponytail. "I'm not special."

"I wasn't talking about being a sentry, and believe me, my dear girl, you are most definitely special." Sebastian winked. "We've known Shane for two hundred years, and through all of that time, I've never seen him with a woman. Oh, don't get me wrong, I knew where his bread was buttered but—"

"What my dear brother is trying to say," Diego interjected, "is that it's quite clear why Shane chose you as his woman."

"I'm not his woman." Maya straightened her back, and guilt tugged at her when she saw the look on their faces. "I'm sorry, I don't mean to be rude, but I've got more pressing matters to deal with. Can you direct me to the underground tunnels so that I can start heading back to New York? I'd like to cover some ground before sundown."

"Of course," Sebastian murmured. Linking his arm in hers, he guided her to the elevator. "But shouldn't you wait for Quesada? I realize that he may not be at his best at the moment, but if memory serves, you are still a trainee, are you not?"

"Trainee?" Diego laughed and waved off Sebastian's concerns. "The girl is packing enough silver in that coat to take down a stampede of vampires or werewolves. My nostrils are burning just from being near it." He winked at Maya. "See? That's why I could never be a sentry. I'd never get used to the constant stench of silver."

"Speaking of Shane," Maya said evenly as she cast a wide smile. "If he comes looking for me, please don't tell him that I was here." Sensing their apprehension, she added quickly, "Part of my final test to become a sentry is to handle a mission on my own. I'm sure you can understand how eager I am to reach the next level," Maya said, praying they'd believe her lie.

"Of course." Diego tilted his head in deference. "As you wish."

"Thank you." Maya smiled politely and stepped into

the elevator with Diego's comment lingering in the air. She hadn't realized it until he mentioned it, but Maya barely even smelled the silver anymore.

Diego slammed the gate shut, and the gentle hum of the machine surrounded them. Maya kept her attention straight ahead, not wanting to give any hint that she shouldn't be doing what she was doing. It was probably a foolish move to confront Horace on her own, but she had no intention of putting the people she cared about in harm's way.

"I'm finished with training," Maya murmured when the elevator came to a halt. "It's game time."

Shane awoke abruptly from the deep, healing slumber and instantly noticed the glaring absence of Maya's soft, curvy body. He had slept alone for four hundred years—until he'd found Maya—and that was exactly the way he liked it. Solitary. Focused. However, being with her had turned everything upside down, and not having her with him felt *wrong*. He resented the hell out of it. He missed the scent of Ivory soap, the weight of her body against him, and the silky feel of her hair as it drifted over his shoulder.

Shane cursed under his breath, swung his feet over the side of the bed, and ran his fingers through his hair. Growling with frustration, he rested his elbows on his knees and put his head in his hands. This entire situation was his damn fault. If he hadn't gotten close and allowed himself to feel something for her, then he wouldn't be feeling so shitty now.

And he wouldn't have hurt Maya.

He had hurt her. He knew he had, and that wounded look on her face would likely haunt him for the rest of his days. He shoved the guilt aside and kept reminding himself that it was for the best. How could he be with Maya when he was so obviously incapable of thinking clearly whenever he was near her?

Shane's love for Maya blinded him, and that made him a liability. With all the changes that were happening in New York, with the arrival of Olivia and Doug's child, the Presidium didn't need an ineffective sentry in their midst. Neither did Maya. How could he protect her when she made him mad with worry?

After his egregious error with the wolves, Shane realized that loving Maya would mean letting her go. In the long run, she would be better off without him.

Rising to his feet, he stretched and moved his body, grateful to find all of his wounds had completely healed, although the werewolf bites left scars on both his leg and his shoulder. He caught a glimpse of himself in the mirror and made a face of disgust. His clothes were bloody and torn, and he looked downright haggard. Shane pulled the bloodstained shirt off and tossed it aside before inspecting the scar that ran along his neck and shoulder. The scars would fade and eventually be barely noticeable, but at the moment they were still red.

Shane strode out of the room and crossed the hall to the door of Maya's bedroom. He paused for moment before knocking and reached out with his senses to see if she was sleeping. Maya's distinctive energy pattern was nowhere to be found. Frowning, he opened the door and was met with an unexpected sight. The drape had been pulled down and the window was wide open. Maya's sentry uniform was gone, along with several throwing weapons, two guns, and most of the ammunition.

A feeling of dread crept up Shane's back as he ran downstairs calling her name. He burst through the front door and shouted for her but was answered only by the bullfrogs in the bayou. Flying up to the roof, he scanned the entire property, but Maya was nowhere to be seen, heard, or felt.

Shane reached out to Maya with his mind, desperately needing to feel the intimate telepathic connection that only they shared. *Maya? Maya, where are you? Answer me*. Warmth flooded his body when their minds linked, but the connection was stopped swiftly and he knew she'd severed all communication. A deep, aching void filled him from the lack of her presence. Panic. Fear. Anger. All of it flooded him viciously when he realized that she really was gone.

"She ain't here." Lottie's voice drifted up from the kitchen window. "Get off my roof before you fall through it."

Shane jumped from the roof and landed silently in the backyard before running up the back steps into the kitchen. Lottie, who was dressed in her fortune-teller getup for work, looked at Shane with something resembling pity.

"Like I said." Lottie sighed. "Maya ain't here."

"Where did she go?" Shane's fists clenched and unclenched at his sides while an overwhelming sense of inadequacy filled him. "Please," he said, softening his tone. "Do you know where she's gone?"

"Beats the hell outta me. Don't know why you're so surprised that she took off." Lottie grabbed her big leather bag and draped it over her chest. "I may be old, but I ain't deaf, and conversations carry through this empty old house. I heard what you told that poor girl. Why didn't you just rip her heart out and stomp on it? That probably would've hurt less."

"I did what had to be done." Shane's mouth set in a tight line and he folded his arms over his chest, suddenly feeling defensive.

"Don't gimme that shit. You're scared." Lottie wagged a finger at him. "You are a big, fat fraidy cat. You love that girl. I know you do. So why the hell are you doing your damnedest to lose her?"

"It's better for everyone this way."

"Bullshit," Lottie shot back. "Better for who? You? I don't think so, because you look like warmed-over alligator bait. You obviously love that girl, so I don't know why you are pushing her away. The only reason I can come up with is good old-fashioned cowardice."

"It's complicated," Shane said tightly.

"I don't really think it is. When she showed up here with you that first day, she was a different person. Scared and unsure of herself, and in so many ways, Maya was lost. Now…well…she found herself, and I think much of that is thanks to you."

"Maya will be fine." Shane knew how hollow the words sounded, but he hoped if he kept telling himself that, it would eventually be true. "Her life will be better off without me in it."

"Well, I guess she would be fine." Lottie nodded her head and pursed her lips together and looked him up and down. "She's tough and resilient. Yes, sir, that girl finally got her past figured out, and until you threw that curveball at her, she thought her future was straightened out too."

"Maya's future will be as it should." Shane straightened his back and kept his gaze on Lottie. "She can go back to her life at The Coven."

"No, she can't," Lottie whispered. "No more than you can go back to living a solitary existence—and don't give me that shit about it's better for her. You're scared and loving her makes you feel out of control. You did this for *you*—not her." Shane flinched at Lottie's unsettlingly perceptive observations. "That girl needs you, Shane, and you need her. She might have gypsy blood, but she's not meant for the solitary, isolated life of a gypsy like I am. Maya's got a fire in her belly about something, and based on the way she flew out of here last night, I'd say it's burning her up."

"Last night?" Shane's chest tightened. "She left before sunrise?"

"Yes, sir." Removing her car keys from the bag she shrugged. "Not surprised you didn't notice. You were pretty banged up from those nasty wolf bites. Anyway, yes. She flew right past my window not long before sunup. Why are you so freaked out? Can't you do that blood tracking thing to find her?"

"No." Shane ran his hand over his jaw, wracking his brain trying to figure out where the hell Maya would have gone. "Her gypsy power hid her memories, and unfortunately, it also seems to shield her location."

"If I had to make a bet, I'd say that stubborn girl is off to prove a point."

Wrapped up in his own thoughts, Shane didn't even notice that Lottie had left the house. He ran up to their room and put on his sentry uniform, making quick work of arming himself with what Maya had left behind. Launching himself into the night, one thought ran through his mind.

Where the hell did she go?

Given that there had been little darkness left when Maya flew off, he suspected she went either to Bayou Escape or The Den. She was unfamiliar with the entrances to the underground tunnels in this area, so she'd have to take refuge from the sun somewhere familiar. He checked with Lillian and Boris, but they hadn't seen or heard from Maya, which meant she must have gone to see Sebastian and Diego.

Fury and frustration filled every fiber of Shane's body, and he strode right past the hostess at Bayou Escape. He scanned the restaurant for the two men, but they weren't there. Ignoring the hostess's pleas to stop, Shane took the elevator down to the vampire club. His fangs hummed and erupted when he detected a faint but familiar scent. "Maya," he whispered.

The smooth, seductive jazz music drifted over Shane, and memories of his time here with Maya came roaring to the forefront, which only served to heighten his level of agitation. The club was packed with vampires, but tonight everyone was dressed like they'd come straight from the Roaring Twenties. The men wore old-fashioned tuxedos, and the women were clad in flapper dresses. Sitting in the middle of it all like two proud peacocks were Sebastian and Diego.

Dressed in white ties and tails, the brothers waved him over to their table. Sipping out of crystal flutes, they snapped their fingers, which brought two scantily clad human women over to the table. Both of the women approached Shane and look disappointed when he waved them off, refusing their advances.

"That sentry uniform is not exactly in line with our theme this evening," Diego said, watching the girls flounce away. "It's our annual Prohibition Party, and you aren't dressed for it."

"I'm not here for the party." Shane leveled a stern glare at the two men and didn't miss the curious stares from some of the clubgoers. "And you know it."

"Why so grumpy?" Sebastian asked, placing his crystal flute on the table. He rolled the delicate stem between his fingers, glancing from Shane to Diego. "Lose something?"

"Cut the crap, Sebastian," Shane growled. "I know Maya was here, so don't even try to deny it. Where is she?"

"Sorry." Diego sighed and rose to his feet. "She asked us not to tell you, and as you know, we have a reputation for providing discreet service to our customers. We won't start breaking that rule, not even for you."

In the blink of an eye, Shane placed both hands on the table in front of the two vampires, getting right in their faces. The club was bustling around them. Shane had no desire to make a scene, and drawing attention to himself was unwise. Wrestling for control over his temper, he kept his voice low.

"Discreet?" He leaned closer, his fangs in plain sight. "Perhaps you should have been more discreet around Otto. Would either of you happen to know how he found out where Maya and I were staying so he could send his pack of assassins after us?"

"We didn't have anything to do with that," Sebastian said. "We'll never allow him in here again. I swear it."

Sebastian and Diego shook their heads as they looked at Shane through wide, fearful eyes. Someone to the left moved, but Shane flicked his head in that direction and hissed a warning at one of the waiters who stopped and thought better about interrupting.

"Now, let's try this again." Shane stood tall and folded his hands in front of himself, keeping his voice even. "When did Maya leave and where did she go?"

"She said she had to do this task on her own to complete her sentry training," Diego sputtered. "She was adamant that we not tell you anything."

"Well I'm adamant that you do," Shane ground out. "Where. Is. Maya."

"We can't tell you," Diego pleaded.

"Oh, I think you better." Shane lowered his voice further and flashed his fangs. "Because if anything happens to Maya, I will hold both of you personally responsible."

"She came here looking for Otto," Sebastian babbled, and Diego's face fell as his brother told Shane everything. "Maya called him. She said that she had what Otto wanted and that she knew who he was working for. She told him to have his boss meet her at some bridge in Central Park at midnight. Then we let her into the underground tunnels so she could start going back to the city before dark."

"A-and she told him to come alone," Diego added. "That's it, Shane. We swear. And I'll never let another filthy werewolf in one of our places again."

Fear flickered up Shane's back as he realized what Maya was planning to do. She was going to meet Horace and his pack, all by herself. A knot of dread formed in his gut, and without another word, he left.

All he could think about was getting to Maya.

Riding up in the elevator, he reminded himself to be reasonable and focus on the facts. Maya was heavily armed, a naturally strong fighter, and she wore the necklace that could turn a wolf mortal. On the flip side, she'd also been flying all night and hadn't slept, which meant she'd be in a weakened state. The only reason Shane wasn't freaking out completely was because he knew Maya wasn't as fast as he was. She'd take far longer to get back to New York, especially using the lengthy and circuitous network of tunnels.

Shane had age and experience on his side, and it was nighttime. Flying at night was always faster, but he was going to need an extra edge. Stepping out onto the street, he surveyed the humans in the area and spotted a young man walking alone. That was exactly what he needed. Live feeds provided more energy than bottle feeds, and Shane needed all the help he could get.

He made eye contact with the drunkard, glamoured him, and quickly pulled him into a dark alley. Shane fed, and energy surged through his body like a jolt of lightning. Sensing he was at risk of taking too much, Shane released the man. He was a sailor on leave and intent on finding a hooker. Shane licked the wound closed and sent the sailor on his way with a fabricated memory of being pleasured by a bevy of beauties.

Shane's body hummed with the rejuvenating pulse of a live feed, and it took him a moment to realize that the cell phone in his pocket was vibrating. He yanked the phone from his coat and swore when he saw Olivia's phone number scrolled across the screen.

"Yes?" Shane answered curtly, before shooting into the sky.

"You can come home," Olivia said. "Although you can leave that shitty attitude in New Orleans. I have a baby now, and I'm really not in the mood to placate a cranky four-hundred-year-old vampire."

"Apologies." Shane pressed his fingers against his eyes and struggled for patience. "I am on my way back and should be there in a few hours. There have been some new *developments*."

"Really?" Olivia let out an ironic laugh. "Well, we've had some of our own. King Heinrich and his oldest son, Killian, arrived in the city last night. When I met with them, I tried to apologize about what happened with Horace, but the king waved it off and said he's the one who should be apologizing for his kid. I guess Horace is the black sheep of the werewolves."

"Has King Heinrich taken control over his son?" Shane stilled, praying that by some miracle Horace was out of the picture. "Is Horace with his father now?"

"Nope. Horace and his pack are MIA. The king went to see his son last night and they had some kind of blow-out. Killian tried to speak with his kid brother again this morning, but Horace had checked out of the hotel. As of right now, he's fallen off the grid. We checked out Rat's club, but so far, we can't find 'em."

"I'm betting that slippery son of a bitch Rat knows exactly where Horace is."

"Maybe." Olivia sighed. "He swears up and down he doesn't. Horace isn't just avoiding us. It looks like he's avoiding his family too. I suggested that maybe he left the city, but his brother seems adamant that the guy is still here. I think Killian knows something that he's not sharing with the rest of the class."

Shane tensed and processed what Olivia was saying. It seemed unlikely that the king was involved, but could Killian be in league with his brother to overthrow their father? Shane knew that whatever choice he made now, the information he shared with the czar would directly impact the delicate relationship between the two races.

Even though telling Olivia about the power of Maya's necklace could create more problems and maybe even anger the king, it didn't matter. All that mattered was that the woman he loved was going to meet a pack of wolves alone. Vampire and werewolf relations could explode in a fiery blaze for all he cared. Maya's safety was his only concern.

"Shane?" Olivia asked. "Hello? Did you hear me? How's Maya doing? Is she there?"

"No," Shane responded solemnly while he sliced through the air like an arrow. "She's on her way to meet Horace."

Chapter 16

MAYA RAN THROUGH THE DANK, DIRTY SEWER TUNnels during the daylight hours and then took to the sky when the sun set. Watching the sliver of orange sink into the horizon, Maya could practically hear it when it was swallowed up by the darkness. Whipping through the crisp night as fast as she could, she hadn't been in the air for more than a few minutes when Shane's panicked voice touched her mind.

Maya! Where are you? Answer me, Maya!

Guilt filled her as she ignored his pleas, and she slammed her mind shut, preventing any further communication. Even though Maya hated shutting him out, she knew that it was for the best. She was the one with the werewolf whammy necklace, and that meant that it was her problem to deal with. Besides that, she was still pissed at him for pushing her away.

She was exhausted, and since she hadn't slept, the trip was taking her far longer than it had when she was with Shane. After what felt like forever, the iconic New York City skyline came into sight. Maya's belly clenched as her nerves began to get the best of her. Glancing at her watch, she saw that she had a few hours until it was time to meet Horace.

Her gut instinct was to seek comfort from her coven—her family—but if she did that, then she'd probably have to tell them what she was doing, and one of two things would happen. They would either try to stop her or insist on coming with her, and neither choice was viable. She had to do this on her own.

So, with nowhere else to go, Maya went to the one place where she loved to sit quietly and collect her thoughts.

Landing in the torch of the Statue of Liberty, she sat down on the ledge, grateful for a few hours of quiet before the storm. She closed her eyes and used the time to go over and over the different fight moves Shane had taught her. But no matter how hard she tried, she couldn't focus because the sound of Shane's wounded, worried voice continued to haunt her.

Maya's eyes fluttered open. Smiling, she stared out over the beautiful sparkling lights of Manhattan. It really was a beautiful city. But even the glittering skyline couldn't stop her thoughts from drifting back to Shane and the girls in her coven. No matter how many times she went over it, she always returned to the same conclusion. Going back to The Coven would mean dragging her family into this mess.

The smell of the water filled her head, and the mournful wail of a boat's horn blared, shattered the quiet. Maya wasn't blind or stupid. She knew that she'd caused her fair share of trouble since she arrived on the scene, and she didn't want tonight to be yet another example of her causing problems for the coven.

"You are totally fuckin' predictable," laughed a familiar feminine voice.

Maya swore loudly and shot into the air, before flipping over and landing on her feet in a battle-ready stance. Her fists were raised and her eyes wild, but her body relaxed when she saw she wasn't facing enemies.

"Trixie?" Maya said in a wavering tone of disbelief. Her fangs retracted and she lowered her fists, gaping from Trixie to Sadie. Both of them were dressed in black from head to toe, and Trixie had dyed her hair almost ebony. Gone were the spiked pink locks. Sadie's hair was tied back tightly, and the two women looked ready for a fight. "Sadie? What are you two doing here?"

Before Maya could say another word, her sisters flew over and gathered her up in a massive hug. Maya clung to them and kissed their cheeks repeatedly, laughing through her tears. After a long hug, the three of them looked at each other and laughed while wiping at their wet cheeks.

"How did you know I was here?" Maya asked.

"Are you kidding?" Trixie asked incredulously. "You always come up here when you need some space or when you're sulking because you're pissed at me." Trixie winked and cracked her skull-ring-studded knuckles. "You're not as slick as you think you are."

"No." Maya shook her head and looked from one sister to the other with obvious confusion. "I mean, how did you know I was back in New York?"

"Shane," Sadie said evenly. She hopped on the ledge, folded her hands in her lap, and leveled a serious look at May. "You must really be crazy to think that any of us would let you face those wolves on your own. We're your family, Maya, and family sticks together."

"He told Olivia everything?" Maya asked with dread.

"Yup. Your man spilled the beans to Olivia, and then she sent us out to look for you." Trixie rolled her eyes when she saw the annoyed expression on Maya's face. "Oh, don't start, okay? The guy obviously loves you."

"I thought he did," Maya whispered.

"Well, he does. He's flying up here like a bat out of hell, but don't be surprised if he bites your damn head off once he gets here. When Olivia was on the phone with him, I could hear him flipping out from all the way across the room. The boy is pissed."

"This isn't his problem. He was supposed to get me out of town until the situation with the wolves was smoothed over and train me to fight. He did both, so his job is done."

"You're not going to meet Horace and his cronies all by yourself, so just forget it." Trixie shook her head adamantly. "I don't care how badass you think you are now."

"You don't understand," Maya said, stepping closer to her sisters. Her hand drifted to the necklace hidden beneath her sentry uniform. "If I don't give him this necklace, then they'll never stop. The wolves won't stop until they get it. This whole stupid mess started because of me, and I don't want anyone else to get hurt." Her voice quivered, but she bit back the tears. "They killed my parents when they were trying to get this damned thing, and I won't let them hurt anyone else that I love. Contrary to what everyone thinks of me, I'm not a selfish, stupid little girl. I don't need babysitters or bodyguards. I can take care of myself."

"We know that, Maya," Sadie said in her signature calm, soothing tone. "You can do all of those things, and if you absolutely had to, you could take care of yourself. That's not why we're here."

"I don't understand," Maya said quietly.

"The point is that you don't have to do this by yourself.

We're your family, Maya, and we love you, no matter what…and it's okay." She and Trixie exchanged a knowing look. "We heard about what happened in New Orleans—what you did to that werewolf, or what your necklace did."

"That's pretty freakin' cool." Trixie jutted her chin at Maya and gave her a look of approval. "I never heard of a gypsy-vampire before, but for some reason, I'm not surprised that it's you."

"Why?" Maya asked hesitantly.

"Why? Because you're special, Maya. You always were. From the minute Olivia brought you into the coven, it was obvious that you weren't like the rest of us, y'know? I mean your turn did take five freakin' days." Trixie punched her playfully on the shoulder. "I guess we can't call you Baby Vamp anymore."

"Baby! Oh my gosh," Maya exclaimed. "How's Olivia doing—and the baby?"

"Great," Sadie said with a smile. "Xavier has appointed himself temporary nanny during the meeting. Emily is beautiful, Maya. Wait until you see her. She's got Doug's eyes, Olivia's red hair. She's a beauty. You should have seen Doug waiting out in the hallway during the birth. The dude freaked the fuck out."

"Really?" Maya asked, sadness tugging at her. "I guess I missed a lot while I was away."

"Nah," Trixie said, waving it off. "You have plenty of time to catch up. One thing's for sure, though, Olivia and Doug have no shortage of babysitters. We've all been fightin' over Emily since she was born." Trixie saw Maya's expression and quickly changed the subject. "Come on. Everyone's waiting for us back at the

Presidium, even the freaking werewolf king and his son. It's like a really awkward class reunion or something."

"Horace?" Maya balked and stopped dead in her tracks.

"No, dopey." Trixie rolled her eyes. "His oldest kid, Prince Killian. By the way, I'm not into werewolves, but holy crap is he a hottie. Totally gorgeous and built like a tank. I bet he's got one down to his—"

"Oh please." Sadie rolled her eyes and cut off Trixie's rant. "He's an arrogant, gruff caveman who probably chases his tail whenever there's a full moon."

"See?" Trixie winked. "Even Sadie likes him."

In spite of the situation that loomed in front of them, Maya couldn't stop the chuckle that bubbled up. Shaking with laughter, she gathered her sisters in another warm, lingering hug before they shot into the sky and headed to the Presidium. With her sisters by her side, Maya knew she could handle anything…even letting Shane go.

The three women landed silently in the gardens of The Cloisters and were immediately greeted by the club's bouncer, Damien. Dressed all in black, he emerged from the shadows behind an archway of stone. He flashed Maya a fang-filled smile before slinging his rifle over his shoulder and sweeping her up in one of his signature bear hugs.

"Hey, little sister." His deep baritone rumbled around her like a comforting blanket as he placed her back on her feet. "Good to have you home."

"Thanks, Damien." Maya smiled and squeezed his hand. "It's good to be back, but if you're here, then who's bouncing at the club?"

"Olivia closed the place for a few days. She figured

that it would be best to keep all of us focused on the current situation with the wolves."

"Right." Maya nodded her understanding, though she couldn't help feeling guilty. Olivia hated closing the club. Yet another item Maya could add to the list of things that were her fault.

"Everyone is waiting for you down in Olivia's office, and the museum's human guard is in a glamour sleep, so you don't have to worry about dodging him tonight."

"Everyone?" Maya asked hopefully. She wanted to see Shane. In spite of how angry she was, Maya loved him desperately. "Is Shane here yet?"

"He got here a few minutes ago." Damien glanced briefly at Trixie and Sadie. "He grunted something that resembled a hello and went right downstairs. He's pissed."

"Yeah?" Maya's jaw set determinedly. "Well, he can join the club."

Without waiting for a response, Maya walked past Damien and pushed open the heavy, wooden door. The heels of her boots echoed through the halls of the cavernous museum and seemed even louder when she walked into the Tapestry Room. Willing her nerves to settle and with Sadie and Trixie right behind her, Maya stepped up to the massive fireplace. Standing in front of the six-foot opening, she pulled the thick iron spoke and the back wall of the hearth swung open.

The three women strode swiftly through the maze of secret corridors until they finally came to the newly renovated Presidium offices that were occupied by the czars. When Maya and her sisters reached the enormous stainless-steel doors of the office entrances, Sadie pushed past Maya and pressed her thumb to the black panel. Moments later, the lush offices of the Presidium were revealed.

The circular space was carpeted in warm tones of beige and burgundy, and the walls were lined with beautiful pieces of artwork Olivia had acquired over the years. To the left was Suzie's reception desk, and to the right were comfortable couches and coffee tables with ceramic lamps that gave off soft, welcoming lighting. It looked like the lobby of any successful corporate office in Manhattan, and Maya couldn't help but smile.

Olivia and Doug had brought the Presidium into the twenty-first century.

Suzie was dressed in a simple gray suit with her pale blond hair tied back in a tight bun. She shrieked with delight when she saw Maya and flew out from behind her desk. Before Maya could utter a sound, Suzie had wrapped her up in a hug that vaguely resembled a choke hold.

"Wow," Maya said quietly as Suzie reluctantly released her. "I guess you missed me, huh?"

"Of course I did." Suzie sniffled and wiped her eyes with the back of her hand. "I'm just so glad that you're okay. Olivia told us about what happened and I kind of saw some of this coming, but I didn't want to say anything because I can't always decipher the visions. Sometimes it's just a bunch of upside-down nonsense."

"You saw the thing with the necklace?" Maya asked warily. Ever since Suzie was turned, she had gotten visions of the future, but she rarely spoke about them. "You saw what I did to that man?"

"Not exactly." Suzie lifted one shoulder. Looking

away from Maya, she scurried back to her desk. "But now what I saw makes sense."

Maya wanted to pepper her sister with questions, but before she could, the double doors on the other side of the room swung open and everything inside her stilled when she found herself staring at Shane. His dark eyes glared at her from beneath inky brows, but it was the harsh look carved into his features that set her on edge.

"Everyone is waiting," he bit out. Shane turned on his heels and went back inside, leaving the doors open behind him.

"I see that getting laid didn't do much to improve his mood," Trixie quipped.

Maya shot her sister a look, and the three women followed Shane into the conference room. At the center of the room was a long mahogany conference table, complete with a phone and audiovisual setup, and lined with several black leather chairs—four of which were occupied.

The necklace hummed against Maya's chest and that familiar pull tugged at her gut. Maya knew the two men seated across from one another, on either side of Doug and Olivia, were King Heinrich and his son Killian. Both men had thick, muscular builds like Horace, although they were much taller than he was.

There was no mistaking their relationship. They had the same piercing, intelligent eyes, and other than some graying hair at the temples and a full beard on the king, he and Killian were strikingly alike. Both men rose to their feet when the women entered the room and bowed their heads in deference.

"Maya, this is King Heinrich and his son Killian,"

Olivia said evenly. She kept her intense green-eyed gaze on Maya and gestured for everyone to sit. "Shane was kind enough to fill us in on what happened in New Orleans, and we know you came here with the intention of giving the necklace to Horace but—"

"Wait." Maya rose to her feet and fought to keep her voice from shaking. "Before you say anything, I would like apologize."

"Maya—" Doug began.

"No." Maya held up her hand, removed her gloves, and shot a glance at Shane before continuing. "I owe everyone in this room an apology. My actions were stupid, reckless, and childish, and those actions have brought us to this point." She unzipped the top portion of her catsuit to expose the necklace and reached around to unclasp it. The cool metal and stone fell into the palm of her hand, and she cradled it against her chest. Killian and Heinrich were fixated. "I have no interest in being a werewolf hunter like my Vanator ancestors, and I have no desire to cause any more trouble for my family or the vampire community."

"Maya," Olivia said insistently. "Hold on a second. King Heinrich would like to say something." She gestured to the king. "The floor is yours, Your Majesty."

"Thank you." Heinrich tilted his head in gratitude before turning his serious expression to Maya. He folded his hands on the table and looked her up and down before he spoke, which made her feel like a bug under a microscope. "My son is the one who should be apologizing. Horace may be my son, but I am not blind to his *shortcomings*." Sadness rimmed his eyes. "Horace has been troubled since he was a child. My wife would say it is simply his nature. I, however, am of the belief that we have a choice in how we behave. I believe that Sentry Quesada acted the way he did to protect you. It would not be the first time that my son behaved badly with a beautiful woman. In addition, I do not hold you responsible for what you did to that young werewolf, any more than you would hold me responsible for the wolves that attacked your ancestors. You were defending yourself and so were they," he said solemnly.

Maya tried not to look at Shane, who was standing at the head of the table behind Olivia and Doug, but it was impossible. The man was magnetic. Tall. Powerful. Domineering. His penetrating gaze didn't move from Maya's face while King Heinrich spoke.

Choices? Choices were all well and good, except for love. If only she could choose not to love Shane.

"My grandfather told me stories of the Vanator gypsies and the power that they wielded. The Vanators hunted down and destroyed hundreds of our people over the centuries with that necklace, so you can imagine what someone like Horace could do with it."

"My brother thinks he can use it to overthrow my father," Killian interrupted. "You must hand it over."

"Who died and made you king?" Sadie asked incredulously. She remained seated to Maya's right but kept her big, brown eyes on Killian. "Last time I checked, you're not in charge," she said, jutting her thumb toward the king. "He is."

"Enough," Olivia said wearily as she shot Sadie a look. "Apologies, we're all a bit on edge."

"No problem," Killian said with a wink. "I like a woman with some moxie."

"Oh please." Sadie rolled her eyes.

"Maya," Olivia said gently. "The necklace is your family heirloom, and I have explained to King Heinrich that I will not force you to hand it over. However, given the circumstances, I'm sure you can agree that it would be best to give it to the wolves."

"Yes," Maya whispered. She looked down at the necklace in her palm and ran one finger over the smooth, brilliant green emerald. "It vibrates when wolves are close by, and when it's not lying against my skin… well…see for yourself."

Maya held it by the chain and allowed the stone to dangle in the air. When it began to glow, everyone let out a gasp. Killian and Heinrich's eyes flickered to orange and they growled. "It's just letting me know that there are wolves in the vicinity. I don't think it can hurt you like this," Maya said quickly. "I think I have to be wearing it, and when I took that boy's wolf away, I had both hands on his chest."

"Yes," King Heinrich murmured. His eyes flickered back to their human state. "According to the legend, the Vanator gypsy women who wielded the dark magic were always wearing that necklace."

"My brother saw a picture of all of you online. The advertisement for the club, that one with all four of you." Killian pointed to the necklace. "Maya, you were wearing it in the photo. That's why he came to New York."

You could have cut the tension in the room with a knife while everyone watched and waited to see what Maya would do. Rubbing the stone between her fingers, she looked at each of them but lingered on Shane. *We all have choices*, she whispered into his mind. *Don't we, Shane?*

"Here." Maya leaned across the table and placed the necklace at the center. "It's yours." She flicked a glance to Shane who had moved closer to Killian but kept his intense gaze on Maya. "Like you said, King Heinrich, we all have choices, and this is mine."

"Thank you," Heinrich said in a voice edged with relief. "You are exactly the way Sentry Quesada described you." Maya flicked her confused eyes to Shane but the king continued speaking. "I have already informed the czars that Killian and I will meet Horace tonight at the bridge, instead of you, and we will escort him and his friends out of the city."

"Thank you," Olivia said as she and Doug rose to their feet. She shook hands across the table with both werewolves and gave them a charming smile. "Our two sentries, Shane and Pete, will be in the area and can provide additional assistance if necessary."

"That's generous of you," Killian said with a wide grin. "But I'm sure we can handle this family matter on our own."

"I insist," Olivia said through a tight smile.

The tension level in the room ratcheted up a few notches while the leaders of both races smiling politely at one another. King Heinrich finally broke the silence.

"Very well." He looked at his son and held up one hand to prevent him from interrupting. "We would be grateful for their assistance. You have been gracious hosts, and we wouldn't want to seem ungrateful. Would we, Killian?"

"Aw, man," Trixie whined and cracked her knuckles. "I was looking for a chance to practice the fighting skills that Pete taught us."

"Another time," Sadie said with a glance at Killian. "Something tells me we'll have other opportunities."

"What are you going to do with the necklace?" Shane asked the king while he continued looking at Maya.

"Destroy it," the king whispered.

He removed a black velvet bag from his pocket, reached across the table, and used it to pick up the necklace. Maya took an involuntary step back. Her movement didn't go unnoticed by anyone, especially Shane, who seemed more agitated than usual. Without a word, Heinrich dropped the bag on the ground and stomped on it repeatedly with incredible force. The room shook as the werewolf king pummeled the bag, turning the stone into dust and the chain into clinking pieces of broken metal.

Maya's hand flew to her mouth while she watched the king transform her necklace into a bag of junk. Her stomach churning, she backed away from the scene. She was prepared to give them the necklace, but she definitely hadn't expected them to destroy it right in front of her. Images of her grandmother flickered through her head and she squeezed her eyes shut, attempting to get herself together as pain flared deep in her gut.

"Maya?" Olivia moved across the room and stood next to Maya. "Are you alright? You look like you're going to faint."

"Oh man," Trixie moaned. "She's not knocked up, too, is she?"

"Trixie," Olivia warned.

"What?" Trixie said with pure exasperation. "She and Quesada are bloodmates like you and Doug, so it's not exactly outside the realm of possibility."

"Is this true?" King Heinrich asked, looking from Shane to Maya. "There is another bloodmate vampire couple? Are they daywalkers, too?"

"No," Shane said tightly. "Maya and I have decided not to commit to the bloodmate bond. I will be transferring to the European offices as soon as possible. Like you said, King Heinrich, we all have choices."

"It ain't exactly something you choose," Doug said. Olivia shot him a look and he quickly added, "But I wouldn't have it any other way. Right, babe?"

"You're not going anywhere, Quesada," Olivia said firmly. She placed both hands on Maya's arms and lowered her voice to gentler tones. "Maya? What's going on?"

"I—I didn't think they'd destroy it," she whispered through shaking lips.

"I'm sorry," King Heinrich said earnestly with a bow of his head. "I shouldn't have done that in front of you, Maya. It was thoughtless of me. Please accept my apologies."

"It's fine," Maya bit out. "I'll be fine." She hardened her expression and looked at Shane briefly. "I'm not pregnant. Shane and I aren't daywalkers, and I'm not a werewolf hunter. I'm merely an exhausted vampire who hasn't slept in twenty-four hours, and I'd really like to go back to my apartment and get some rest."

"You're not going back alone," Olivia said with a quick look at Shane. "Shane will take you home."

"No," Maya said a bit too sharply. She shook her head and plastered on a smile, trying to laugh off her reaction. "I flew all the way back from New Orleans by myself, I think I can handle going back to the apartment."

"Right." Olivia kissed her warmly on the cheek.

"Then humor me and let Sadie and Trixie walk you back, okay?"

Maya nodded wordlessly and cast one last glance at Shane before leaving with her sisters, but he looked away. He didn't insist on coming with her and made no attempt to telepath. A sob choked Maya when the doors closed behind them because Shane's choice was heartbreakingly clear.

Chapter 17

MAYA WANTED NOTHING MORE THAN TO SLEEP. To drift into the leaden slumber of a vampire and hide—but sleep wasn't coming. Clad in her favorite pink tank top and yoga pants, she lay on her bed tossing and turning but found no relief. She glanced at the clock on the nightstand and saw that it was well past one in the morning. The meeting with Horace had apparently gone off without a hitch, and according to the call she got from Olivia, the wolves were headed to Kennedy Airport for their flight back to Alaska.

There was still no word from Shane.

Grumbling, Maya kicked her blankets off and made her way out to the living room. Maybe some mindless television would help her get her mind off everything. She snagged the clicker off the couch and flopped onto the pink and white fabric. Shane's comment about not decorating their place in shades of bubble gum came roaring back. Fresh tears stung her eyes when she realized that would never happen. There would be no apartment with him…no life with him.

The ring of the telephone interrupted her thoughts and made her yelp in surprise. It was probably Olivia or one of her sisters calling to check up on her. Again. Tossing the remote on the table, she padded quietly across the hardwood floor to the kitchen and picked up the cordless phone.

It wasn't her sisters or Olivia. It was Rat.

"Is this my absentee employee?" he asked playfully.

"Rat?" Maya went back to the couch and sat down. She pulled her bare feet up under her. "Is this about work? Actually, I was going to come see you tomorrow night and let you know that I won't be working for you anymore. Since I didn't show up for the past week, I'm probably fired anyway."

"You're not fired," he simpered. "But I can't say I'm surprised that you quit. I heard you were back in town, and I just wanted to let you know that I have your money from the night you worked. In addition to your pay, you get a cut of the dancers' tips. I'd come by the club and give it to you, but Olivia is still sore with me for having the wolves at my place. I was only trying to be a good host but I can't win for losing, I guess." He let out a beleaguered sigh. "So when can you come by?"

"How about tonight?" Maya asked wearily. "I can't sleep anyway, and staring at the walls isn't helping."

"Yeah, sure. I'm here all night, but do me a favor and leave the boyfriend at home," Rat griped. "Quesada is a fuckin' killjoy and he makes my customers nervous."

"He's not my boyfriend, Rat," Maya snapped. "I'll be there in a little while."

She hung up the phone then quickly dialed Sadie's cell phone. The old Maya would have run off on her own without thinking about the consequences, but not anymore. She knew it would piss off everyone if she went out tonight by herself, so she decided to ask Sadie to come along.

"This really couldn't wait until tomorrow night?" Sadie asked as they strode across the street, dodging cars along the way. "You don't need the money that badly, do you?"

"No." Maya laughed and linked her arm through Sadie's before stepping onto the cracked sidewalk in front of The Dollhouse. "I couldn't sleep so why not do something productive, right?"

"I guess," Sadie said doubtfully. She grimaced when they approached the strip club's door. "These places gross me out. A bunch of slobbering, horny guys stuffing money in a half-naked woman's pants? No thanks."

"Don't be such a prude," Maya teased.

"I am not a prude," Sadie protested. "I love sex and I've had lots of it, but this whole setup feels icky."

"TJ, the bouncer, isn't out here," Maya murmured. She looked around, her senses suddenly on high alert. "That's strange."

"What?" Sadie unlinked her arm from Maya and scanned the area with her sister. "Maybe we shouldn't go in."

"It's probably nothing," Maya said, tugging the door open. "We'll make it quick."

Stepping into the dark club, Maya was surprised to see that the entire club was empty. The lights were on and music was blaring, but there wasn't a customer or an employee in sight. There was, however, the pungent aroma of blood, which made Maya's fangs break free and sent her hunting instincts into overdrive.

"Do you smell that?" Sadie whispered.

Maya nodded, glanced to the left, and moved toward the bar, where the smell was strongest. There was a pile of dead bodies and the unmistakable residue of vampires who had been dusted. Something glinted in a pile of dust, and Maya squatted down to pick it up. It was a gold tooth.

"Oh my God," Maya murmured. She showed the tooth to Sadie and rose to her feet. "Rat."

Stepping away from the carnage, Maya felt a familiar, aching bloom in her gut, and her body shook uncontrollably. She turned her wide, frightened eyes to Sadie and whispered, "Werewolves. Run."

"Come on," Sadie whispered harshly and grabbed Maya's hand.

When the two women turned around, a delicate but deadly net of sterling silver drifted over them in a deceptively gentle manner. They screamed when the silver seared their exposed skin, and both women fell to the ground in a writhing heap. Maya's vision blurred from the pain, and the last image she saw before she passed out was Horace's smiling face.

Shane sat on top of the George Washington Bridge and watched the lights of the cars below while the humans made their way from one end to the other. The wolves were at the airport waiting for their plane back to Alaska and a war had been averted. The summit had gone remarkably well, and the Emperor had put the supernatural leaders' minds at ease regarding the changes in the vampire community.

All was right in the world.

Unless your name was Shane Quesada.

In that case, the world was turned completely on its ear and nothing made sense anymore.

After an hour of back and forth, he had finally convinced Olivia and Doug to have him transferred to Europe. Lost in his thoughts, he barely noticed the new sentry when he landed next to Shane on the bridge.

"You are supposed to be patrolling Brooklyn," Shane said without looking at the younger vampire. "This is not Brooklyn."

"No shit." Dakota sat down next to Shane. "I know you're supposed to be a badass, but all you look like to me is pussy whipped."

"What I look like is none of your concern." Shane stilled and turned his head slowly before locking eyes with the underling. "Leave."

"Damn," Dakota said through a laugh. He took a lollipop out of his coat pocket, unwrapped it, and stuck it in his mouth. "Pete told me you were uptight."

"Human candy?" Shane looked at him like he was crazy.

"What?" Dakota shrugged. "I still like how the cinnamon ones taste."

"Do you have any reason for being here other than to irritate me?" Shane asked dryly.

"Not really," Dakota said with a shrug. "I did a pass of Brooklyn and got bored. So I came to see where you wanted me to go next. Pete is back on paternity leave now that the wolves are headed out of town, so you are my go-to guy. So, where do I go? The sun is gonna be up in a little while."

Before Shane could tell him to go to hell, the phone in his pocket buzzed. It was Doug's number.

"Yes?"

"We have a problem," Doug bit out. "Horace gave his father the slip at the airport. He told him he was going to use the can, but he never came back. Killian insisted his father go home with the others, but he's staying behind to deal with his little brother. Looks like he doesn't want the old man to have any blood on his hands."

"When?" Tension radiated up Shane's back along with an impending sense of doom.

The line was silent for a beat or two before Doug said, "Over an hour ago." Shane swore loudly, but Doug shouted over him. "Killian just called me, man. He tried to find him on his own first but the trail went cold. He's embarrassed, and I can't say that I blame him."

"Where is Maya?" Shane asked, leaping to his feet. Panic and fear filled him, recalling the look of outright fury on Horace's face at the bridge. He was outraged when he realized that he'd been duped and Maya wasn't coming to meet him. "Is she safe?"

"I'm heading over to the apartments now to check on her." Doug's voice was edged with frustration. "Olivia and the baby are finally sleeping, and I'd like to get this situation handled before she has to worry about it. Got me? I have Damien standing guard at the Presidium. You and Dakota head over to Rat's place now because chances are that little shit, Horace, will try and hide out there. I told Killian to get a cab over to The Dollhouse, and I'll meet you there once I check on the girls. Even if Horace isn't there, Rat may know where he's gone."

"Understood." Shane hung up and stuck the phone in his pocket. He flicked his furious gaze to Dakota and ground out, "Horace is back in the city." Shane reached inside his coat, pulled out two magazines of ammunition, and handed them to Dakota who looked at him with curiosity. "These are liquid silver bullets. They'll drop a vamp or wolf in a matter of seconds. It's a guaranteed kill shot."

"Far out," Dakota rasped, making quick work of refilling his guns. "Pete was right. You aren't a guy to fuck with." He checked the mag and smirked at Shane. "This Maya broad must be somethin' else if she's got you all fired up like this."

"She's not a broad," Shane bit out as he stuck the guns back in the holster. His jaw clenched and he pressed his lips together when reality hit him like a lead weight. No matter where he went or what he did, Shane would love Maya. It wouldn't matter if he was in Europe or on the damn moon. Nothing he did or said would alter his feelings for her, and he felt like a Class-A fool for trying to deny it—to deny them. He only hoped that he would have the chance to make it up to her. "Maya is my mate."

"Then I don't know what you're doin' out here on a bridge all alone holding your dick in your hand." Dakota smacked Shane on the shoulder and snorted. "You might be old, but you could stand to learn a thing or two, brother."

Shane shot him a doubtful look before whisking into the sky. They flew swiftly and silently through the dark Manhattan night with Shane barely able to control his burgeoning anger. Dakota at least had the good sense to keep his mouth shut and followed Shane without asking any questions.

The two men landed in the alley next to The Dollhouse, and when they slipped along the sidewalk, Shane was grateful there were few humans in the vicinity. He stopped outside the club and held up his hand to keep Dakota from moving. Leaning against the door, he closed his eyes and reached out with the finely tuned senses of a sentry. When his eyes flicked open, three distinct scents filled his head with horrifying clarity. Amid the potent stench of blood and werewolves, he detected the fresh, feminine scent of Maya, and every fiber of his being hummed with rage.

Without thinking, he flung the door open and flew inside with his gun drawn. The club was empty, but he quickly spotted the pile of dead bodies behind the bar and remnants of at least two dead vampires. Dakota stood next to Shane with his gun drawn and pointed toward the stage. Written in blood on the white wall was one word…"Roof."

Armed to the teeth, Shane and Dakota made their way up the narrow staircase toward the roof. When they reached the rooftop door, Shane pressed his finger to his lips and gestured for Dakota to hang back.

Shane threw a prayer to the universe, turned the doorknob, and slowly pushed the creaking metal door open. The sky had brightened considerably, and though he could feel the warning pull of the sun, Shane barely felt it because all he could see was Maya.

Maya was staked to the roof by her arms and her legs with chains of silver wrapped around her wrists and ankles. Aside from being able to smell her flesh burning, he could see wisps of smoke drifting up from the wounds. Sadie was staked out the same way, and Horace sat cross-legged between them with a gun against Maya's temple. Every muscle in Shane's body hummed with barely contained violent rage, and though he wanted to shoot Horace full of liquid silver, the gun at Maya's temple gave him pause.

"If you want to live, then I suggest you let the women go," Shane bit out.

"Let me think," Horace said dramatically. "Nope. I took care of that scumbag, Rat, and his whore dancers. He was helpful at first but then he turned into a whiny pain in the ass, so he outlived his usefulness."

"Shane," Maya whimpered and winced in pain.

The sound stabbed at Shane's heart like a knife, and he flicked his attention to her tearstained face. "It will be alright, youngling."

Dakota stepped forward, raised his gun, and fired but Horace dodged the bullet, pulled a gun with his other hand, and fired two shots. One hit Shane and the other slammed into Dakota, who was sent flying down the stairs. Shane struggled to stay on his feet, but the silver bullet remained lodged in his chest. Although it missed his heart, the damage was severe. Pain burned through his veins when the silver festered in his body. He blinked and his vision blurred, but he kept his gun trained on Horace, who was kneeling between the two women.

The sun crept higher and Shane knew their time was running short.

Shane stumbled and fell to his knees. His left arm hung uselessly at his side, and he fought to keep the gun in his right hand, focused on Horace.

"Let the women go," Shane sputtered and bit back the bone-melting pain. "You can have me instead. I'm a sentry for the Presidium, and killing me will be a much bigger coup for you than eliminating a couple of women."

"I'm sick of bitches like her trying to make me look

stupid." Horace rose to his feet slowly. "Besides, killing all of you will make trouble for my old man and that's fine by me. I hate the old fucker and my brother with his holier-than-thou attitude. They don't deserve to have the power of the wolf because they fucking tamed it. Men like them are holding our race back when we could be ruling the world." He snorted. "Why am I even wasting my time talking to you?"

The world wavered and Shane steeled his strength before taking a shot at Horace. The bullet bounced off the edge of the building, missing his target completely. Horace's bullet, however, did not. Two more rounds of silver penetrated Shane's torso and sent him to the ground in a useless heap. He landed next to Maya and could feel whatever life he had draining from him along with the blood. With his last bit of strength, Shane turned his head so that the last sight he would see on this earth would be the woman he loved.

Blistering pain seared through Maya's body from the silver burning her flesh, but nothing wounded her more than watching Shane get shot. She watched the life began to fade from his eyes and the sight turned her pain to rage. Her fangs erupted and she screamed with pure, unadulterated fury, which only elicited a laugh from Horace. Tugging on the chains at her wrists and with pain shooting up her arms, Maya screamed against the pain and kept trying to break free.

"I think I'm going to fuck you quick before I go," Horace said in an almost matter-of-fact voice.

He placed the gun on the ground and began to undo

his pants while he stood over Maya. She flicked her gaze down to see that he was fully aroused. He shed the rest of his clothing and tossed it aside. Dropping to his knees, he kissed her cheek and looked at Shane while Maya continued to pull against the chains.

"I bet you like to watch." Horace scraped his fingers over Maya's arms.

With his unwelcome touch and his disgusting erection pressing against her hip, every ounce of anger inside of Maya erupted. With a primal scream, she pulled the restraints out of the roof and rammed her hands onto Horace's chest. A massive surge of energy, just like the one that night in the bayou, gathered in her chest, shot up her arms, and blasted into Horace. The look of shock on his face was almost as satisfying as watching him fly naked through the air and slam against the building chimney. He tumbled to the tar roof in a pathetic heap before pushing himself to a sitting position. A look of terror covered his face while he pressed his hands to his chest.

"What the fuck?" Horace whimpered. He ran his hands over his hairy torso, as though looking for something he lost. "You fucking gypsy whore. What did you do to me?"

Shuddering with pain, adrenaline, and fury, Maya ignored his babbling and pulled the silver off her wrists and ankles, not even feeling the burns to her fingers. Frantic, she looked at the sky blazing orange along the horizon and she knew she had to get Sadie inside. Weakened from the silver burns, Sadie wouldn't survive even the smallest amount of sunlight.

Doug landed on the roof next to Maya just before

Killian came bounding up the steps and burst through the door. Maya whimpered with relief at Doug's arrival and crawled over to sit by Shane.

"She took my wolf, Killian," Horace babbled from the other side of the roof. "That gypsy vampire bitch made me mortal."

"You took his wolf," Killian murmured, looking from Horace to Maya. "The magic wasn't in the necklace at all…it's you."

"We can figure that out later," Maya said quickly. "We have to help them."

"Holy shit cakes," Doug blurted out while running a hand over his short blond hair. Wasting no time, he went over to Sadie and, with gloved hands, yanked the silver off her wrists and ankles. "We've got to get her inside. The sun is coming up fast. Watch him, Killian." Pointing at Horace, he said, "Better yet, just get him the fuck out of my city."

"He's no longer one of us," Killian said with a voice edged in sadness. "But perhaps he never was."

"What do you mean I'm not one of you?" Horace spat. "I'm your fucking brother."

"You are an embarrassment," Killian said tightly.

Maya cradled Shane's head in her lap and encouraged him to drink from her. Killian stood by and watched the two of them, which was probably why he didn't notice Horace had picked up the discarded gun. Screaming with blind fury, Horace squeezed off two rounds as he charged across the roof stark naked, but neither hit their marks.

The gun jammed and before Horace could shoot again, Killian shifted into an enormous black and brown wolf. With a rumbling growl, he leaped onto his brother's chest. Horace flailed helplessly while Killian snapped his neck with a sickening crunch. Blood sprayed through the air, and Killian lifted his head and let out a mournful howl that ricocheted around the Manhattan skyline.

"Fuckin' A, Killian," Dakota grunted. Stumbling through the door, he grimaced in pain before leaning against the wall and sliding down to the floor. "Remind me never to piss you off, man."

"Come on, you gotta get up, kid," Doug shouted to Dakota. He had Sadie, moaning in pain, draped over his shoulder and was pulling Dakota to his feet with his other hand. "I have to get them inside. Maya, I'll be right back for you and Shane." He gave a concerned glance toward the brightening sky. "Just sit tight."

Still in his wolf form, Killian whined and lowered his blood-covered muzzle before trotting over to Shane and Maya. In a shimmer of light, he shifted back to his human form, snagged his ripped jeans, and pulled them on before kneeling next to Shane and Maya. He held his wrist out and nodded. "Here."

"Are you sure?" Maya asked through a choking sob. She knew it was against the law to feed from a werewolf, but with the amount of silver in his body, Shane could die without it, and saving him was all that mattered.

"It's the least I can do," Killian said somberly. "After all the trouble my brother has caused."

"Thank you," she whispered.

Maya took Killian's wrist in her hand and made a small incision before holding it to Shane's mouth. Eyes closed and starving once the blood touched his lips, Shane grabbed Killian's arm and drank ferociously.

Maya watched with fascination when the three bullets emerged and tumbled to the ground, the bleeding slowed, and the wounds closed. After a few minutes, Maya gently pulled Killian's arm from Shane's grasp and licked the wound on his wrist closed.

"Am I dreaming?" Shane's eyes fluttered open and he locked gazes with Maya. He reached up and cradled her face in his hand. "Or have I died and gone to heaven?"

"Nope. But that's a really cheesy pickup line. Sure sounds like New York to me." Smiling, she leaned down and captured his lips with hers, kissing him tenderly. When she broke the kiss, she ran her thumb over the beard scruff on his cheek as he sat up slowly to face her. "So, I thought you couldn't love me."

"I've been a fool, Maya," Shane said flatly. He winced, leaning one hand on the roof to keep himself in a sitting position. "But I promise that for the rest of eternity, I will make it my full-time job to make it up to you. I do love you, Maya. I am hopelessly, uncontrollably, irrevocably in love with you. Can you forgive an old vampire for his foolishness?"

"I knew it." She leaned in and kissed him again, reveling in the taste of him. Her hand fluttered over his shoulder, and Maya stilled when she realized that they were bathed in the bright, warm, golden light of the morning sun. "Shane," she whispered in awe, holding her up hand in a ray of sunshine. "We're daywalkers."

"Bloodmate legend or not…" Shane murmured. He placed a kiss at the corner of her mouth and rested his forehead against hers. "Walking in the sun or an eternity of darkness, if I have you by my side…I will walk anywhere."

"I was wondering when you two were going to notice that," Doug said from the doorway of the stairwell. "Looks like this pesky bloodmate legend is more than just some fluke. Welcome to the club, kids."

"Two more daywalkers are now in the vampire ranks." Sitting on the ledge, Killian was staring at his brother's body with an expression that Maya couldn't quite decipher. He flicked his serious gaze to Maya. "I will have to let my father know about the latest…developments."

Maya scrambled to her feet with Shane at her side and snuggled against him, looking from Killian to Doug. Killian may have dealt the deathblow, but Maya was the one who took Horace's wolf and rendered him mortal. She recalled what the king had done to the necklace, and studying Horace's broken body, Maya wondered if a similar fate awaited her.

"I would never use my power except in self-defense, Killian," Maya said adamantly. "I swear it!"

"What power?" Killian rose to his feet and looked at his brother's dead body before giving Maya a sad smile. "My brother challenged me to a fight, and when an alpha is challenged, it is a fight to the death. That is what I will be reporting. That and nothing else."

"How can we be sure that you won't suddenly regain your memory?" Doug asked. He came out into the sunlight and stood next to Shane and Maya. "Not to sound ungrateful or anything but you know…shit happens."

"He can be trusted," Shane murmured with a steady stare at Killian. Maya looked between the two men and saw a glimmer of respect for Killian in Shane's eyes, one she hadn't seen before. He bowed his head in deference to the werewolf prince. "Thank you, Your

Highness. You are a man of duty and honor. If you are ever in need of my assistance, you need only ask."

"I thought you were gonna be in Europe protecting the Eurotrash," Doug said with a pointed glance at Shane.

"I will remain here in New York—if you have no objections, that is."

"Me?" Doug shrugged. "I got no objections, but now Olivia is gonna have to redo a bunch of paperwork, and that is a bitch. So in exchange, you and Maya owe us some babysitting time."

Shane opened his mouth to protest, but Maya wrapped her arms around his neck and kissed the thought right out of him.

Emily gurgled happily in Shane's lap, and Maya could swear her ovaries actually buzzed with excitement. What was it about the sight of a big, strong man going gaga over a baby that was such a turn-on? Emily had one pudgy hand wrapped around Shane's index finger while he bounced her on his knee and sang her "This Is the Way the Horses Ride" for the eight hundredth time. Her big blue eyes smiled at him, and her soft, red curls bounced while he pretended to gallop with her.

The Christmas tree in the corner was decorated with red bows and twinkling lights, and though Christmas was still a few days away, presents were piled high underneath. Most were for her and Shane, but there were several for baby Emily too. Other than spending time with Shane, there was nothing Maya enjoyed more than spoiling that cute little girl. Though Emily was only a year old, Maya had a hard time remembering what life was like without her…or Shane.

She knew the likelihood of getting pregnant like Olivia did probably was nonexistent but, hey, a girl could dream. Olivia and Doug were under the impression that Doug's angel bloodline was the key to Emily's conception. She could eat both human food and vampire fare, but she seemed to be partial to human food—Cheerios in particular.

Maya finished cleaning the dishes in the sink of their newly renovated apartment. Gone was the tapestry of pink. It had been replaced with cool tones of green and blue. Now that they were daywalkers, she and Shane could have found an apartment in a regular apartment building but Maya liked being here—with her family.

She smiled wistfully. Funny how just a year ago she was crawling the walls, and now there was nowhere else on earth she would rather be.

Life had changed significantly over the past year. Not only were she and Shane fully bonded and daywalkers, but her power had grown significantly. So much so that she could sense a werewolf within two miles. The only reason she'd figured that out was because Killian and some of his pack had moved to New York.

Killian told Olivia and Doug he wanted to expand his business on the East Coast, but they were convinced he wanted to keep an eye on Maya. Killian may not have told anyone else about Maya's power, but the knowledge of it clearly haunted him. Maya wondered if he secretly blamed her for his brother's death.

A few minutes later, Olivia and Doug swept into the apartment, both dressed elegantly from a night out at the theater. Emily laughed and clapped when Olivia gathered her daughter up in a flurry of hugs and kisses. That left Shane looking mildly dejected. He rose to his feet and shook hands with Doug before walking them to the door. After a few minutes of chitchat—all about Emily, of course—the czars left with their tiny charge giggling all the way out the door.

Maya waved and let out a sound of contentment as she went back to the sink. Shane's arms linked around her waist, preventing her from doing more work, and he nibbled kisses down the length of her neck. She let out a sound of pleasure when he ran his hands down her arms and tangled their fingers together.

"Just what do you think you're doing?" Maya murmured.

"I'm trying to get fresh," Shane said between kisses. Spinning her around, he hoisted her onto the edge of the sink. "But you seem oddly preoccupied with the dishes."

"Well, perhaps I could be persuaded," she said with a smile. "But…there's something else I'd like to do first."

With a wicked grin, Maya pushed Shane back, the muscles of his chest flexing beneath her fingers, and she slipped off the counter. "Come with me."

Flying through the crisp night sky hand in hand, Maya giggled and Shane kept bugging her to tell him where they were going. When they approached Midtown, the series of lit-up snowflakes that lined Fifth Avenue came into view. Moments later, Rockefeller Center came into view and the massive tree twinkled brightly at the center of it all.

It was three in the morning and this part of the city was oddly quiet, which was exactly what Maya needed for what she wanted to do. They landed on the ice in the skating rink at the center of Rockefeller Center, and Shane looked around with more than a little curiosity.

"What are we doing here, youngling?" he asked. He linked his fingers with hers and tugged her body against him. "There are many things I would like to do with you and to you, but this place is rather…public."

"I know." Maya linked her arms around his waist and popped up on her toes before kissing his lips lightly. "I didn't bring you here to have sex."

"I see. I won't lie to you. I find that disappointing." Shane frowned briefly, which made Maya laugh and bury her face against his chest. "Did you want to go ice-skating?"

"No." Maya pulled back and looked him in the eyes. "This is one of the most magical places on earth, and I wanted to be sure you remember what I'm about to say."

"Alright," he said warily.

"I never said thank you." Maya fiddled with the buttons on his shirt and squeezed her eyes shut for a moment before looking him in the eyes again. He started to say something but she pressed one finger to his lips, which he promptly kissed.

"I'm listening," he murmured. Shane's hands settled along the top of her butt and pulled her closer, almost imperceptibly. "Go on."

"You saved me, Shane. I know you tell me all the time that I saved myself, but I couldn't have done it without you." Her fingers curled against his chest. She gazed at him through wide, earnest violet-blue eyes, her voice wavering with emotion. "You helped me rediscover my past, accept my present, and embrace my future. I'm a pain in the ass. I'm stubborn. Pigheaded and sometimes hotheaded. I think before I speak and leap before I look. I'm rash, impulsive, and occasionally childish. A lot of guys would have run the other way. So…thank you. Thank you for loving me."

"I see." Shane nodded and looked at her seriously. "You forgot a few things."

"I'm a werewolf hunter?" she asked nervously.

"Maya." Shane laughed and cradled her face in both hands. "Those qualities you listed are just a few of the reasons why I love you. But you're forgetting a few things."

"Like what?"

"You are loving, devoted, and fiercely protective of the people you care for. You are driven by loyalty and honor…and you are a wildcat in the sack," he said, wiggling his eyebrows at her.

"Hey." Maya smacked his arm playfully. "I'm being serious."

"So am I," Shane growled before capturing his lips with hers. He angled her head so he could delve deep. Maya's stomach fluttered when his tongue rasped along hers. Far too quickly, Shane broke the kiss and suckled her bottom lip. "I love you, Maya, and you should know that *you* saved *me*."

"Let's call it even," she whispered.

The snow began to fall, and cold, white flakes fluttered over them gently. Maya giggled and tried to catch some on her tongue before Shane swept her up in his arms and shot up into the sky. He carried her all the way home, and later that night while they lay tangled in the sheets, one thought went through Maya's mind.

They had saved each other.

Hunter by Night

by Elisabeth Staab

She wants out

Party girl Alexia Blackburn is only hanging around the vampire compound until her best friend—the queen—has her baby. After that, nothing is going to stop Alexia from getting back to daylight, safety, and feeling like a normal human being. But leaving the vampire world has one big catch…

He needs her to stay

Head of vampire security Lee Goram has hated and distrusted humans for centuries. Feeding on vampire blood has kept him strong…but now it's killing him—and he's horrified to discover that Alexia may hold the key to his cure. He'd rather die defending his king than admit his weakness, but time is running out for the great vampire warrior…

"Brilliantly written. Everything came together perfectly for a super-fast read that I did not want to put down."—*The Romance Reviews*

For more Elisabeth Staab, visit:

www.sourcebooks.com

Kissing with Fangs

by Ashlyn Chase

There's something he's never told her...

When her workplace burned down, Claudia should've taken it as a sign to move on—and not just professionally. She's been secretly lusting after her mysterious boss, Anthony Cross, for years. There's no way she should agree to help him rebuild if she wants to keep her heart intact, and yet it's impossible to stay away...

The flames that destroyed Anthony Cross's beloved bar are nothing compared to the heat he feels every time he lays eyes on Claudia. But he can't have her—it's against paranormal law for a vampire to date a human. Besides, he has some dangerous enemies, and one in particular already has her sights on Claudia. He owes her the truth—both about his feelings and his vampire nature—which means their lives are about to get hotter than ever...

"Chase constructs a cast of intriguing characters set amidst a flurry of paranormal activity."—*RT Book Reviews*

"A fast-paced, entertaining paranormal romance with interesting characters while taking on a fresh story line to keep you intrigued."—*Tome Tender*

For more Ashlyn Chase, visit:

www.sourcebooks.com

Jaguar Hunt

by Terry Spear

USA Today Bestselling Author

Two deadly predators...

As a feline Enforcer, Tammy Anderson has one objective: locate the missing jaguar and return it to the States. She doesn't have time for distractions, and she definitely doesn't have time for sexy shifters with more muscles than sense.

One hot mission...

Everyone and their brother has warned JAG agent David Patterson that Tammy is Ms. Hands-Off...which only makes him more determined to get very hands-on. But things heat up in the steamy jungles of Belize and their simple mission gets a whole lot more complicated. Now it's going to take everything David's got to protect the gorgeous she-cat who somehow managed to claw her way past his defenses...and into his heart.

Praise for *Jaguar Fever*:

"Readers will enjoy this thrilling tale as love and danger collide."—*Midwest Book Review*

"Spear's writing style, as usual, is very detailed and descriptive. A must-read for lovers of paranormal romance."—*Romancing the Book*

For more Terry Spear, visit:

www.sourcebooks.com

About the Author

Sara Humphreys is a graduate of Marist College with a BA degree in English literature and theater. Her initial career path after college was as a professional actress. Some of her television credits include A&E *Biography*, *Guiding Light*, *Another World*, *As the World Turns*, and *Rescue Me*. Recently, Sara joined the Happily Ever After blog at *USA Today* as a contributor, and her novel *Untamed* won two PRISM awards—Dark Paranormal and Best of the Best. Her sci-fi, fantasy, romance obsession began years ago with the TV series *Star Trek* and an enormous crush on Captain Kirk. That sci-fi obsession soon evolved into a love of all types of fantasy and paranormal—vampires, ghosts, werewolves, and of course shapeshifters. Sara is married to her college sweetheart, Will. They live in New York with their four teenage boys. Life is busy but never dull. She loves to hear from her readers, so stop by her website and say hello.

www.sarahumphreys.com